IN THE SHADOW OF Vargas

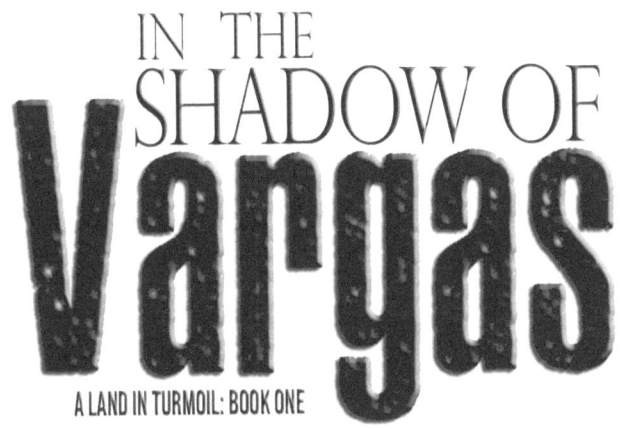

A LAND IN TURMOIL: BOOK ONE

E. PAUL BERGERON

SPANISH TERRITORY-1820

William MacLeod eased out of his saddle onto the rocky trail and sidestepped his way to the little bay mare at the end of the string of pack animals. "See here, little lady, I know you don't like being at the end of the line, but you don't like being in front either. If we're ever going to catch up to those damned Frenchmen, you got to stop trying to toss your load."

He snugged up the hitch and pushed her nose away as she tried rubbing the side of her face on his coat. "We're so damned far behind now, it'll be nightfall before we catch up. I swear I'll sell you to the first Indian I see. Soon as he finds out what a mean-tempered little cuss you are, he'll have you for dinner. Then you'll be wishing you hadn't gone and upset me."

Ahead, the trail climbed into a thick blanket of clouds. He picked up the lead rope and kneed his horse. Somewhere up ahead the others led their own string of heavily burdened pack animals.

"I'll bet they're so busy dreaming about St. Louis they haven't once looked behind to see if I'm following," MacLeod muttered. "Stay together, they kept telling me. Don't get separated. What in heck did they expect when they saddled me with this string of half-broke crow fodder?"

The clunk of the horses' hooves against the rocks and their constant blowing spoke of the weight they carried into the thinning air.

Fifteen minutes later he broke out of the clouds and climbed the short distance to a saddle between two thinly wooded peaks. MacLeod stopped to let the animals catch their breath. A pile of dung, still steaming, lay at his feet. He swiveled in his saddle and checked the loads again. Twenty-four full packs of furs. He and his partners had talked about what the furs might bring in St. Louis. Prices had been good when they left, but they worried that Manuel Lisa might have ruined the market. MacLeod chuckled, recalling the talk about Lisa. They all had cursed him and his Missouri Fur Company. MacLeod found himself doing the same—and he had never even met the man.

The warm sun baked his back after the chill of the fog. He took one last look around. Fir-covered peaks poked their heads out of the clouds, looking like so many rocks in a field of new snow. His mare snorted. She seemed to echo his worries.

The faint markings left by Charbonneau, Stewart, and Belanger led across the narrow saddle and back down into the fog. The stock resisted moving out of the warm sunshine, but MacLeod had no intention of spending any more time admiring the landscape. Still, he couldn't help taking a moment to gaze off to his left at the massive bulk of a mountain pushing aside the clouds and wondering if it was the mountain General Pike spoke of. The one he had come west to see. But he had no way to know.

MacLeod figured the others would have waited for him there on top of the pass if they were going to wait anywhere. He pulled his collar up around his ears to ward off the dampness and kneed his dun gelding into the fog.

Half an hour later the sun burnt through the fog and bathed the canyon in warn sunshine. A thick stand of golden-yellow aspen cloaked the valley floor and up one side of the canyon, a sure sign that some years back an avalanche cleaned out the fir trees.

The gelding dipped his nose to drink from the water trickled out from between the rocks and spread across the trail. He leaned forward in the saddle to let him drink. That's when he noticed the other set of tracks.

The tracks led across the wet ground and down the far side of the canyon; not fresh, maybe a week or so old, he figured. He wondered if the others had seen them.

It wasn't the first Indian sign they had seen. A man couldn't spend a year or so in the mountains and not see sign. Belanger was always seeing tracks, and Indians. The others laughed at him, but MacLeod didn't. If he had he would find himself pinned to the ground with the little Frenchman sitting on his chest, his skinning knife tickling his cheek, just to remind him who was a trapper and who was just the camp tender. But this was the first sign he had seen in a while.

MacLeod checked the pistol stuffed under the sash around his waist and dropped his hand to the scarred stock of the .50 caliber Kentucky rifle his mother had given him when he left. He ran the back of his hand over suddenly dry lips and stripped off his heavy coat, tying it behind the saddle. *No need to get all worked up about them. If the others were worried, they would have waited up.*

The heavy boom of a rifle echoed off the canyon walls, followed quickly by a half dozen more. He urged the big dun forward, dropping the lead rope to let the string follow on its own while running through his mind a plan for what he would do if the others had encountered a party of hostile Indians.

He heard cries, unlike anything he had ever heard before, followed by more shots. Ahead, the canyon narrowed, forcing any fight into an area of intermittent aspen and pine. He had no idea how far the sounds carried as he warily kneed his horse into the trees. Another cry, long and wailing, followed by a series of shorter ones sent chills up his spine.

Ahead, the two sets of tracks converged, leading through a small landslide of boulders before crossing the creek. The dun plunged into the icy waters, churning his legs to gather himself for the leap up the other bank. MacLeod held his rifle over his head to keep the water from fouling his powder and clung to his saddle as the horse lunged over the lip of the far bank. Two unfamiliar horses broke out of the trees and raced toward him. Neither had a rider.

The chill he had felt intensified. He knew death lay up ahead, something nothing had prepared him for. With a degree of awareness he had never experienced before, MacLeod pushed through the shrubbery and into a heavy stand of aspen. Before him lay a scene of battle that spoke of a sudden, unexpected confrontation.

Stewart's body laid to his left, riddled with arrows, his head glistening red where his hair had once been. The bodies of two Indians sprawled close by.

Another cry broke through the silence, startling him. He whipped his rifle to his shoulder, his eyes sweeping the tree line, his breath coming in short gasps. He saw a string of loose pack animals milling about among bodies, then movement beneath their legs. He dropped to the ground and crept forward.

Beneath the belly of Belanger's big black mule MacLeod saw two Indians feverishly hacking at a body. He crawled forward to get a better view when one stood, blood dripping from his finger-tips, and turned to face MacLeod, his mouth opening to scream a warning.

Without thinking MacLeod dropped the iron sights onto the Indian's chest and pulled the trigger. The body tumbled backward over the man's companion, still sitting astride Belanger's body. MacLeod pulled his knife from its sheath and, shrieking out his own challenge, raced across the twenty paces separating them.

The Indian rose as MacLeod's arm swept through a semi-circle, the razor-edged blade slicing open the Indian's throat. Pulsating hot blood gushed out and onto the front of MacLeod's leather shirt. For an instant their eyes locked. MacLeod saw a look of puzzlement in the black eyes before they went blank. He pushed the Indian's body aside and saw the mutilated body of Belanger, his friend and teacher. MacLeod fell to his knees and vomited until he gagged from the effort.

Another shot rang out from farther down the canyon. He had forgotten about Charbonneau. He retrieved his rifle, poured powder down the barrel and rammed home a ball, then added a pinch more powder to the pan, whispering a silent prayer that he wasn't too late.

More loose animals streaked past, followed by two Indian ponies, their sides streaked with blood. He crawled forward, keeping as close as he could to a belt of waist-high rocks. He held his breath and waited. No sound came up the canyon. As quietly as he could he moved out of the trees to the edge of a small clearing. Between the spot where he knelt and the creek, he spotted three more Indian bodies, a sign his friends had not died easily.

His heart felt like a hammer beating the inside of his chest. He took a deep breath and sprinted across the clearing to the shelter of a fallen log and froze as he caught sight of movement off to his left.

He could see Charbonneau sitting with his back against a tree, attempting to reload his rifle with one hand, an arrow protruding from his shoulder. The effort to ram a ball down the barrel caused blood to flow down the shaft of the arrow and darken the front of his buckskin shirt.

MacLeod held his breath while he searched the trees behind Charbonneau. Two birds burst from the branches of a tall fir about forty yards ahead and MacLeod saw the low-slung branches slowly part. A brown body emerged and began working its way toward

Charbonneau. MacLeod slowly raised his rifle and took a bead on the unsuspecting Indian. Before he could fire, another figure rose from the ground less than thirty feet away, his bow bent. MacLeod quickly switched his aim to the new threat. He fired a fraction before the Indian, his ball causing arrow to plow into the tree trunk a fraction above Charbonneau's head.

The first buck charged across the short distance separating them. MacLeod pulled his pistol from his belt, holding it in both hands and firing point blank into the Indian's stomach. The Indian fell and lay thrashing in the dirt. MacLeod tried to reload his rifle, but his hands shook so badly little of the powder appeared to go down the barrel.

A minute passed. Charbonneau moaned, but MacLeod waited, his eyes sweeping over the tree line for any sign of movement. He heard nothing but the nervous stomping of the stock as they milled about.

Satisfied there was no further threat, he picked up his rifle and empty pistol and jogged over to where Charbonneau sat propped up against a tree. "How bad you hurt, Mr. Charbonneau?"

Charbonneau bit down on the ends of his long mustache. "Bad enough, I think."

MacLeod knelt. "What do you want me to do?"

"You must take it out," Charbonneau whispered through gritted teeth.

MacLeod shook his head. "I don't know if I can. I ain't never done anything like that before."

"*Mon dieu!* I can't ride all the way to St. Louis like this. You build a fire and then you make the hot water. You find my whiskey and then you take this arrow out."

As MacLeod started to rise, Charbonneau laid a hand on his arm. "What about the others?"

MacLeod shook his head, unable to say the words.

Charbonneau nodded. "And the furs?"

"I'll see about them up after I take care of you." He gathered a handful of dry grass together, sprinkled a little gunpowder on it and touched off a spark with his flint. He fed the flame with small sticks lying on the ground.

"You must bury the others before it get dark."

MacLeod ignored him as glanced around, spotting Charbonneau's horse nearby. The little bay mare rubbed her head on MacLeod's shoulder when he reached for her lead rope. He pulled a battered flask out of Charbonneau's coat pocket, walked back and held the flask to Charbonneau's lips. "Not much more than a swallow left."

Charbonneau drained the flask and coughed.

"Better you take it out now. You do it quick. Then you wash it good, and then I sleep some."

The tip of the arrow had barely broken through the back of Charbonneau's shirt. MacLeod knew only one way to get it out. He cut the shirt away from the shaft and said. "You ready?"

"Do it quick and don't stop, no matter what."

MacLeod grasped the shaft below the fletching and shoved it hard, pushing the arrowhead through the skin and out another six inches. Charbonneau screamed, but MacLeod knew he had to finish it. He broke off the arrowhead and in one motion pulled the shaft from the wound, hoping he wasn't leaving any splinters behind.

After bathing and wrapping the wound with an old cotton shirt, he gently laid Charbonneau back and covered him with a buffalo robe. He fed more sticks into the fire before rounding up the loose stock. He passed the crumpled bodies and felt his stomach churn again when he saw the damage done by a .50 caliber ball at close range. He wondered how long it would be before some warriors were sent out in search of the war party, or if they would accept the loss and grieve in their own way.

Eleven men lay dead in the narrow canyon. Eleven men who happened to take the wrong trail at the wrong time and whose bones would lie there forever. MacLeod shook his head. Their worst fears had caught up with them.

Flies formed in frenzied clouds above the pools of drying blood. MacLeod worked quickly, scratching out shallow graves in the thin soil and wrapping the bodies of his friends in their blankets. Alive, they had laughed and cajoled and taught him the lessons of life and war. Belanger, the short, stocky French Canadian who possessed a gift of laughter and a temper to match his ability with his knife. A man born too late to be the Coeur de Bois he saw himself as, who dreamed of roaming the Canadian woods and paddling his canoe through the treacherous waters of the Lachine rapids, who once confided to MacLeod that he was a descendent of the legendary Pierre-Esprit Radisson.

Of Stewart, MacLeod knew little. In their few frank discussions, Stewart sometimes talked about the years he spent in the British army, but only in vague generalities. However, he had shared with MacLeod his experience with both rifle and pistol, drilling him in their use until MacLeod could load and fire either weapon quicker and more accurately than he ever dreamed possible. How could such a man be caught unprepared as he obviously had? Of Stewart's personal background MacLeod knew little, only that he had sailed from England in a hurry and that it involved a woman, an officer's wife.

MacLeod picked up Stewart's pistol from beside his body. A beautiful English flintlock made by Bates of London, in .60 caliber. He remembered the first time he had seen it. He was sweeping the floor of the Charbonneau Mercantile in St. Louis, and Stewart was showing it to Charbonneau. It seemed so long ago, MacLeod thought, yet it couldn't be more than about eighteen months ago, if his calculations weren't too far off. He figured it was pretty close because about that time of the year he stood on the street in front of the dry goods store, wondering if was ever going to eat again. Charbonneau stepped out wearing an apron and carrying a broom, and he began sweeping. Without thinking, MacLeod had taken the broom from Charbonneau and began sweeping the accumulated dirt and refuse off the wooden walk and onto the muddy street. That night he slept in the back room of the store, his stomach full for the first time in weeks. And that was when it all began; well, part of it anyway.

He shook his head at the memory and began the gruesome job of burying his friends.

After completing the task of building rock cairns over the bodies, MacLeod carried Stewart's Harper's Ferry musket over to the little mare and tucked it under the covering robe. The .54 caliber half-stocked rifle made a solid back-up weapon, although he had never grown to like its heavy recoil.

As the shadows crept across the valley floor, a pair of mountain chickadees sang their hoarse song. Life in the canyon began returning to normal. Death of one sort or another happened every day in the canyon, part of life's natural cycle. MacLeod wondered how long it would take for his life to return to normal, or if it ever would.

Dusk had settled by the time he rounded up the pack animals and stripped of their loads. MacLeod soaked a piece of jerky in boiling water and fed Charbonneau a cup of the hot broth. He covered his friend with a fur robe, then made sure both the rifle and musket were close at hand. He leaned back against a log and closed his eyes.

The visions refused to die and neither did the questions. What if they had stayed together? Would that have helped? Or would his body now lie among the others? It all seemed unreal. Four bodies lay nearby, the result of his actions. In total eleven had died, and

Charbonneau with an arrow hole in his shoulder. Only MacLeod was left in one piece.

He saw Charbonneau watching him from across the fire. "I should've kept up. I tried. Why didn't you wait?"

Charbonneau shrugged.

"Who were they, the Indians I mean?"

"I think maybe they Utes. It doesn't matter who."

"I never killed anyone before, Mr. Charbonneau. Don't think I like the feeling."

Charbonneau reached into his pocket and brought out his pipe. "Fix me a smoke, then we talk."

MacLeod took the pipe, along with the waterproof packet that protected what remained of Charbonneau's precious supply of tobacco. He emptied it into the pipe and packed it down, and held a fire brand over it while Charbonneau sucked it into life.

"Sometime these things they happen, either them or you. Now we go to St. Louis, that what we do now."

"What about the furs?"

"We take them with us."

MacLeod thought about it a moment. Eight pack animals with three packs a piece and each pack weighing close to ninety pounds. They had done the numbers many times and it still came out to eight thousand dollars at St. Louis prices when they left.

Charbonneau pulled on his pipe and watched MacLeod. "We leave all the traps and gear. We use all the animals and pack them lighter, and we travel faster that way."

MacLeod stirred the fire and added a branch. "It'll take me half the morning to pack those dumb brutes, and a spell to unpack and picket them at night."

"I give you one of the others share of the furs, maybe more, we see. You make fifteen hundred dollars, if we make it. What you think, eh?"

What could he think? Fifteen hundred dollars was more money than his father made in all the time he could remember. "Guess I could try it for a day or two, see how it goes."

In the morning, MacLeod sorted the loads and cached the traps in a niche between some large boulders. He made a mark on two trees nearby but doubted he could ever find the place again. By the time the string stood packed, and Charbonneau hoisted into his saddle, the sun sat overhead. He led them out through the aspen trees alongside bushy blue columbine, the white and blue flowers offering themselves to fluttering butterflies. MacLeod closed his eye and said a silent prayer for his former friends, wishing he knew where he had packed the Bible his mother had slipped into his hand before he left the farm outside Boston. Trust her to think of his soul needing reinforcement.

By late afternoon MacLeod stopped and made camp, not far from a small creek where he could get water and maybe a deer or elk would come down to drink at dusk. Between having to stop to check on Charbonneau, and the constant conflict of contentious stock, they had managed only five or six miles for the day. St. Louis seemed a long way off, and the long string of pack animals made them easy to spot by any Indians looking for trouble.

Dawn broke through heavy cloud cover as MacLeod rolled over and sat up. He reached over and stirred up the ashes of the previous night's fire. Spotting the glow of a hot coal in the ash, he tossed a handful of dry grass and sticks on top. He blew on the coal until the grass flamed up, then fed dry sticks into the flame. It would make some smoke, but if he kept the fire small, the smoke would dissipate in the trees.

"How you doing this morning, Mr. Charbonneau," MacLeod called out, as he stood up and stretched. He walked over and knelt beside Charbonneau and shook him gently. "I'll get some water going and maybe make us a cup of hot broth. About all we got till I see something to shoot. I didn't have any luck last night."

Charbonneau moaned.

MacLeod laid his hand on Charbonneau's head and felt the fever. He knew then they would not be travelling for a spell. He bathed Charbonneau's shoulder and wrapped it with pieces from a torn blanket, then spent half of the morning rounding up the loose stock and driving them back to the camp. Sooner or later he would have to picket them all to let them feed or let them graze and hope they didn't travel too far in the night.

He picked up his rifle. Unless he saw some game to shoot MacLeod figured it would be one of the horses in the cook pot, or his moccasins. They were down to nothing and St. Louis wasn't getting any closer. As he glanced around, looking for any sign of trouble, Charbonneau groaned. MacLeod went to his side and placed a wet cloth for his forehead. He didn't have much to go on but one thing he knew for sure, his employer was awful sick and needed more help than Macleod had to offer. He made the decision that he had been putting off since it happened.

I know you're going to give me a heap of argument when you wake up, but there just isn't any other way.

MacLeod strode across to the pile of gear under the trees, found the axe and camp shovel and went looking for a place to begin digging.

Three days later, Charbonneau sat up and surveyed the camp. "Where are the furs.?"

"Mr. Charbonneau, I guess the fever broke last night, but that shoulder looks awful bad. You need a doctor."

"I see a doctor when we get to St. Louis. What have you done with the furs?""I cached them over yonder."

"They will be ruined for certain," Charbonneau said. "I will be ruined if I cannot take them to St. Louis."

"Well, sir, I'm begging your pardon, but you won't make it to St. Louis. You need to have someone who knows what they're doing look at that shoulder. I figure there's got to be someone in Mexico knows what to do. Soon as you're fit to ride again, we can go to St. Louis and get ourselves more horses and come and get these furs. I dug those holes deep, lined them with sticks and such, and wrapped everything in those extra skins we had. I drew us a pretty good map, but I figure I can find this place without it. When we come back here, these furs should be as good as new."

A cough racked Charbonneau. He doubled over, then straightened up and shook his head. "You dig them up and we go to St. Louis. I will make it all right. *Oui.*"

"Fraid not sir. There's no way I can round up these critters every morning, take them to water, pack them all while I'm dogging their hooves, and then lead them all the way to St. Louis. Why, you said yourself it must be close to a thousand miles. Maybe if we're marching along over nice flat grassy territory, with no Indians anywhere, and these mutton heads finally decide it's alright to follow the one in front, we could make it in three, four months maybe. But we got a string of half-broke stock who go berserk at every other creek crossing or the sight of rattlesnake."

Macleod walked off, his back to Charbonneau. "No, sir. I just up and killed four men, and I figure I'm in charge now, with you being the way you are, so you can let me handle this or you can fire me, seeing as you hired me. Now, I'm going down to the creek and fetch some water so I can clean that shoulder again while you think it over."

MacLeod shooed some of the stock away and dipped water from the creek. He had turned all the horses loose except for his horse and Charbonneau's, Belanger's big black mule, and the little bay mare as a back-up pack animal. The rest of the stock would wander away eventually, or get jumped by a grizzly. Nothing he could do about it.

"You know how to get to Mexico?"

"I figure we head south, along the line of these mountains. I think they're called the Sangre de Cristos. We keep going we'll find them, or they'll find us. Same thing. We'll take along a couple of packs of furs for trade. Reckon we ought to make up a story about the rest of the furs, otherwise they'll be wanting them too, just like they did with Mr. DeMunn and Chouteau."

"Listen to me," Charbonneau said, beckoning MacLeod to come closer. "Maybe I make it and you not worry, but in St. Louis the name Charbonneau has great respect. My daughters, Rose and Jeanette, they hope to make good marriages someday. I watch Manuel Lisa make great profits with his furs, and I saw it as my only chance. I sell my business to buy supplies and equipment for this trip."

"What happens to your family if we don't make it back?"

Charbonneau's body seemed to deflate. "I guess they go to her family in Montreal. The girls will not marry then, for sure nobody want to marry into ruined family."

"So what is it you want from me?"

"You promise you will come back soon and take the furs back to my family, if anything happen to me."

"Nothing's going to happen to you," MacLeod said, but seeing Charbonneau weaken more each day, he wasn't convinced.

Charbonneau doubled over as a cough gripped his body. When he could talk he said, "I had a dream."

MacLeod threw a stick in the fire. "You and your damned dreams. All right, I promise, but we're both going home, I can feel it," MacLeod said, but his words were far different from what he felt.

SANGRE DE CRISTO MOUNTAINS

The fresh breeze flowed down off the mountain, chilling the morning air. "You ready?" MacLeod said, studying Charbonneau.

Charbonneau nodded and pulled himself upright. "I will be better in the saddle."

"We best be going then."

MacLeod picked up the lead rope of Belanger's black mule and mounted his horse. He had decided to retrace their route over the narrow pass and drop back down to the Rio Grande and follow it south. It was risk they would have to take, if Charbonneau were to survive.

He recounted some of the stories of the others who had ended up jailed in Santa Fe, or Chihuahua, or were never heard from again. Some said the ones that never came back were enticed into staying by the fine, well-rounded señoritas one could meet in Santa Fe. Belanger had spoken of it several times. MacLeod knew Belanger had never been in Mexico, but he knew better than to contradict the man.

"How you doing back there?" MacLeod called over his shoulder. When Charbonneau failed to answer, he knew it was time to find a place to rest.

This was not what MacLeod had dreamed about while sitting in Charbonneau's parlor in St. Louis and listening to Belanger's tales of French fur trappers from Canada who had explored lands never before seen by white men. Across the smoke-filled room, the glistening eyes and jet-black ringlets of Charbonneau's sixteen-year-old daughter Jeanette beckoned. He wondered if the money he stood to make from the furs might increase his standing in her eyes, and how did Charbonneau view him as a suitor? They never spoke of it, or about Jeanette, and MacLeod knew he would have to join their church to be considered eligible, something his Presbyterian relations would surely frown upon.

They rode through a landscape of scattered junipers rising tall and straight alongside the short, bushy pinion pine that dotted the land. The rich green of the trees accented the rust-red soil. A pair of rock squirrels camped on an outcropping, their cheeks packed with pinion nuts, and watched until the procession had passed. A half-mile or so ahead he spotted a grove of trees that looked like a good place to stop.

"We'll rest a spell in the shade up ahead," MacLeod said. He led the pack animals down the steep bank of an arroyo and across a dry creek bed, watching for a spot to climb the far bank. He saw a break between two junipers and headed his horse toward it.

Charbonneau's voice caused MacLeod to turn. "I think maybe someone is also there."

When MacLeod topped the bank of the arroyo he saw them. A large party of men and horses milled about among the trees close by the shore of a small lake. The sounds of laughter and shouts of men carried across the distance to where MacLeod and Charbonneau sat on their horses.

I'm going to get a little closer," MacLeod said, urging his horse toward a small thicket of bushes that would shield him from those in the trees below. Charbonneau followed.

A sudden piercing scream came from the trees, then ceased with the crack of a pistol. MacLeod reined in the dun and watched as men on horses forced a group of people over to one side of the trees and corral them.

"Got to be Mexicans," MacLeod said.

Charbonneau moved up alongside MacLeod and grunted. "Others come by the lake. I think maybe they Apache."

MacLeod shivered. General Pike said he had seen large portions of New Mexico devastated by the Apache when he rode south to Chihuahua. "Looks like they're expected."

As they watched, two men chased a woman into the open beyond the fringe of trees. She stumbled and fell. As she rose, one of her pursuers knocked her to the ground and straddled her. The woman struggled until the man hit her with his fist. She lay quiet while both tore off her clothing.

Others laughed at the scene, but their grins disappeared as a ragged volley of shots rang out. MacLeod watched as the group surrounded by the men on horseback toppled to the ground.

MacLeod stepped from his horse and slid his rifle out from under the gear. "It ain't right."

"No," Charbonneau said. "There are too many of them."

6

Miguel Griego, captain of the *urbanos*, the New Mexico governor's hand-picked militia, sat on his horse and reflected on his situation. His gambling debts were forcing him to take too many chances and that could lead to more trouble with his father, the only man he feared.

"Mon Capitan, you want this one?" a grinning, pimple-faced member of his squad asked as he wrestled with the kicking body of a young Indian girl he held under his arm.

Griego shook his head and pointed to another captive. "That one. She is mine."

"That one she will need a strong hand," the squad member said, looking over at the young Navajo woman who stood beside an old man and apart from the other captives.

Griego watched the men satisfy their urges. It was better than having to pay them, and they rode with him expecting such entertainment. They would have to share the other young girls, but the tall angry one would be his, and he had no intention of sharing her.

"What will we do with the old ones?" asked Gomez, Griego's second in command.

"The Apaches will only pay for the young ones. The others have seen us. You know what to do with them."

He watched as six of Romero's Mescalero Apache approached through the trees, coming to buy what he had to sell. They would not be happy there were so few. They expected more, but the village he raided was made up of mostly old men and women.

Griego eased himself out of his saddle and settled his feet on the ground. He scratched his groin, anticipating the relief he expected soon, and started for the captive he had chosen for himself. She looked much better than some of those women in Santa Fe he spent so much of his time with. What a shame he could not keep her awhile.

As he waddled toward the woman, he wondered why the old man beside her was not with the other old ones. He would be dealt with later.

The woman stepped back as he approached, then spun around and raced out of the trees, followed by the old man.

Griego stood in the shade of a large cottonwood and screamed out orders for someone to bring them back. The two spent soldiers rose sullenly, their pants at their ankles, and swore at their companions who refused to give up their turn with the captives. With Griego's threats of violent reprisal hanging over their heads, the two *urbanos* located their muskets and went in search of their horses.

Moments later, the first squad member galloped out of the trees in pursuit of the girl and the old man, followed by the other.

MacLeod peered through the branches of a scrub mesquite bush. "Why do you figure they shot those people? Don't appear to be Indians, and look at those coming around the edge of the lake. They're Indians for sure and those others down in the trees don't seem too worked up about it. Doesn't make sense."

From behind him MacLeod heard Charbonneau sigh. "Maybe we go now and no one see us."

"Don't think we can move out of this draw without being spotted. Maybe if we stay put till they go," MacLeod said, glancing back at Charbonneau. He knew he needed to get him help soon or he would be burying him.

He moved to the other side of the bushes to get a better view. "The one in that fancy-looking outfit and the big hat seems to be in charge. He's been prancing around on that big white horse and appears to be telling the others what to do."

The black mule pushed past MacLeod and clambered up the shallow bank of the arroyo, drawn to a bunch of grama grass. The little bay mare followed. MacLeod cursed softly and edged away from the shelter of the mesquite toward the trailing lead rope. He grabbed the rope and led the animals back into the arroyo.

"Damn," MacLeod muttered, after hearing a shout from below and seeing the man on the white horse point up in their direction. "I hope they're friendly, 'cause we sure aren't in any condition to do any running."

A moment later MacLeod saw what the shouting was about. A figure had bolted out of the trees and was racing up the arroyo toward him and Charbonneau. He realized there was no way they would not be spotted. He moved out from the bushes and led the pack string over to Charbonneau. He sure didn't want any more trouble, but those among the trees had already shown they would kill with ease.

"It's a woman," MacLeod said. "Must be one of those that weren't shot."

"Another one coming, too," Charbonneau said.

MacLeod had been so intent on watching the woman approach he had not seen the second person about fifty yards behind. Shouts from the grove of trees brought his attention back to the small, white-clad figure springing after the woman.

The woman seemed to hear the shouts and stopped. She turned and beckoned to the one behind, then ran on, her path angling away from where MacLeod stood watching.

Charbonneau pointed back at the trees. "They send others."

The lead rider quickly overtook the small figure and knocked him to the ground with the butt of his gun as he rode past. The woman turned to see her pursuer overtaking her.

She reached down and picked something off the ground, then waited until the rider closed the distance. She threw whatever she had picked up at the rider, striking the horse and causing it to rear back. She bent down again and picked up another projectile.

Without thinking, MacLeod dropped to his knees, estimating the distance at about a hundred and fifty yards, and brought his rifle to his shoulder.

Below, the rider kneed his horse toward the woman, backing her up into a mesquite bush and raised his gun.

The loud retort of MacLeod's rifle rolled across the high desert and down into the group gathered in the trees. The rider slumped in his saddle, then fell to the ground. MacLeod quickly poured powder down the barrel and seated a ball, then tapped a little powder into the pan. He turned to see the second rider point his gun at the small figure lying on the ground. MacLeod fired a second time, and the rider slid from his saddle and lay still.

A scattering of shots came from the tree line. MacLeod stood for a moment, wondering what to do next. He watched the group below to see if others would emerge to pick up the bodies. More weak-sounding shots followed. He saw the figure on the white horse edge back among the trees while still seeming to be shouting orders and pointing in Macleod's direction.

Charbonneau moved up beside Macleod. "Now there is more trouble, I think."

"Didn't seem right, Mr. Charbonneau, even if they're only Indians. Besides, those men had already shot those others."

"I think maybe they shoot us too," Charbonneau mumbled.

Macleod saw the woman run back to the one who had been knocked to the ground. He started toward them. "Can't just off and leave them now. The others are sure to shoot them." He jogged through the scattered clumps of brush toward the two figures in the dry wash.

The woman leapt to her feet as he approached, a combination of fear and defiance on her face. An old man lay at her side, a rivulet of blood training down his face. MacLeod heard a high-pitched cry off to his left, but paid no attention to it, picking up the reins of one of the loose horses and handing them to the woman. As the old man struggled to his feet and reached out to take the reins, MacLeod heard thundering hooves. He stepped out from behind the horse and saw an Indian astride a small, thick-bodied horse racing toward them. The Indian clung to the mane of the horse with one hand, a long lance in the other, his heels hammering the sides of the pony. MacLeod stood still, awed by the display of bravery in charging someone who had just killed two armed men. He had heard the stories of Indians charging their enemies in order to touch them and count coup to prove their individual bravery. But how would anyone know what was in the mind of this Indian, and the lance held in the Indian's hand did not look like something MacLeod wanted to be touched with.

Both the young Indian woman and the old man had turned to flee. MacLeod knew he had no time to recharge his rifle. The Indian pushed himself upright on his horse and drew the lance back, screaming a challenge. MacLeod realized he had waited too long. He transferred the rifle to his left hand and drew the pistol from his sash. The Indian's charge never slackened.

Suddenly the old man seized MacLeod's rifle and stepped in front of MacLeod, raising the rifle like a club. The Indian's face contorted in rage. He let out a long piercing cry as his horse raced over the last twenty yards.

MacLeod realized the Indian was not much more than a boy, but as deadly at that range as any man. MacLeod's arm swept up and he took aim on the Indian's body. The sharp retort of the pistol cut off the Indian's cry. MacLeod pulled the old man out of the path of the horse as it swept past. The young body hung over the horse's neck for a dozen strides before tumbling to the ground and rolling into the roots of a mesquite bush.

Silence lay over the high desert like a cloud. MacLeod stood beside the old man and shook his head, asking himself, why?

The Indian woman stepped to MacLeod's side, took the reins of the horse and spoke to him. He had no idea what she said, but he gathered she was urging them to hurry. He came out of his trance at the sound of more scattered shots coming from the trees. A spent musket ball glanced off a nearby rock and rolled past him as he turned to follow the woman up the arroyo.

Then he felt himself falling to the ground.

HACIENDA OUTSIDE RANCHO DE TAOS

MacLeod's head throbbed. He touched the spot where, apparently, a musket ball had grazed it. He squinted through the pounding ache and tried to focus his thoughts but could not remember much after shooting the young Indian. He followed the woman and the old man, wondering where they were heading but too dazed to ask or argue.

Two hours later the woman led him and Charbonneau' into a small clearing beside a stream. Belanger's black mule and the little bay mare followed. The old man helped Charbonneau from his horse and laid him on the ground, and helped the woman peel away the French man's blood-soaked shirt.

"*Mon Dieu*," Charbonneau cried out, knocking her hand away.

She grunted and pulled his knife from his belt. With a single stroke she slit the shirt to exposed the wound. MacLeod leaned his back against a tree and watched as she gathered dry sticks and pine needles and started a fire. She went through their gear and found a pot and filled it from the stream, then, while the water heated, she walked along the edge of the stream and uprooted a handful of plants. She returned to the fire and placed the plants in the pot.

"What she doing?" Charbonneau questioned.

"Can't really tell, but whatever it is it can't do us any more harm than I've already done. I'm sure sorry I went and shot those two men. Don't know what's got into me lately except for all the wrong things them fellas were doing, shooting all those people even if they were only Indians. Don't seem right."

"Maybe the Indians try to kill them first," Charbonneau said.

After the woman finished cleaning Charbonneau's wound, she applied a paste from the plants, holding it in place with his shirt. When she finished with Charbonneau, she cleaned the wound on MacLeod's scalp and smeared what was left of the paste on it.

As night fell in the canyon, the woman fed Charbonneau with a thin broth made from the few strips of meat they had left, then she covered him with a robe and gave the rest of the food to the old man. They huddled close to fire as light rain began to fall and mist shrouded the trees.

They rose before the sun and descended out of the mountains, traveling west. Charbonneau's blanket-wrapped body lay snug on a pole travois the old man had lashed together. The old man ran ahead, his tireless pace eating up the miles.

Near the mouth of a winding canyon, the thick green underbrush gave way to a drier red earth. The trees were stunted and grew farther apart. MacLeod took a deep breath and smelled the tang of sage growing among the orange-red flowers they called desert paintbrush. Far to the west the gray-blue of distant mountain ranges bordered the far side of a vast, high valley.

MacLeod knew Charbonneau's strength could not last much longer. He motioned to the woman, hoping she understood he wanted to know how much further they had to travel. She pointed to a long green line of trees in the distance.

In the late afternoon, they rode through fields of crops tended by Indians. Small children carrying leafless branches kept chickens and sheep away from the vegetable patches. Macleod also detected a run of pigs from the smell that drifted to him on the breeze.

Half a mile away, the green line of cottonwoods marked a river, feeding countless irrigations ditches. Small adobe buildings were scattered around a high wall, the complex resembling a small town easily defended if attacked.

Those tending the crops and animals stopped their chores and watched as the old man led the party through the gates in the wall and into the courtyard.

9

Maria De Cordero sat beside the slow-moving waters of the river that fed their irrigation ditches and the needs of the hacienda. She liked this time alone, away from the constant activity in the kitchen and courtyard. Even *siesta* time had its interruptions. She leaned back against the trunk of a cottonwood and closed her eyes. Visions of the last *baille* in Santa Fe played before her eyes. It did not have the same dash and excitement as those she remembered from her childhood in Vera Cruz, but at least it helped break up the endless boredom of hacienda life.

She opened her eyes for a moment as a gentle breeze brought her the scent of the sage, still wet from a heavy morning dew. She should be married; she was in her eighteenth year and would soon be beyond the age when most young women marry. Many of her friends had two or three children, and their bodies showed the effects of childbearing and too much of the rich foods served daily. Of course, offers of marriage had been made to her father—many in fact—but nothing that might bring a happy union.   They   seldom   came from younger men or their families. Those shied away because Maria made men feel insecure and inadequate in many ways. Many had attempted to parade themselves before her, but gaudy clothing or prancing horses, with heavily adorned silver trimmings on saddles, or on the admirers themselves, failed to impress her. She ached for conversations beyond that of the bitter gossip she heard among the women. Is being beautiful and being someone who has knowledge beyond the religious teachings or household gossip so bad, she wondered?

When she attempted to question others about why certain things were the way they were, or why the Church, or the governor, did what they did, the others shrugged and told her she should forget such questions, those were the arenas of men. Sometimes she wished she had never sat in on the lessons her brother received from the tutor in Vera Cruz.

A wavering line of ducks dropped out of a clean, blue sky and settled near the river's edge. From her spot beneath the tree, Maria watched as her father walked to his horse and spoke to one of the Indian servants. He mounted and rode out of the gate toward the spot where she sat. Maria thought it strange that he should do so, but it gave her a moment to watch him as he approached. He was far more handsome than the average man in New Mexico; at least that was her opinion. A tall, thin man who carried himself with an air of nobility, yet did not display the arrogance that some full-blooded Spanish *peninsulars* did. Unlike most of the others, Don Cordero had been born in Spain, which made him a member of the ruling class, if he so chose to be. He did not make an issue of it, even though he was a *rico* and a very rich one. She noticed the gray in his beard and the lines around his eyes, somewhat deeper than before. Much had changed in him since the death of her brother, Francisco. Only she seemed to notice the difference, and he sometimes let a small amount of emotion show when they were alone.

"Father, will you sit with me a moment, it is such a beautiful day."

"You should not be here alone. I have told you this; it is not safe."

"I am sorry father, but my horse is there, as you can see."

It was unlike him to sit on his horse and talk like that. Maria wondered if it had anything to do with the messenger who had arrived at the hacienda the day before.

"I wish to speak with you," Don Cordero said, stepping down from the saddle.

Something inside her turned over. She knew by his manner it would be difficult for him to say.

"I have received an offer of marriage for you. It came only yesterday, but I have not had the opportunity to speak with you alone."

"From whom did you receive it?" Maria asked, knowing in her heart she would not like the answer. In her mind she ran through the names of those whose offers had been refused.

"The offer came from Don Antonio Griego, for his son Miguel."

Maria lowered her face into her hands and shook from side to side. "Oh God in heaven no, father. Please tell me you will refuse," she pleaded. "I would rather die. You cannot do this to me."

Don Cordero threw his hands in the air and stalked to his horse, then whirled around to face her. "There is no one in all of New Mexico who would suit you. I have been more patient than all the saints in Rome. What more can you ask?"

Maria wiped the tears from her eyes and gazed out over the muddy waters of the river. She could not imagine marrying Miguel Griego. He of all the men who had approached her father was the worst. She remembered the last time he took her out of the arms of another to dance with her. She could not help recalling his foul breath and the way he had thrust himself against her, crushing her breasts against his body. She remembered the unveiled lust in his eyes, more open than any of the others, more animal-like.

"Have you made your decision?"

"No, I am still considering it. I will decide if this offer is a good one for you. You must prepare yourself in any case."

Maria took her father's hands in her own. "I ask you, father, please turn down this request. I cannot marry such a man. He is a vile pig."

"Maria, you will not say such things. The Griego family is respected. It has owned land here in New Mexico for a hundred years."

"He is a pig. Do you not know of the things he has done?"

"They are but rumors," Don Cordero replied.

"Rumors? They are not rumors. Ask the Indian families whose people he has stolen, or murdered. Ask anyone who knows anything of him."

"Many rumors fly off the tongues of people without knowledge. His father is the *alcalde mayore.*"

"He is his father's son. His father has his position because he knows things about our governors that they wish no one to hear."

"You speak these things that you cannot know for certain, Maria. You must learn to keep your tongue," Don Cordero said.

"I did not know that allowing you to associate with Francisco's teacher would produce a woman whose knowledge surpasses those whom she might marry. You have driven off good men with your biting remarks and opinions. This is not Vera Cruz. There is a limit to the men available to be your husband."

"Why must I marry at all? I would rather not marry than be the property of such a man as Miguel Griego."

"You must marry."

"Why?"

"Where would you go when our Father decides my time has come? What would you do? Who would care for our lands and look after your mother?"

"I am able," Maria said.

Don Cordero shook his head. "You are only a woman. What do you know of such things? You must marry so that your husband may take care of these lands and these peons who depend on us. Don't you see it is the way it is, it is our way?"

"Then perhaps our way is not always the right way," she answered.

"I will not debate you, Maria. I will say it is our way. You will marry when I decide and that is my decision only."

"But father."

"Enough." Don Cordero mounted his horse and wheeled around, touching his spurs to the stallion's flank and racing back toward the hacienda.

Maria laid her cheek against the bark of the tree and wept.

MacLeod's straightened in the saddle and sniffed the air, then smiled. The smell of food cooking surrounded him in a cloud of unfamiliar yet pleasant aromas, and he recalled how often a full belly meant only endless strips of tasteless jerky washed down by mountain stream water.

He studied the structure as they walked their horses through the heavy wooden gate hung on massive iron hinges. It appeared to be a continuous room, with doors opening out onto a courtyard, built to enclose the entire area, except for gates at each end of the adobe enclosure. An overhanging porch-like roof provided shade for each room, and combined with a number of large leafy trees, gave relief from the sun.

Chickens scratched in the dirt at the feet of a heavy-faced Indian woman who watched as the horses walked to the center of the courtyard and stopped.

MacLeod eased himself off his horse and waited a moment for the pain in his head to ease. He walked over to Charbonneau and knelt beside his liter. "How you feeling?"

Charbonneau grimaced. "Where is this place?"

"Not sure, but it's not Santa Fe. I just hope somebody here speaks our language."

"You are at my hacienda. I am Don Augustin de Cordero and I speak your language."

MacLeod rose slowly to his feet. "My name is William Wallace MacLeod, sir, and this here is Mr. Lucien Charbonneau, from St. Louis."

MacLeod became aware of how they must look in the presence of this tall, bearded man who carried himself with such an air of authority. While he waited, the man spoke with the old Indian who had brought them.

"This is Sebastian," Don Cordero said. "He has told me what happened. You must sit here in the shade while I see to your friend, and then you can tell me why you have come to *Nuevo Mexico*."

A shallow-faced, young girl appeared with a gourd of water. MacLeod took a long drink, surprised at its coolness. He thanked her and watched as she scurried off to the giggles of other Indian women peeking out of the open doorways.

MacLeod seated himself in the cool shade beneath the thatched roof of the porch while Charbonneau was carried inside. Soon others arrived with buckets of water and linen. An old woman, older than MacLeod thought possible, shooed children away from the doorway. They returned with a tree stump and placed it beneath a narrow window and climbed up to peer into the room. MacLeod laughed to himself. If nothing else, the children here were the same as those in New England.

"Your friend is being cared for. The Indian woman is a noted healer. She will see that his wounds are treated, and when she is done, she will look at yours."

MacLeod jumped up at the sound of Don Cordero's voice. "Thank you, sir. I've been mighty anxious about him."

"Now, perhaps you will tell me what brought you here to our country."

"Well, my friends and I...there were four of us when we started...we've been trapping beaver somewhere north of here for quite a spell."

"Beaver?

"Yes sir, beaver, for their pelts."

"And these beaver furs have value that would make you come this far?"

"In St. Louis they bring as much as five dollars apiece. We figured we had close to eight thousand dollars' worth, all told."

"And you say you were north of here?" Don Cordero said, pointing to the mountain range MacLeod could see through the gate. "How far to the north. Were you in Mexico at the time?"

"Don't believe so. We were trapping the head waters of the Arkansas down as far as the Rio Grande."

Don Cordero ran his hand over his short beard, shaking his head as he did. "Please continue."

"I reckon we somehow got a mite careless and ran smack into a party of Indians. The others got themselves killed, and Mr. Charbonneau here with an arrow through him."

"And you, how did you manage to escape being killed," Don Cordero asked,

"I was somewhat behind and came on them late, and there were only three or four of them left. The others being dead."

"What happened to the Indians you say were still alive?"

"Afraid I had to kill them."

Don Cordero's jaw dropped. "You killed them?"

"Yes, sir. It weren't an easy thing to do, and I never done such a thing before, but I had to do it. They were fixing to finish off Mr. Charbonneau. Afterwards, I buried the others and cached the furs, figuring we'd come back in the spring for them. Then we ran into that pack of scoundrels two days ago."

"I see," Don Cordero said, "and then you shot those that chased Sebastian and the woman?"

"Afraid that's true, sir. Didn't think it was right, them shooting those people like that. Figured they'd do the same to that woman and old man."

Don Cordero pointed to the old man who was leading the horses away. "He has served my household for many years. He is Navajo, the woman also. She is my daughter's servant. Most of the men and women you see working the fields and in the household are Indian, Navajo or Pueblo. I am thankful for their lives if what you are saying is as it seems. You are welcome in my home."

"Sir, who were those men at the lake?"

"Possibly slave traders, or Comanchero. We have something of a problem with them. They steal women and children, and trade them for money, or horses, or anything of value. They have no set rules."

"Why were the others killed?"

"It could be they were too old. The men will not adapt to the tribe, and if the women are too old to produce children, they are of no use. What those men want is the young women and children. The children will be brought up as if they were their own, and the women will soon become with child and will not want to leave without the child. In our society, the women would not be taken back after living with the Indians.

"Ours either," MacLeod said, remembering how a woman from his own town was treated after being rescued from an Indian village.

"How far is it to Santa Fe? That's where we were going to try and get a doctor for Mr. Charbonneau."

"Santa Fe is south, about two days ride," Don Cordero said. "Here you are close to San Fernando de Taos. But you will not find a doctor in Santa Fe, at least not one who will care for your friend any better than he can be cared for here."

"In that case, I guess I'd be obliged if we could stay a spell, until Mr. Charbonneau can travel."

"Of course. A room will be prepared, and there is hot water. You will also find clothing to wear while your own are being washed. You will eat as soon as you are done."

"Thank you, Don Cordero," MacLeod said

"If you will excuse me now, I have work that needs to be done," Don Cordero said. "But there is one more thing I must warn you of. We are a long way from Santa Fe, and it is rare that we see the governor or any of his troops, but they occasionally come through this area. You must remember that you are a foreigner in New Mexico and foreigners are not welcome."

MacLeod interrupted. "But we thought we were still in the United States of America when we were trapping. There are those that believe everything east of the Rio Grande belongs to the United States. They say President Jefferson bought it when he purchased Louisiana from Napoleon."

Don Cordero bristled. "They are mistaken. What your Jefferson bought does not include any of this." He swept his arm over everything in all directions. "This all belongs to Spain, and it was illegal for Napoleon to sell it in the first place. He made an agreement with the King of Spain not to sell it to the United States."

"I was only trying to explain why we never thought we were intruding on Spain's land."

"Nevertheless, that is not how Governor Melgares will see it. You have shot two of his soldiers. He would arrest you and in all probability send you to Chihuahua, to the Commandant General."

"Why would he do that after I explained what happened to us."

"Because I doubt he will believe your story of these slave traders. He has denied they still exist. Now I must excuse myself."

The old woman who had tended to Charbonneau tugged on MacLeod's sleeve and led him into a cool, dark room. Charbonneau lay on a pile of furs beneath a narrow slit of a window. On the wall above hung the crude wooden image of a bleeding Christ and in the far corner of the room a steaming tub of water sat on the earthen floor beside a mattress of straw and furs.

As MacLeod stripped off his greasy, bloodstained, deerskin clothing, he realized he had not taken a hot bath in more than a year.

He stepped into and squatted down, sighing with pleasure as the warm bath water enveloped him. He leaned back and spread his arms along the edge of the tub, wondering how long it would take for Charbonneau's wounds to heal enough for them to travel. If what Don Cordero said was true, they needed to get out of Mexico soon.

The room reflected its occupant. Maria de Cordero sat on a low stool while her Navajo servant, Peche, combed out the tangles in Maria's waist-length hair. A few sticks of wood burned in the corner fireplace, sending flickering shadows across the whitewashed walls. Across the room, on a heavy wooden chest, a pair of candles illuminated a crude carving of the crucifixion.

"You must tell what it is that happened with you, and then you must let me tell you what my father spoke of today."

While Peche ran the brush through Maria's hair, she told Maria the story of her capture, along with that of Sebastian and of being taken, along with the other captives, through mountains to the waters of a shallow lake. "They were Indians that took you?"

"No, señorita, they were your people."

Maria shook her head. "I cannot believe that. You must be mistaken."

"No, it is true, but we run and then the one with the hair like the grass in summer comes to us."

"These are the men that you brought here? My father says they are *Americanos*?" Maria stood up and walked to the comforting warmth of the fire. I do not understand why they did not chase after you?"

"Señorita, I do not know. Maybe they did not want to catch us."

Firelight danced in Maria's eyes. She tried putting aside the thought of her possible marriage. "What are these strangers like?"

"I do not know much. I do not understand their talk. One is old."

"And the other?"

Peche's eyes lit up. "He is young like you. He has eye like the sky, but he is very dirty and there is a strange smell on both of them. Sebastian says it is the smell of the beaver."

"Yes, I heard that Sebastian burned their clothing."

"What do you think your father will do with them?"

Maria shrugged. "I have not spoken to him."

"Sebastian say he would not want to be the enemy of the one with that gun."

"That is much to say of someone so young. I must meet him sometime, but now you must hear what my father has said to me."

Maria often shared her thoughts and worries with her servant, not in the hope of receiving advice but to have someone to talk to. "Someone has made my father an offer of marriage for me," Maria said. As she spoke she watched the heavy wooden gates swing shut to seal the hacienda into its nighttime cocoon.

"Is that not wonderful?"

"No, it is a terrible thing." Maria bit her lip to hold back her grief. "Because of who this offer is from."

"It is marriage, is it not?"

"Yes, but not one I will want to live for. I will never go through with it."

"But it is your father's wish," Peche said.

The tears had faded from Maria's eyes when she turned from the window. "No matter, I will find an answer if I must, but I cannot believe my father will accept such an offer. I would hope to have some love for the man I marry."

"What is this love you speak of?" Peche asked.

"How can I explain it? It is wanting to be with someone, to touch them, to know they respect you and want you the same way," Maria explained. Have you not felt that way for someone?"

"No. My people only wish to have someone to share the work with and to bring in food. Nothing else is needed."

Gazing across the plaza, Maria watched the dancing light from the candle through the window of the room where the foreigners slept. She wondered if love was a part of their customs.

Peche picked up the nightly things and walked toward the door. "If you speak to your father about this, you will make him angry will it not?"

Maria mulled the question for a moment. "Yes, I must wait for the proper moment."

Santa Fe

Miguel Griego rode into the square in front of the Governor's Palace. For two days he had thought of what Romero would do when his son's body was returned to him. He needed these intruders caught as a bargaining chip to deal with Romero and as a means to pacify his own anger at the insult he suffered in front of his men. But what could he have done against such a weapon, and how many others might have been hiding in the arroyo waiting for him to leave the cover of the trees? At least that was the story he planned on telling the governor.

The cool morning air held the scent of spice from the breakfast fires, reminding him he had not eaten. Time for that later. He turned his horse over to a sleepy guard and brushed the dust from his jacket and pants. He pushed past several peons waiting outside the governor's door and entered the dingy interior of the palace. Griegos had lived in the vicinity of Santa Fe for a hundred and fifty years. They seldom waited for permission to enter.

Governor Facunda Melgares sat at a desk beneath a narrow window signing a stack of papers with a flourish. His aide, *Teniente* Zavalda, stood by his side, directing him to where his signature was required. They both looked up as Griego strode into the room.

"My Governor," Griego said with the barest hint of a bow.

Governor Melgares tilted his head in acknowledgement. "Señor Griego, we have missed your presence here lately. How is your father, Don Antonio?"

"He is well," Griego said, but in fact had not seen his father in weeks, and had no intention of doing so soon.

The governor continued to talk through his smile. "You will conduct my blessings to your beloved father."

"Most certainly. I will do so when I see him next, you can be certain. However, I have come to you with a most important matter." For the past two days Griego had wrestled with the story he would tell the governor, who never asked where he went when he took the governor's *urbanos* out of Santa Fe for long periods of time. He knew the governor never asked because the man did not want to know the answer.

The governor put his pen aside and glanced at his aide. It was known that he did not like surprises.

Griego began his well-rehearsed story. "I have just returned from the north, where we were chasing a band of Apaches, when we were suddenly attacked by a large party of foreigners."

The governor leaped up, sending his heavy chair toppling over. His mouth hung open.

Griego continued. "Before I was able to repulse this attack, two of my men were killed. I am afraid I was unable to bring the bodies of these brave men back for proper burial."

"Foreigners. What were they doing in my country? How many, tell me? Are they still here?"

"There appeared to be about ten of these men, but I believe they could be a scouting party for a much larger force." Griego knew no one, other than those who rode with him, could contradict his story.

"It is impossible, Melgares said, looking to his aide for guidance. He paced behind his desk, his hands fluttering about. "And how far away is this army. Did they follow you? If Santa Fe is in danger, we must get help from Chihuahua."

His aide held up a calming hand. "Surely, Your Excellency, there is still time. After all, if we send messengers to the Commandant General seeking help, he will most certainly have doubts about your ability to govern. You remember how easily he panics."

Governor Melgares rubbed his chin. "Perhaps you are right."

"Señor Griego," Zavalda interjected, "you said you and your troops were able to beat back this attack."

Griego couldn't be sure where Zavalda was going with his questions, but he had no choice but to follow along. "Yes, that is true."

Zavalda smiled. "And would you not think these intruders need time to lick their wounds before they attempt another attack?"

"Yes, that is certainly a possibility," Griego said. This fabrication would put him in Zavalda's debt, but he had no other choice.

With his hands resting on the top of his desk, the governor nodded his head in agreement. "I had the same thoughts, but when this very big army has, as you put it, licked their wounds, they will want to take revenge, do you not think? Then Santa Fe itself will be in danger," Governor Melgares said, beginning to pace again.

"There is one other thing, Your Excellency. During this attack, the Apaches we were chasing believed they were also under attack. One of them was killed," Griego said.

"That is good, is it not?" Melgares asked.

"Yes, that is true, but we believe the one killed was the son of the Mescalero, Romero."

It took a moment for the governor to grasp the implications. He ceased his pacing and looked for a place to sit. Zavalda righted his chair and placed it behind him. "Is this, Romero, not the one who has laid waste to many of the small villages along the river? I have reports all over my desk here of the destruction and death he has caused to happen to my citizens. Is this the same Apache?"

Griego nodded. "He is the one, and he will want to take his revenge against anyone he believes was involved."

Griego felt the time was right. "If I can be of service, governor. Allow me to return to the north in search of those responsible. If I am successful, there is the possibility we can use those I capture to appease the Apache."

"Yes, that might be the answer. You are already in possession of knowledge of their whereabouts, are you not?"

"Yes, I believe I know where to find them."

"Perfect." He turned to his aide. "Write a paper there on your desk and give Senor Griego my authority to do this."

"Could you also issue a ration of gun powder? Our supply is very low."

The yearly allotment of gunpowder came from Mexico and was stored in the presidio arsenal. Griego knew Melgares hoarded the gunpowder and sold it privately to some of the *ricos.*

Governor Melgares pursed his lips and opened a drawer in his desk. "Yes, of course. I can allow you a few pounds, but I must keep the rest of it for the defense of our city." He handed the key to Zavalda and held up four fingers. "I have given you the title of *Commandant de Armas* while you are on this mission for me. I wish you to make all speed to find these foreigners and report back to me immediately," Melgares said.

"Thank you, Governor. I will be away as soon as I can provision my troops. I promise you I will attend to your wishes as quickly as possible."

Outside the palace, Griego hoisted himself into his saddle and gazed northward into the clear and cool air. A smiled parted his lips as he urged his horse forward and headed toward Rosalita's gambling and bedding house. He needed the comfort of warm and willing bodies before he returned to the north.

HACIENDA OF DON AUGUSTIN DE CORDERO

MacLeod opened his eyes to the morning sounds of the hacienda. He swung his legs out of the bed and felt a twinge of guilt. The image of his mother in his dream made him aware of the worry she must feel for the lack of any news from him. He wrote his last letter the night before they left St. Louis. How long has it been, two years?

"What you think so funny, eh?"

"Had a dream, that's all."

"Me, too, but I dream we open the cache and the furs no good," Charbonneau said.

MacLeod knew Charbonneau set great store on his dreams, and he would be dragging his jaw on the floor for days if he were not convinced otherwise. "There's no way. No one is going to find them, and when we come back, they'll be as dry as a chipmunk in a tree."

"Maybe you say so, but how you find them for sure, huh?"

"I'll find them, don't worry. In fact, since I know exactly where I buried them, I'll give you the map I drew. We'll come back with some help and plenty of horses, take those packs back to St. Louis, and march them right past Manuel Lisa. You best put your mind to getting well enough to travel and not worrying," MacLeod said.

He pulled on the unfamiliar clothing given to them by Don Cordero and stuck his head out of the door. He watched an Indian woman waddle across the courtyard, balancing bowls of food on her head. If it was anything like the previous night's food, MacLeod knew it would be a battle between hunger and how long he could stand the burning in his mouth and throat from the spicy dishes.

The woman placed the steaming bowls of beans and red peppers on the dirt floor, along with a platter of round, thin pancakes. Bite-sized chunks of meat floated in the bowls. After surviving the last few weeks on hard jerky and water, this mouth-watering food would be a feast. If only he could overcome the heat.

With no spoon to eat the mixture, MacLeod followed the instructions from the night before. He peeled one of the pancake-like flapjacks from the pile and folded it in half to make a scoop. With this, he shoveled the spicy food into his mouth. It took a moment for the peppers to take effect and by that time MacLeod had eaten four or five large mouthfuls. At first his mouth and throat began to burn, then the sensation spread to his cheeks and eyes. He blew out great gasps of air and lunged for the jug of water, but Charbonneau had ignored the pain in his shoulder and beaten him to the cooling water.

"Quick, the water," MacLeod gasped.

"*Sacré bleu, ce tres chaud*," Charbonneau wheezed. "I bet you could melt ice with dis." Charbonneau drank water from the gourd and handed it to MacLeod.

Between gulps of water, MacLeod wiped the sweat from his forehead. "We best be getting home soon, or we'll be nothing but cinders. How do these people do it?"

"After the fire go out, she pretty good. Better I think than we have for great long time."

MacLeod scooped another portion into his mouth and took another drink of water. He wiped his mouth with the back of his hand. "Damn, even my teeth hurt."

They ate in silence as the sounds of the hacienda floated into their room. Chickens gossiped outside their window while clawing at the dirt for loose seed. The occasional snort of a horse waiting for its rider blended with the hacienda Indians calling to one another while going about their assigned chores.

MacLeod sensed a change in Charbonneau's mood. "How's the shoulder today?"

Charbonneau shrugged.

"I figure we stay until you get better, then maybe we can get out of here before winter snows us in, or we get caught up by the authorities."

Charbonneau pushed his dish to one side. "Who are these authorities?"

"It seems the stories we heard were true. Don Cordero said they would probably send us to Mexico, like they did with the others, if they catch us here."

While they talked MacLeod, looked through the open doorway out onto the courtyard. He watched the Indian women placidly going about their daily chores, then, from the far side, the slender figure of a tall woman emerged from the main living quarters and walked across the courtyard. She wore a dark scarf over her hair, her face hidden from MacLeod's view. He had the feeling she did not want to be seen by them. He moved closer to the door as she approached, a slim hand holding the scarf across the side of her face. As she passed she turned her head slightly. For an instant, their eyes met, then she quickly turned her head and walked past.

MacLeod watched her entered a room and disappear. He backed away from the window and tried to take a deep breath. "You ever see someone, a woman I mean, who kind of grabs you so hard you feel you don't dare take a breath because you know you can't?"

Charbonneau remained silent.

"I only saw her for a moment, and she had this scarf-like-thing pulled over part of her face, but it seemed like I never saw anyone so pretty before."

MacLeod returned to the window, knowing he had to see her again. "I was thinking we should see about getting our rifles back. I feel kind of naked without them. She can't be one of the servants, so she probably knows where I can find this Don Cordero."

He left Charbonneau muttering to himself and followed the shade of the overhang to the door he had seen her enter. He ran his hand over his beard, wishing he had shaved it off when he took the bath.

The woman suddenly emerged carrying a basket and almost collided with MacLeod. Both took a step back and stared at each other.

"Sorry, ma'am," MacLeod said. "I'm looking for Mr. Cordero. Could you tell me where I might find him?"

She stood looking at him, her black eyes never wavering, a slight rise in one eyebrow, and the barest hint of displeasure on her face. She gave no indication that she understood his question. MacLeod had the feeling he had been found wanting.

She handed the basket to a passing woman and pulled her shawl together. With a shrug, she brushed past him and crossed the courtyard to the main living area.

Was she Cordero's wife? MacLeod wondered. He felt a twinge of jealousy at the thought.

Tiny specs of dust drifted lazily through the narrow shafts of light to settle on Maria de Cordero's embroidered bed covering. She sat with her feet tucked under her and her head resting in her arms. It was her thinking position, she liked to say, and that day she felt she had more to think about than all the times before. Her father's announcement had pushed everything else from her mind, as it should have, until she ran into the *Americano*. What was it about him that took her mind off Miguel Griego's marriage proposal?

It had to be the eyes, so blue, and they looked at her in a different way. They did not travel all over her body like all the others, but gazed into her own eyes. She could almost feel them penetrate into her thoughts as if they asked the same questions she posed. She shook her head. There was no one for her to ask about these feelings, certainly not her mother who spent the majority of her time either shouting at the servants or praying for forgiveness for only producing two offspring. She stood and gazed out the window.

Could it have been the soft voice that spoke to her in such a respectful manner? She could not be sure, but she knew she wanted to know what he looked like beneath the beard. She blushed. "Enough of this foolishness," she said to an empty room. She knew somehow she needed to convince her father he must refuse this marriage offer he had received.

Through the open gates of the hacienda, Maria saw her father pull his horse to a stop and converse with the man who supervised the peons in the fields. It would be better to speak with him when he was alone. She pulled her *reboso* over her shoulders and walked out to meet him.

"How is your day, Father?"

Don Cordero frowned. "It is well."

"The *Americano* asked for you. He said he wished to inquire about their weapons. I did not let him know I understood."

"I will attend to them in time."

Maria felt his aloofness. "You do not approve of them?"

"They are in our country illegally, and I have yet to know why they are here," Don Cordero said as he turned his horse over to one of the servants.

"Did they not tell you why they are here?"

"They claimed to be trapping for some animal skins."

"Why?"

"They say these furs are of great value in America."

"And do you not believe them?" Maria asked.

"I am not convinced, but I have told them they are welcome until the older one is able to travel. I am taking a great risk in allowing them to remain. It is against our law to be here without a passport," he said.

"You have said in the past you do not approve of their country. Why is that?" Maria asked.

"Maria, you ask such questions. It is not for a woman to bother with such things. You should be thinking other thoughts. This one time I will answer your questions, but this is one of the reasons it is so difficult to arrange a marriage for you. Your husband will not care what you know of America, he will know nothing himself."

"I am sorry father, but you know of my curiosity about such things," she said.

Don Cordero placed his hands on her shoulders, a gesture he often did when talking with his headstrong daughter. "You must understand," he said. "Our system of government has survived for a thousand years. Our church also, and to these great powers we owe our allegiance. These *Americanos* have a hatred for the King of England and all monarchies."

He took his hands from her shoulders and seemed to marshal his thoughts. "Their government is chosen by the people themselves and that means all of the people, even those without name or property, and their leaders can be changed at the will of the people. It is a form of government doomed to failure."

"But do they not have a church like we do, to guide them in their decisions?"

"Yes, of course. Some are of the One Great Church, but most practice other thoughts. But that is not all. They have no respect for those of nobility; they have none of their own. I spoke with some of their great men many years ago. They said their respect was held for those who earned it. These are great disadvantages to a young country. Who can they look to for guidance?"

"Are we at war with these *Americanos*?" Maria asked.

"No, but they are a very aggressive people, and while we thought our borders were insulated from them by large areas of land, the French leader, Bonaparte, sold the very land to the Americans. This was contrary to an agreement he had with our king. Enough," Cordero said, shaking his head. "I must go now."

Maria felt the time to bring up the marriage proposal could not be postponed. "Father, I wish to speak to you again of the offer you received from Don Griego," she said.

Don Cordero held his hand up as if to stop her from continuing.

"No, please, Father, let me continue," Maria pleaded.

He nodded slowly. "Very well."

"When we spoke, you said I must marry so there will be someone to manage our lands when you are no longer able. It is necessary, therefore, that this man I marry should be capable of such things, is it not?"

"He must take my place, yes," Don Cordero said.

"Then, Father, you must allow me a little more time to find such a man."

In a gesture of impatience, Don Cordero threw his hands in the air. "We have spoken of this before, Maria, and you have made these same promises."

"Father, please," she said. "I ask for but one more chance. Miguel Griego is not the man. You have said you do not approve of his father, Don Griego. What makes you think his son is any different?" Tears began to streak her cheeks.

"Enough. I have told you this is not your concern."

Don Cordero's taught expression told her she had spoken more than she should have, but the overwhelming realization of what his decision meant overshadowed her ability to control her emotions. Sobs wracked her slender body. She felt hope drain from her and confronted her father with a last attempt. "Then allow me to return to Mexico. I will enter our church and give my life to His teachings. Surely you cannot refuse me this request."

Don Cordero once again took her by the shoulders and shook her gently. "Do not be the child. Have you not been raised to marry the one chosen for you? Do you think I have not thought of your welfare? Miguel Griego may not be your Don Diego de Vargas that Fray Alvarez has filled your head with, but he will surely give you a home and you will have many children. What more do you want?"

Maria broke from his grip and turned her back on her father. Her life would become one of virtual servitude and constant pregnancy. She knew she had already overstepped her bounds, but she could not restrain herself from one last word. "And what are you paying them to have me? How much do you have to give Miguel Griego to have me?" she cried.

Don Cordero reacted as if he had been slapped. "You will return to the house and remain in your room until I return. You have no respect for my decisions, and it is not in your place to question them. He stepped up into his saddle and jerked his horse around in a tight circle. "I will go to Don Griego myself. I doubt Miguel Griego knows what he will be getting in you, but I imagine he will need a heavy hand."

Maria sank to the ground and wept while thirty paces away MacLeod stood shielded from view by a high-wheeled cart.

15

He had not seen her again and, feeling restless, and getting only blank stares from everyone he spoke to, MacLeod wandered through the gate of the hacienda wall and was struck by the vastness of the valley that lay before him. At his back rose the high peaks of the rugged mountains and below a gently sloping, red-tinged land ran down to the green line that marked the path of a river. He walked through the patches of crops tended by the seemingly tireless workers, crossing the frequent ditches that carried water to the fields. He stopped at the bank of the river, his mind struggling with the image of the girl lying in the dirt as her father mounted his horse and rode off.

The sound of a hoof stomping the soft earth appeared to come from behind an ancient cottonwood whose roots were slowly losing their battle against the encroaching waters. He walked carefully toward the sound and edged around the tree. A saddled roan mare nibbled at the tufts of grass growing between the roots. The mare raised its head and stepped aside as he moved past, into a ring of boulders that formed an enclave, cutting off the view of the hacienda.

MacLeod suddenly found himself within a few feet of the girl, who sat with her chin on her drawn-up knees, her arms wrapped around her legs. Both drew in their breaths.

"Excuse me, ma'am," MacLeod managed to blurt out, quickly backing away.

The girl leaped to her feet and edged her way toward the mare.

He felt foolish in the white pantaloons and shirt he had been given to wear. "I didn't mean to startle you. ma'am. It's just that I saw your horse and I thought maybe it had wandered away from the house."

His words appeared to reassure her. She stopped backing away, a hint of a smile creasing the edges of her mouth. Her eyes moved over him.

"Reckon I look a sight different, what with the beard gone and all." He knew she couldn't understand him, but he kept talking, hoping she wouldn't decide to run off. He held his arms out to the side and his shirtsleeves stopped at his elbows. "Don't look like much, but I reckon they burnt my other clothes. I sure hope I can find someone to make me something that fits proper."

As he spoke, she turned her head to look toward the hacienda, giving MacLeod a glimpse of the profile he remembered from their first meeting. Her long, black hair hung across the front of a beaded leather vest. The black, wool skirt halted a few inches above a pair of soft leather boots, held at a narrow waist by a silver buckle. A pair of doeskin gloves lay on the ground beside her.

MacLeod shook his head and muttered just a shade over a whisper, glad again that she couldn't understand him. "Ma'am, you are the prettiest thing I ever recall seeing. I'm sure sorry about what happened the other day with your father. I hope it wasn't on account of us."

Fire leapt into her eyes. She clenched her teeth together and brushed past him, striding toward the mare as she wrenched on her gloves.

"Wait. Where are you going? What did I do?" he begged with a questioning gesture. "Please don't leave."

She spun around and pointed a gloved finger at him. "It was not for you to hide and listen to others?" she said with the barest hint of a British accent.

MacLeod's jaw dropped. He stood looking at her as if he had been caught peeking in a window, then his own anger rose to match hers. "You've been standing there listening to me jaw away like a damned jay and all this time you knew everything I said. Why didn't you let on you understood?"

"At least I did not hide. What was said with my father was something between us only. You had no right to listen," Maria said with her hands planted defiantly on her hips.

"Well, at least I didn't know what was being said."

"And how do I know that?" she asked.

"I guess you don't, other than I said so, and I don't tell lies."

She spun around and walked back to the river's edge, gazing across the water while MacLeod wondered if he should leave.

"Did you mean those things you said?" she asked after a time.

"What things?"

"What you said about me. Did you mean them?"

MacLeod felt his face begin to burn. "I guess I do. I mean, they were true," he mumbled.

Minutes passed. She turned to face him, her arms crossed. "I suppose you *Americanos* say this to all women they meet?"

He couldn't remember any girl being so direct. It took him a moment before he could answer. "No, ma'am, I never said it to anyone before. I'm sorry, I just sort of blurted it out."

"Thank you, if you meant it," she said. "I am Maria de Cordero, and who are you?"

"William Wallace MacLeod, ma'am, and if it's not being too direct, can I ask, are you this Mr. Cordero's wife?"

She laughed and shook her head. "No, but what kind of a name is that, William Wallace MacLeod?" she teased.

Lord, he thought, *she sure can be direct.* "The MacLeod's, ma'am, are from Scotland. William Wallace fought and defeated the English and the MacLeod's fought alongside him."

She tilted her head in acknowledgement and led him through a stand of willows. She found a place to sit in the warmth of the sun, spreading her skirt and sitting on her legs. MacLeod sank to the ground, unable to take his eyes off of her.

"Now, I want to know about this place you come from, this land of America," she said.

MacLeod loved the way she struggled to find the right words. His curiosity got the better of him. "Where did you learn to speak English? Your father does, but I can't figure he has much reason to use it."

She gazed across the river at the valley below for some time before she spoke. "We come from Vera Cruz. It is a long way from here. I had a brother, Francisco. He was younger than me. I loved him very much. But he was never strong like other boys. My father hired this man from the country of England to tutor Francisco. My father wanted him to learn your language. He hoped to send Francisco to other countries, to learn how others lived, and he believed this language would help him."

"Is he there now, in another country?" MacLeod asked.

"I used to sit with him and help him with his lessons. This man was kind and very patient with Francisco," she continued, as if she hadn't heard his question. She wrapped her arms around her knees and rested her head on them. "Francisco died. I think of him always."

"I'm sorry," MacLeod said, wishing he could think of something else to say.

"That is how I learned your language. My father and I speak it occasionally if we desire to keep certain things to ourselves." She rose and brushed the grass from her skirt. "But now I would like to walk while you tell me of this place you come from and why my people seem to fear it so. My father says your type of government cannot last."

As the afternoon wore on, they strolled beside the winding river as it worked its way through the fields of crops, Maria reaching for his hand when necessary to cross a feeder stream, and holding it for a brief period until it became awkward to continue. The sun inched toward the western mountains while they talked of everything that came to mind. MacLeod, for the first time, lost his awkwardness in the presence of a young woman who laughed when she could not find the right words to ask her question.

"You are different from the men I know. I do not feel the need to guard my words at all times, but I have a question if you will answer me."

"I will if I can," MacLeod said.

Maria paused a moment as if to put her thoughts into the proper order. "In your country does, one marry for love or does your family make these arrangements for you?"

MacLeod couldn't help being flustered by the intimate question. He just wasn't used to young women being so forward, as his mother would say. "Well now, ma'am it's pretty much you meet somebody, and you both decide that's what you want to do. I never heard of anybody being forced into it," he said, although he knew of some who pretty much had to, after what maybe happened.

"Do you have someone waiting for you?"

"I don't suppose so, leastwise not so you could say as much." He had no intention of bringing up Jeanette Charbonneau, who might or might not be waiting, because they never really talked about anything like that. In fact, they never talked much at all. Mostly it been his daydreaming.

"I must tell you about us," Maria said. "My father and mother were born in Spain; they are called *peninsulars*. The ruling class of all of Mexico are *peninsulars*, people born in Spain. I was born in Mexico, and although I am of pure Spanish blood, I am considered a *criollus*. If I were in Vera Cruz, I would be married to someone who is also a *criollus*, unless, of course, someone from Spain wished to reduce himself to my level to marry me. Then you have those that are not so pure and are called mestizos, with the possibility of some less than pure Indian blood in their veins."

MacLeod remembered men being called half-breeds and supposed it was the same. "Are there many of those?"

Maria laughed. "More than you might think. There are times when the women of some of our better families have children who appear somewhat darker than others. It is never admitted, of course, and these children find homes with another mother, possibly one among the hacienda workers. But it is a way of returning the favor for the beatings by drunken husbands. And what husband would wish it known his wife found her pleasure with an Indian?"

"I don't understand why you're telling me this," MacLeod said.

"So you will know something of the ways of our country," Maria said and walked a few feet away. "My father has decided I am to marry a man I cannot love. In our country, this is the way it is. All marriages of the *ricos* are decided by the father. When you heard us arguing it was because of this."

The thought of her being promised to someone caused a flush of foolish jealousy to sweep over him. "And you have to go ahead and marry this man?" He wondered who these *ricos* were.

"Yes, once the agreements has been reached, there is little I can do about it," Maria said.

"This man," MacLeod asked. "Is he someone you know? He must be if you despise him so?"

"He is a pig. He is everything I loath, but I do not wish to speak more of it with you."

They walked back to the cottonwood where her horse grazed on the short grass along the river's edge. "I am sorry, I should never have said some of these things to you," she said, picking up the braided reins. "But there is no one else I can speak with, and you will be gone soon. Now I must go."

"Wait," MacLeod said holding up his hands. "How soon will this happen, this marriage?"

Maria mounted her horse with ease. "That will be determined by the man, but once my father accepts the offer of marriage, I will be watched to see that a meeting such as this never again takes place. I will not be permitted to be alone with a man; it might reflect on the honor of my betrothed." She laughed. "He, however, can do as he pleases, and you can be sure he will."

The mare pranced in a tight half circle, held in check by Maria's gloved hands. "I am happy we have met. I hope your friend recovers quickly and you can return to your country."

MacLeod put his hands on the mare's neck. "Will I see you again, before we go?"

She checked the mare, a sad smile creasing her face. "Perhaps, perhaps not," she said, guiding the mare through the opening in the rocks and touching its sides with her heels.

MacLeod stood and watch her retreat. "But perhaps I will," he said, and followed on foot.

HACIENDA OF DON ANTONIO GRIEGO

Miguel Griego opened his eyes and swore to the saints he would kill whoever was pounding on his door and causing him such pain.

"Miguel, if you are in there, you must open the door. Don Antonio has sent me."

Griego swung his feet out onto the cold dirt floor and waited a moment for his head to cease its spinning. When he felt he could stand unaided, he pushed himself to his feet and stumbled to the door. "What is it you want, you imbecile," he whispered, sending piercing shafts of pain into the recesses of his head.

"Your father said to bring you to him." The man looked over Griego's shoulder at the naked bulk sprawled on the bed. He grinned. "She is much woman, that. She is as fat as a large cow."

"Shut up, fool," Griego growled, scratching his stomach where a family of lice had taken up residence. He had planned to have gone in search of the intruders by then, and be out of his father's reach. Those who held his gambling debts believed he had left Santa Fe days before.

Still standing naked at the open door, Griego tried to cut through the alcoholic fog and bring his thoughts into focus. "What is the day?"

The messenger from Don Antonio Griego shrugged. "Who knows. It is unimportant. Your father wishes to see you and that is all that matters."

Griego silently chastised himself for the fear his father's demand produced. Don Antonio Griego held his son's life in his hands, and blood did not prevent him from seeking his vengeance when upset. As he had told Miguel on more than one occasion, his older brother had already produced two males for the Griego bloodline. Miguel could consider himself expendable.

"I have important work to do for the governor. Tell my father I will attend him when it is completed," he said, attempting to close the door but finding it blocked by a spurred boot.

The man shrugged again and indicated the three men who sat on their horses watching. "Don Antonio sent us to bring you to him. We must not return without you."

The woman on the mattress rolled over onto her back and pushed aside the blankets, yawning as she scratched at the red bite marks on her belly and groin. She farted.

The messenger shook his head and grinned as Griego went in search of his pants.

The party rode out of Santa Fe and took the road southwest toward the Griego hacienda. A mile outside of town, one of Griego's *urbanos* caught up with them.

"What is it?" Griego demanded.

"The governor is frantic. We have looked everywhere for you," the man said.

One of the men sent by Don Antonio Griego laughed. "He is not hard to find if you know which whore he has not used lately. He owes money to all the others."

Griego bristled. "If you did not work for my father, your life would be worthless." He turned back to the *urbano*. "Tell the governor I have been summoned by my father. I will leave as soon as my business with him is complete."

"*Sí*, Miguel, I will tell him, but he is very much angry that you have delayed. It is four days since you returned."

"Four days? Impossible. It cannot be four days," Griego said, but he had no way of knowing how long he had been drunk.

Late that afternoon they approached the rambling huts and various buildings surrounding the Griego hacienda. Sober-faced

Indians worked the nearby fields under the watchful gaze of Don Griego's guards.

Miguel entered the courtyard of the hacienda, the smell of urine and garbage lying heavy in the still air. A group of pigs rutted through the refuse, turning it over for the flocks of chickens that followed.

The room Don Griego used for dispensing his duties opened onto a wide, shaded patio. Two heavy, high-backed chairs sat beneath spreading branches. He sat smoking in one of the chairs, his bulk hanging over the edges of the seat. The legs of both chairs had been cut down to allow his feet to touch the ground when he was seated. Miguel's brother, Guadalupe, a mirror image of his father, sat in the second chair.

"Why have you sent these fools to bring me here," Miguel Griego said.

Don Griego knocked the ash from his cigar and contemplated the glowing end a moment, letting Miguel wait before answering. "I wished to speak with you on my time, not yours."

The hint of a smile briefly touched the face of Guadalupe Griego.

"You have brought me here," Miguel said. "What is it you want? I have orders from the Governor."

"*Americanos* are marching in force toward Santa Fe, I am told, and the governor has put you in charge of the defense of *Nuevo Mexico*?" Don Griego asked in disbelief. "Do you think I am a fool? I have spoken with one of your followers. When we are done, you may go in search of these phantom intruders. You will at least convince our stupid governor he is safe. I have had you brought before me because of these," Don Antonio Griego said, taking a packet of papers from his vest pocket. "Do you know what these are? These are your debts that I have paid."

"There was no need to bring them to you. I would have taken care of them in time," Miguel said.

"Close your mouth and listen. I know of your whoring and gambling. I know of the cheap women you bed and the debts that others fear collecting because you are a Griego."

Don Griego pushed his bulk from the chair and stood to his full five feet in height. "If you choose to fool the stupid governor, that is up to you, but I know why you went off to the north. I know about your raiding and selling of these people you steal."

Guadalupe Griego could not resist the chance to offer his own observations. "Father, the Church has ordered the slave trade to cease. Fray Alvarez has the ear of the bishop."

"This Fray Alvarez is a dangerous man, yes," Don Griego said. "He has values and ideas that are not in agreement with what I want, and he cannot be bought. And if that is not enough, the governor is also afraid of the Bishop. So you see, all of this makes your selling of slaves a danger to my position and that makes you a danger to me. If you were not the result of a night in your mother's bed, I would have you shipped off to California."

Miguel Griego ran through the names of his *urbanos*, trying to figure out which one had betrayed him, and for how much. When he found out, the man would be fed to the coyotes.

"You are as worthless as an old woman," Don Griego continued. "Look at your brother. He may be as stupid as sheep, but at least he is of some use to me."

Guadalupe Griego stared at his feet.

"And now you have made an enemy of this blood-letting savage, this Romero. You are the cause of his son's death, and we will pay a price for it. Already I have had to hire extra men to guard the hacienda. Your mother and sisters are afraid he will come here and rape them," Don Griego said. He stood up and paced the shaded area beneath the patio roofing.

The sun beat down on Miguel, who stood with his hat in his hands.

"Can you imagine it, this Romero riding here to rape your mother and sisters?" Don Griego shook his head as he returned to his chair and sank slowly into the depths of its cushion. "Why he would want to come here to rape them, I do not know. If he knew them, he would look elsewhere, but they are afraid, and I will get no peace until armed men who are sworn to protect their honor surround them. I wonder who will protect these men from your sisters."

Don Griego gingered his cigar as he spoke. "But I have finally found a use for you after all these years. Yesterday, while you lay with your foul whore in Santa Fe, Don Cordero came here to my home. He rode here on his fine horse, and he said to me, Don Antonio Griego, I accept the marriage proposal that you have made for my daughter Maria. This man of such noble blood came here to my home to accept this offer," Don Griego continued. "This man, this *peninsular* who has never acknowledged my existence before."

Miguel felt his knees weaken. His father had to be mistaken, perhaps referring to another woman of the same name. Maria de Cordero, the one woman who caused him such pain when he thought of her. Maria de Cordero in his bed, every night, available to him whenever he wanted. Then his thoughts strayed to the property she was sure to bring. Enough, he calculated, to maintain his way of life without the hassles of the slave trade. He would miss those young captives. He brushed the flies from his face, drawn to him by the sweat from being made to stand in the sun "Father, when will this marriage take place?"

"Have you not been listening? Has the swelling in your pants squeezed the last ounce of your brain until there is nothing left with which to think? You will be married when Don Cordero delivers to me the deeds of the land that comes with his daughter, and the silver. The silver will pay off the debts you owe. The land is another matter. If I were a younger man, I might send your mother to Mexico and take this woman myself. You have done nothing to earn such a treasure," Don Griego said with a grin. "But this woman, she is much smarter than you, and such a tongue. You will be lucky if she doesn't talk you to death."

The old man heaved himself out of his chair and approached Miguel. He waved the cigar in his face. "When you leave here, you will run back to Santa Fe and celebrate your good fortune and think of this woman in your bed and all the trinkets her money will buy. Think of this also."

Miguel waited for his father to finish his speech. He knew nothing but word that his dinner waited would make him hurry.

The old man waddled to the far edge of the shade. "Do you remember when you were a child and I took you to see how many sheep were up in the mountains? What was it, two days we rode? And you cried because you wanted to leave and there was nothing up there but sheep shit and cactus. Do you remember that?"

"I remember this, but why do you ask me. It was so long ago it is not important."

"But it is of very great importance because that is where I will send you to live if you foul up this opportunity. If you manage to ruin this chance, you will sit on your fat ass and watch sheep fornicate for the rest of your life."

HACIENDA OF DON AUGUSTIN DE CORDERO

MacLeod sat beside the water, staring at the high mountains to the east, which were shrouded in heavy clouds. The air in the valley felt cold and damp, and along the river bank, the cottonwoods rustled in the afternoon breeze. He wondered how much longer it would be before Charbonneau could travel, and how soon before the mountain passes would be blocked with snow and ice. The only other way out led south past Santa Fe and around the southern edge of the mountains. He doubted that route was an option, especially without the required travel permits.

The sound of a horse approaching made him jump to his feet. He had waited by the river each day, but Maria had not appeared. He turned away from the river, hoping it would be her. He smiled when he saw his wish had been granted.

She held out her arms and let him help her out of the saddle, the feel of her strong body intensifying his excitement.

"I did not think I could come," she said.

"I was hoping you would. I guess you know that?"

"I am glad," she said. Her raven hair was rolled in a coil and pinned behind her head. She slipped off a glove and laid her bare hand on his arm. "We have little time and there is much about you still that I do not know."

"Why so little time?"

"My father is expected to return shortly. He has gone to see Don Griego about the marriage. He will be very angry if he discovers we are meeting."

"We've done nothing wrong. Why would he be angry?"

"For the same reason we could not talk if we met in the courtyard. It will be as if I were already married. To be seen alone with a man is to question my honor, can't you see that?" Maria said.

"That's crazy."

"Please understand this, it is our way. But let us talk of other things while there is time. Tell me more about you," Maria said.

"I told you most everything, about Ma still living on the farm back in New England. Pa died fighting the British at some place called York alongside General Pike."

"I have heard that name before, is that not strange?"

"General Pike came through here back in oh six. They arrested him and his men and sent them to Mexico. Afterwards he came back and stayed in the army. My father brought him to our home a few times, and he used to tell stories about his trip out here. I wanted to come and see for myself."

"So you came out here to see what we looked like," Maria teased.

"Hadn't planned on coming to Mexico. Mostly came to see the mountains he talked about. Never figured anything like this would happen."

"You said there were others with you. You did not want to speak of them before. Will you tell me about them now?"

With her hand still resting on his arm, MacLeod told her the story from the beginning.

"These men that died, they were good friends?" she asked.

"I guess they were more like my teachers. I knew nothing when I joined them in St. Louis. Stewart came from England."

"And the other one?"

"Belanger," MacLeod said, grinning. "He came from Canada, French Canada. I miss them, and now I've got to look after Charbonneau. They were supposed to be the ones looking after me. What about you?" he asked. "Why did you leave this Vera Cruz?"

"My father did not like some of the leaders of our country, especially the one called Antonio Lopez de Santa Anna. My father's life was threatened, and after Francisco died he felt we must leave the country."

MacLeod slipped his arm around her and held her close. "What will you do, Maria, if your father makes you marry this man?"

"I will tell you a story first. Many years ago the Indians of *Nuevo Mexico* rose up against the Spanish and drove the governor and the people out. The churches were desecrated and many of the priests were killed, then a man was sent to try to convince the Indians that we would return and that they should surrender peacefully. His name was Don Diego de Vargas Zapata Lujan Ponce de Leon, and he appeared before the Indians in Santa Fe and told them he would not hurt them if they surrendered and came back to the Church. With Don Diego on this journey was a wooden statue of the Virgin Mary. It had been rescued from the church in Santa Fe when the people fled. They took her to El Paso, and there she remained until Don Diego brought her back to Santa Fe. On the journey he showed her to the Indians and told them they should live in peace because their Mother loved them all. She is called *La Conquistadora,* Our Lady of the Conquest. If you visit my church in Santa Fe you would see her."

"What happened to the Indians?"

"For a time they lived in peace, but then they rebelled again and Don Diego was forced to defeat them," Maria said. She walked away from him and gazed out toward the darkening mountains. They said he was tall and handsome, and he spoke with a soft voice. They say he was just and kind."

"What happened to him?"

"He died shortly after and he is buried beneath the floor of the church in Santa Fe. Father Alvarez showed me the place. Don Diego had great patience and great faith. It is his example I will follow." She turned to MacLeod and smiled. "Perhaps someday someone like Don Diego will come and rescue me."

"I wish I could be the one," MacLeod said, feeling his face flush when he realized what he had said.

Maria held his face in her hands while tears ran down her cheeks. "I wish you could, too," she said and leaned forward to brush his lips with her own.

"Someone's coming," MacLeod said, releasing her and stepping out from behind the trees as a rider approached at a gallop.

Maria recognized the man. "Juan, what is it?"

"Señorita, you must come at once. Your father has returned and wishes to speak with you."

"Is something wrong?"

"No, but he is very angry."

"Thank you, Juan. I will come at once."

MacLeod helped her mount. "Suppose it would be better if I stayed behind a spell, so we aren't seen together like you said."

"It is too late. Someone must have told him. If not he will learn soon enough."

The man appeared reluctant to leave. "Señorita, please hurry."

Maria turned to MacLeod as they neared the rear gate of the hacienda. She held up her hand as he started to speak. "Listen to me, there is little time. It is certain he will refuse to allow me to speak to you again and will have someone watch over me. This time we have spent together is more meaningful than anything in my life. Please, will you remember me always when you have returned?"

"What if I don't leave?" MacLeod blurted without having thought of the consequences.

"You must leave. You are not welcome here in New Mexico. They will arrest you, and I could not bear the thought of what they would do to you." Tears ran down her cheeks. "Promise me."

"I promise."

"Vaya con dios, William Wallace MacLeod."

"Maria, I love you."

With a gloved hand to her lips she spun her horse and galloped into the courtyard.

MacLeod unsaddled his horse and turned it loose in the corral. He heard his name called as he entered the courtyard and turned to see Don Cordero and Maria approach.

"I have been informed my daughter has been meeting you secretly, against my wishes."

"I was not told I could not see her."

"She is to be married, and she knows she must not associate with a man without someone to watch over her."

"Watch over her for what?" MacLeod wanted to know.

"I have explained as much as I am prepared to. I offered you my home and my hospitality while your friend's wounds healed. Now it is time for you to return to your own country. Your horses and enough supplies for you to make it back to your country will be made ready for you in the morning."

The last few weeks MacLeod had spent thinking more about Maria than about leaving. Don Cordero ordering them to leave brought on a problem he had figured he would get to when the time came, and maybe Charbonneau would be well enough to make the decision. He looked to the range of mountains rising high above the valley and knew their only way out would be to retrace the way they came. But would he see her again before they left?

The time they had shared was unlike anything he had ever experienced with Jeanette Charbonneau. In fact, he and Jeanette had never spent any time alone, and had hardly spoken. He watched Don Cordero stride across the courtyard and enter the living quarters. Maria turned for a moment and looked back to where MacLeod stood, then followed her father though the door.

18

MacLeod lay on the thin mattress and listened to the steady drip of rain on the roof.

"I think we get some weather," Charbonneau said from the far side of the room.

"I'm going to round up our horses and gear," MacLeod said, getting to his feet. "I can tell you one thing. I ain't looking forward to packing that damned black mule."

Puddles of rainwater dotted the courtyard. The main household appeared quiet. The big black mule stood on three legs, eyeing MacLeod as if daring him to come within striking distance.

"I never understood why Belanger never gotten rid of you," MacLeod said.

He found their gear and the supplies Don Cordero had promised stacked beneath the overhanging patio. He spoke softly to the black mule as pulled the packsaddle from the pile.

An hour later, the mule and the little bay mare were packed and the horses saddled. MacLeod noted the silent courtyard, as if everyone had been told to stay away from him.

Charbonneau stood by his horse, leaning on Stewart's musket. He handed the gun to MacLeod and waited to be helped into his saddle. His face appeared drawn and painfully thin from his ordeal.

Not the best condition to be attempting the long trip ahead, MacLeod thought. What would he tell Jeanette and her mother if he arrived in St. Louis alone?

"Sure sorry about us having to leave like this. I should have listened to you about the girl. I just couldn't help myself, her being so pretty and all."

"If not the women, then something else, eh? Maybe we stay too long and end up like Chouteau and DeMunn or some of the others. We end up in Mexico in jail. Better we go now. That way we come back sooner for the furs," Charbonneau said with a grimace. "You think about those furs and the money they bring. That make you feel better, like a good drink of whiskey, eh."

MacLeod slid the musket under the tarp on the bay and said, "Yeah, but right now I'd rather be fifty miles from St. Louis on a clear day."

A figure in a long, dark shawl dashed through the rain puddles from the far side of the courtyard. MacLeod knew it was Maria. When she reached him, she pulled something from within the folds of her shawl and handed it to MacLeod.

"Take it, please," she said.

The tiny silver cross and chain lay weightless in his hand. He touched his lips to it and wrapped it tightly in his fist. "Maria, come with us," he blurted.

She shook her head and wiped the tears away with the back of a hand.

"I cannot, William."

As she turned to go the striking figure of Don Cordero appeared in the doorway. He started toward them but halted when a voice called out from the gate.

"It is Señor Griego."

A group of riders burst through the gate and scrambled to a halt in the center of the courtyard. MacLeod watched as a short, thick-bodied man, wearing clothes fancier than any he had ever seen, whirled his horse about and reined it back onto its haunches. The men with him laughed.

"Señor Griego, welcome to my home," Don Cordero said, holding both hands out in greeting.

Despite Don Cordero's words, MacLeod didn't think he was pleased by the display of bravado.

"It is him," Maria whispered. "The one I am to marry. Oh, William, he is also with the authorities."

"Don Cordero, thank you. My father sends his greetings."

"I am sorry he could not bring them himself, but please come and join me in cup of hot chocolate. My wife is famous for her chocolate."

MacLeod watched the man lower himself to the ground. He was built like Belanger but did not carry the weight well. His men had not dismounted but sat looking knowingly at Maria.

MacLeod realized his own rifle and pistol were still in the room. He edged over toward Charbonneau's horse and placed his hand on the stock of the musket, thankful he had taken the time to reload it and change the flint.

Charbonneau moved his horse to conceal MacLeod's movements. "*Mon ami*, there are too many, and maybe they leave us alone."

"They won't like it if Maria comes with us," MacLeod said.

"I must stay. I have told you why."

The only weapons MacLeod could see were the two pistols in Griego's belt. The others carried lances.

Don Cordero said something to Griego and pointed toward MacLeod and Charbonneau. Griego looked as if he had been shot. The others whispered among themselves, their hands instinctively tightening on their lances.

"My father is telling them about your escape from the slave traders and how you came to be here," Maria said.

"Then why does that fellow look so grim?" MacLeod said.

"I do not know."

Miguel Griego began gesturing at MacLeod and Charbonneau as his voice rose in anger.

"He is telling my father that it was you and many others who attacked him and killed two of his men, and the governor has sent him in search of you. Now he is telling my father that the other men you came with were killed by his men, and you ran away when he was preparing to attack."

Don Cordero nodded his head and walked over to MacLeod and Charbonneau. There was no friendship in his voice when he spoke. "I have offered you my home and my hospitality because I believed your story. Now I find it is all a lie."

MacLeod pointed at Griego as he spoke. "If he was there like he says he was, then he's one of them. There were Indians with him, too. I shot one of them. You can ask the old man, he'll tell you."

Don Cordero held up a hand. "Enough. I am convinced you have lied to me. Sebastian was obviously confused about what he saw."

"Begging your pardon, sir, but it would seem kinda hard to be confused about seeing people shot down. Ask the Indian woman. They can't both be confused about somebody bent on killing them."

Movement on his left caused MacLeod to look away from Don Cordero. While they spoke Griego's men had shifted their positions and lowered the tips of their lances.

"The girl is not here, unfortunately. However, I am sure she would agree with the story Señor Griego has related," Don Cordero said.

"But, Father, Peche has told me so. What Señor MacLeod says is true. It must be that Miguel is lying."

"She must be mistaken," Don Cordero, said turning to MacLeod. "The governor has given Señor Griego his permission to search for you and bring you to Santa Fe. You and your friend must go with them immediately."

"I know what happens to people in this country even when they've done no wrong," MacLeod said. He eased the musket out from beneath the tarp, wishing he had his pistol to go along with it.

There were four men, besides Griego, but MacLeod figured the others would not act without Griego's orders. He thumbed the hammer back to full cock and swung the barrel in a smooth arc until it pointed directly at Griego.

Maria cried out, "No, William, please. They will kill you."

As they spoke Miguel Griego shifted sideways trying to move out of the line of fire.

Charbonneau could only watch.

"Tell him to stop moving and stand still," MacLeod said to Don Cordero.

Maria pleaded, "William, please put your gun down. There are too many of them."

"Come with us. You can see my country for yourself."

"I am sorry, it is not possible. I have told you this."

"Then tell those others to drop their weapons or this strutting pheasant will have a hole in him."

Don Cordero spoke to Griego's troops. Reluctantly they dropped their lances in the dirt and backed away. That left Griego standing alone. He pleaded with Don Cordero.

"What's he saying?" MacLeod demanded.

"He is saying that no harm will come to you or your friend," Don Cordero said.

With a look of incredulity on his face MacLeod let out a harsh laugh. "And you believe him? This man ordered those people shot down as they stood there helpless."

"He has denied that," Don Cordero said. "You are obviously mistaken about the situation."

While they argued, Maria stood by MacLeod's side with her hand resting on his arm. "Father, will you personally guarantee that they will reach Santa Fe safely?"

Don Cordero spoke to Miguel Griego. There could be little doubt about the look of hatred on his face. Slowly he nodded his head, glaring at MacLeod.

"You have my word," Don Cordero said. "No harm will come to you and your friend."

Sitting his horse in silence throughout the exchange, Charbonneau finally spoke. "I think we straighten this out with this governor. He will see it is all big mistake."

"You think we should go with them?" MacLeod asked.

"There are too many, and I am not well enough to try to escape. I think maybe this is the only way."

"Please, listen to him," Maria said.

MacLeod looked into her eyes. "Will you be all right when we go?"

"Yes."

Only the restless shuffling of the horses broke the stillness in the courtyard. Finally, MacLeod lowered the rifle and watched Griego scamper off to find his horse.

"I hope your word is as good as you think it is, Don Cordero, otherwise we're dead men"

"You will be safe," Don Cordero said, "But you must give up your guns for now. They will be given back to you when the governor says you may leave."

"What difference is it if I hang onto them?"

"They will not ride with you while you have your weapons," Don Cordero said.

Gently, Maria took the musket from his hands. MacLeod slipped his own rifle out from under the tarp and pulled his pistol from his belt.

"I will keep them for you, until you return. Please go now," she whispered and stood on her toes to kiss his cheek.

Don Cordero grabbed Maria by the arm and hustled her toward the house.

SANTA FE

On the morning of the third day of travel, they got their first view of Santa Fe, although MacLeod had formed his own opinion, based on General Pike's stories. He could see the green of the low shrubs growing alongside the narrow stream running through the town and the rutted cart tracks that constituted a street, edged on both sides by low mud huts. Tall steeples marked the churches, said to constitute half of the ruling government.

Feeling the need to talk, MacLeod urged his horse up alongside Charbonneau's. "Soon as we get to town, we'll see about getting some dry clothes and hot food. It ain't far now."

Ahead, mud houses seemingly built wherever their owner's whim took them, marked the outskirts of the town. Not a tree or shrub grew in sight, and the recent rains had turned the roads into avenues of mud.

As they rode slowly through the town, women with children balanced on their hips called out to the troopers, while emancipated dogs chased bare-footed youngsters. The air reeked of open cesspools and manure, and collided with the smells of cooking emanating from open doorways and windows.

At the intersection of two roads, an old man leaned into the wooden wheel of a cart stuck axle deep in the mud. Motivated by a constant stream of abuse, a team of oxen strained against their yoke. The troopers swore at the man but none offered to help, carefully circling the cart and continuing down the street toward a walled compound in the distance.

Griego had ridden ahead. MacLeod watched him dismount and enter a low doorway to the right of the gate leading into the compound.

The troopers halted in front of a low-roofed, mud building, not much different from the other buildings in town. An uneasy porch roof hung precariously over length of the building, which was shaded by an overhanging cover of branches and thatched stalks. Across the narrow street small shops squeezed themselves between mud homes and smoky saloons, and at the far end of the street, the tall steeples of the church dominated a square where women wrapped in woolen shawls sold various meats and vegetables, while thin chickens fought over scraps tossed aside by the women.

"Maybe she look better in the sun, eh?" Charbonneau said.

"Pretty much like General Pike described it. As long as we get somewhere warm and dry soon, I don't care what the town looks like."

Two of Griego's men came forward and began untying MacLeod's hands as the remaining troops filed through the gate into the walled compound.

While Griego engaged in an animated conversation with a tall, thin man, the pair of troopers pulled MacLeod from his horse and pushed him forward to follow Griego into the building.

Inside a dimly lit room, a short, obese man sat dwarfed behind a heavily scarred plank table being used as a desk. The thin man MacLeod had seen talking to Griego stood to the side of the desk.

MacLeod surveyed his surroundings. The thick adobe walls were similar to those of the Cordero hacienda but had not been whitewashed in some time. Tiny slotted windows laced with fly-filled spider webs let in filtered light. Bear and buffalo hides covered the dirt floor, while the odor of unwashed bodies hung heavy in the air.

Griego approached the desk and offered the hint of a bow to the man seated behind the desk. The man eyed MacLeod with something between fear and fury. He and Griego spoke for a moment before the thin man introduced himself.

"I am Juan de Zavalda, aide to Don Fecunda Melgares, our Most Excellent Governor of Nuevo Mexico. You will tell us your name, and also that of the other man outside, and why you have come here without permission."

MacLeod took a step forward, somewhat awed to be in the presence of the governor. "My name's William Wallace MacLeod, and my friend out there is Mr. Lucien Charbonneau, from St. Louis. We only came to get help for Mr. Charbonneau. Don't know how we could have gotten permission unless we came first, but since we're here, now I expect we could ask you for it now."

The governor did not wait for Zavalda to finish interpreting but leapt to his feet, his face red with rage, and screamed, *"Silencio."*

Zavalda managed to calm the governor while Griego waited his turn. "You have insulted our governor with your lies. We have knowledge you and others came for other reasons," Zavalda said.

MacLeod couldn't believe what he was hearing. "My friend was wounded and needed attention. That's why we came, and if you care you would have someone look to him."

"Your friend will be taken care of in due time. However, the issue before us is why you are in our country where, in case you have lost your memory, you have killed two of our people," Zavalda said, his voice rising in anger.

MacLeod felt they hadn't been listening, or didn't want to hear. "Those fellows I shot had already shot half a dozen of your people, and they were about to kill two more on the orders of this one standing here. He pointed at Griego. "You don't seem to be too upset about that," he shouted.

During Zavalda's explanation to the governor, Griego exploded with outrage. He pointed a finger at MacLeod and shook it in anger.

While both Zavalda and Griego fought for Governor Melgares' attention, MacLeod tried to remember what he had told Don Cordero about the furs.

Zavalda spoke again. "The governor has decided to allow you to tell your story. You will remember that we already are aware of much of it from Señor Griego."

He began the story in St. Louis and explained what had happened on their way home, and why they had decided to try to make it to Santa Fe to get help for Charbonneau.

Governor Melgares rose from his desk and paced the width of the narrow room , while Zavalda continued to relate MacLeod's story, and for some moments afterward.

"I have listened to your explanation with much interest and I am amused at your obvious lies," Zavalda said.

MacLeod exploded. "They aren't lies—"

A guard jabbed him hard with the muzzle of a musket, sending MacLeod to his knees.

Zavalda continued to interpret the governor's response, ignoring MacLeod's outburst. "You are not like you say, our governor says. You say these furs you took from our streams and rivers were stolen by these Indians, yet you attack my militia single-handed. And why did these Indians not steal those furs that our Captain Griego seized and brought here with him. Could you not have driven off a few Indians? How many of you were there, four?" Governor Melgares appeared to be enjoying his harangue as he continued pacing. "It was only because of the bravery of Señor Griego and his men that you have not succeeded in your efforts to attack our people while they slept."

The governor came to a halt behind his desk and smiled while Lieutenant Zavalda continued translating. "No, you are not what you say. You are part of an army sent to build a fort on the Rio de Las Animas. This you cannot deny."

MacLeod could not help but laugh at the absurdity of the governor's remarks. The laugh earned him another jab with the guard's musket and enraged Melgares.

"I know these things. I am the Governor. I was appointed by the King of Spain," Melgares shouted. His face flushed as his anger increased and for a moment his words were unintelligible to Zavalda. Finally, Melgares' temper subsided enough for him to continue. "Yes, you were sent here to build a fort in our country, so that you could support your troops and then steal our silver from our mines. You will never reach Santa Rita and our mines. I have placed myself between your army and our mines, and you will be beaten and destroyed before you reach any of our cities."

MacLeod watched Griego's smirk grow.

"I myself would lead the defense of our proud country as I did many years ago when I was sent to defeat and capture your Lieutenant Pike."

At the mention of Pike, MacLeod couldn't restrain himself. "Beggin' your pardon, Mr. Governor, but you didn't capture General Pike. He came of his own accord after being told he would be welcome. It was only after he and his men put down their arms voluntarily that they were arrested."

As Zavalda explained to Governor Melgares what MacLeod had said, the Governor began pounding his desk. "Lies, lies! It is all lies.

Zavalda barked out an order and the two guards seized MacLeod. Zavalda stood in front of MacLeod, blocking the governor's line of sight. "Let me warn you. Our Governor has the power to do whatever he wishes with you, including having you both shot. Now, do you wish me to inform him that you have called him a liar again?"

MacLeod fought to control his temper. General Pike had related to him the deception they had used to disarm him and his party. He could not find the answers to counter their lies or accusations, and the governor appeared to believe only what he wanted to believe.

The governor sat down at his desk and smiled, motioning to his aide to continue.

"The governor would like you to tell him now, again, why you chose to come to Nuevo Mexico," Zavalda said.

"Like I said before, I thought we could get help in Santa Fe, a doctor or somebody for my friend. There wasn't any other reason."

"So you knew where Santa Fe was?" Zavalda questioned.

"Well, we thought it was somewhere to the south, and we figured we'd eventually run into someone to ask."

"But instead of asking the first people you run into you shot them," Governor Melgares shouted as he stood pounding his fist on his desk.

MacLeod wondered how much longer the charade of Zavalda translating would go on, when it appeared the esteemed governor spoke enough English to communicate by himself. Then he figured it could be for Griego's benefit.

"Excuse me, sir," MacLeod said, "but Don Cordero told me those men were probably slave traders, which makes this one here one of them, in case you didn't know already." MacLeod knew before he finished his outburst he should have held his tongue for once.

The governor smiled and waved his finger at MacLeod, ignoring his accusations against Griego. "Let me clear your mind of these tales you have heard about this trade in slaves. It is so much nonsense. Whenever we recapture some of our children who have been stolen by the Navajo, or the Apache, we hear these stories. Oh, I am sure there may have been a few instances where some Indian children were captured by our people and raised as ours, but were they not better off? Were they not saved from a life of a filthy existence to live a wonderful life as children of our Church? As far as the wild Indians are concerned, what they do amongst themselves is of no concern to me. They will steal or trade their own children if there is a profit to them. This slave business is much like your story—so many stories, so little truth. Now, I have much work to do and this incident has tired me much also."

"Shall I have them taken away?" Zavalda asked.

"*Un momento.* First, I must remind this *Americano* of what he is charged," Melgares said. "You have entered my country without permission and you have killed two of my men. I should have you shot. Maybe I should have you shot twice, such is the extent of your crimes." The governor waved his hands and picked up the paper he had been studying when MacLeod first entered the office. The two guards came forward and seized MacLeod by the arms.

"What about my friend outside? He needs to see a doctor."

"I will think about it, but we have only one man who claims he is a doctor, and he is usually drunk. Perhaps I should question your friend first. Maybe he will be more respectful and truthful with his answers."

"He can't tell you anything that I haven't. Besides, he wasn't involved in the fight."

Governor Melgares leaped to his feet and shook his finger at MacLeod again. "Exactly, and he did not kill any of my people. I may even let him go. Think about that while you sit in my *calabos*. I think our weather is soon to change, and I am told our *calabos* needs repair. We will see how you people who invade our blessed country like Spanish hospitality."

Melgares motioned to the guards. "Take him away and bring me the other one."

MacLeod stared through the barred window at a dismal scene. The governor had been right. The weather had not improved, and for weeks MacLeod watched the people of Santa Fe wallow through the mud as they went about their business.

Nor had the governor been wrong about the condition of the jail, unless he could be accused of understatement in saying it needed repairs. The floor in MacLeod's cell mirrored the streets outside his window, and he had long ago given up attempting to stay dry.

A number of times he asked to see the governor. That brought the sallow-faced guard, who wore the remnants of a uniform and a broken sword stuffed through his belt. The man would come to attention in the mud outside of MacLeod's cell and roll his eyes before announcing that "Governor Fecunda Melgares no Santa Fe," which MacLeod took to mean he was not available.

Night again, but the rain had stopped. MacLeod could see stars between the clouds, and clear nights meant somewhere in town a fandango would be held. The strains of music could be heard above the drunken singing of the revelers. As always, when a fandango began, the guards released the other prisoners and everyone went off to join in the celebration. Hours later, both groups staggered back to their respective places, sometimes the guards carrying the prisoners back to their cells, but just as often the prisoners helped the guards return to their posts.

Two nights later, MacLeod sat on his pallet and listened to the merry making. A key being inserted into the lock on his door alerted him. The door opened and a cloaked figure slipped inside.

"Who is it?"

The figure turned and pushed aside the hood of the cloak, the face illuminated in the pale light of the moon.

"Maria," he said.

She came to him and put her arms around him. They held each other for some time before either spoke.

"What are you doing here?" MacLeod said, not wanting to release her from his arms.

"I came to see Father Alvarez, to ask for his guidance about my marriage, and to see you, of course."

They held each other again. MacLeod found her lips and felt her respond, and for a moment it didn't matter that he was in jail in a foreign country, or that he might be sent to Chihuahua. He pushed himself away and held her at arm's length. "Tell me what this man Alvarez said."

"He said I must do as my father wishes. There is no other way. He said he would pray for me."

"A lot of good his praying for you is going to do if you have to marry that man."

"You must not say those things. Father Alvarez will pray for me, and if there is another way, I will be shown it."

They sat on his pallet and held each other by the hand.

"My guard never leaves for this long at a time. He's sure to be back soon. You best go before he does."

Maria giggled. "He has been distracted. Peche has taken him down by the river. She will keep him there all night. Now, I have also asked Father Alvarez to speak to the governor about you and your friend. He may be able to help."

"I don't even know if Mr. Charbonneau is here. No one wants to tell me where they're keeping him."

"Father Alvarez will find him, and he will come and visit you also."

"Governor Melgares might not allow it."

"Our governor is afraid of the Church.

"What does this Father Alvarez fellow know about us?" MacLeod asked. He did not want to reveal anything to this man that might hurt Maria.

She smiled and laid her hand on MacLeod's face. "He knows my heart is with you, and no one else."

"Maria, tell me what has happened since I left. Has your father told you when you have to marry?"

She pulled her feet up under her and leaned her head on his shoulder. She remained quiet for some time before answering. "Miguel Griego returned to speak with my father about his chasing your friends out of our country and to try to speak to me. I said I could not see him, as I was ill."

"Did your father believe him?"

"I don't think so. He spoke with Sebastian again, the old man you saved. But what is important about Miguel coming to our home is that Peche saw him. When they left, she told me that he was the one who took her and Sebastian."

"You told your father this?"

"Yes. From then on he treated me with more care. I think now he regrets his decision."

MacLeod felt an enormous sense of relief. "He won't make you marry Griego, will he? He'll change his mind."

"No, he cannot go back on his word. He has never done that before."

MacLeod's sense of relief vanished. He could not bring himself to believe the hard headedness of these people, especially her father.

"You're going to marry him even though you know what he's done?" MacLeod said in disbelief.

Maria shook her head and pushed him away. "Listen to me," she said. "Do not to speak until I have finished."

"My father insists that I marry Miguel, and Father Alvarez has said there is nothing else that can be done if it is his wish. I said to you that I would do whatever I had to do, but there are things that even he has no control over. I have decided that when I marry Miguel Griego, I will not be pure as he expects me to be. I will not give him the satisfaction of being the first man I lie with."

She took MacLeod's hand in hers and held it to her cheek. Through the bars of the window the pale moonlight shone upon her face. MacLeod let his fingers caress her face. His own burnt with embarrassment, hearing Maria speak with such openness.

"I don't understand. What is it you're going to do?"

"William," she said, moving closer to him. "I want you to touch me."

She took his hand from her cheek and held it to her hip. "You know the places a man touches a women, do you not?" she whispered.

His breathing grew shallow. Maria reached down to the hem of her long skirt and raised it above her knees. She took his hand again and placed it on her bare thigh.

"Maria, I don't know if I can do this." MacLeod's voice broke.

"This is what I have decided, William. I want you to touch me. You know where. You will be the first."

He felt the warmth of her bare flesh as his hand moved slowly up her thigh. He gasped when his hand reached the firmness of her buttocks, and he realized she was naked beneath her skirt.

She lay back on the straw pallet and drew her skirt up over her hips and held her arms out to him.

Later, when her tears had subsided, and his breathing returned to normal, MacLeod pressed his lips to her cheek. "I told you before that I didn't know what love was. I do now. I'll find a way out of here and come for you, I promise."

She shook her head. "No, once I am married it will be impossible to ever see me again, and you have already made a promise to your friend."

"Nothing's impossible," MacLeod whispered.

"I will think of you always, William. I will think of this night, and I will know that there is such a thing as love."

She lay with her back to him and spoke of those things, which she cherished. She spoke of her visit to the chapel to see the wooden figurine she called *La Conquistadora* and again how the doll had come to Santa Fe with Don Diego de Vargas. She seemed to gain resolve as she talked, and MacLeod listened with his arms wrapped around her.

The first light of dawn woke them.

"I must go," she said, sitting up and brushing the straw from her clothing. She leaned down and kissed him. They clung together until she pushed him away and hurried to the door, where she turned toward him. "Do not wait too long to come."

MacLeod's days were filled with torment over what had transpired. He paced the narrow space between the walls of his cell knowing Maria fought her losing battle with her father. Outside, the guards busied themselves polishing their lone musket and various rusty swords. Such abnormal activity made him realize Governor Melgares had returned.

Two days later the guards escorted MacLeod across the plaza to the governor's Palace.

"*Ah, mi amigo,*" Governor Melgares said, holding up his arms in greeting.

Zavalda, the governor's aide, stepped to the side of the desk and translated. "The governor wishes to apologize for not attending to you sooner. He wishes you to tell him how you have been treated."

MacLeod laughed.

"What does that mean? You have not been treated well? Is the food not plentiful? Is your cot and cell not comfortable? Tell me."

"You can tell your governor the slop he calls food I wouldn't feed my horse, and it wouldn't hurt none if he could find a blanket."

"The governor apologizes for this. He says to tell you we here in Nuevo Mexico are proud of the manner that we treat, our prisoners. He says he is outraged by your treatment and orders me to see those responsible are punished."

MacLeod wondered when this conversation had taken place, since the governor hadn't said a word.

Governor Melgares gave up the pretense of having his aide translate for him and spoke up. "If it were not for so many duties I am expected to fulfill, I would have spoken with you sooner. Surely in your country a person in my position has many people to help him. You would not believe the papers I must fill out each month to send to Mexico, and everything must have two copies made." He groaned and indicated the numerous stacks of papers littering his desk, some held in place by weighted objects. "And do you see anyone else doing this work? No, only I, and of course, *Teniente* Zavalda. Do your men of such important positions do their own work?

"Then there are the inspection tours," Melgares continued, waving his hands in the air. "And the problems with the *alcalde mayores,* and those who I have appointed to collect taxes steal the grain and leave me little or nothing to send to Durango. What do you think they do when I cannot meet my tax quota? They think I steal it. But most of all, I must deal with the Church and their greedy, accusing, threatening…."

Zavalda spoke to the governor, who glanced around to make sure no one else heard his remarks.

"Yes, yes, let us return to other things. He rose from behind his desk and began to pace. "Did you know that your Lieutenant Pike and I became good friends?"

"The general mentioned you," MacLeod said, surprised at the change in direction the conversation had taken.

Melgares looked amazed. "He did? And how do you know this?"

"He and my father were soldiers together. The general stayed overnight at our house whenever he was on his way to Boston."

"And he spoke of his time in Nuevo Mexico, yes? I suppose he never told you he was a spy for General Wilkinson. That he was sent here to witness our strength."

"Well, sir," MacLeod said, figuring he should correct this mistake. "No, but I don't know why General Wilkinson would want to spy on you. There were rumors he took money from the Spanish down there in New Orleans."

Melgares looked stunned. "Impossible. That is another of your lies. He sent your Pike to check our defenses."

"General Pike said he wasn't in Mexico when you met him at his stockade."

"Most absolutely he was. Mexico is all the way to that big river many, many miles from here."

"What big river you referring to?"

"You know the one, it is there," Melgares said, pointing toward the east.

Zavalda decided to explain. "I believe the governor means the Mississippi River."

Melgares sat down and shuffled the few papers on his desk. "But we should not be arguing about such things. We were speaking of Lieutenant Pike. How I remember our trip to Chihuahua. At each town I would send word ahead to arrange for a fandango and for the prettiest girls to come and dance. In El Paso we stayed three days. How was your Lieutenant Pike when you had the good fortune to see him last?"

"It was General Pike, Governor, and he died in the battle of York a few years ago."

"You are sure of this?"

"Yes, sir. My father was with him. They were both killed when a powder magazine blew up."

For some reason it seemed to upset the governor. He flopped into his chair and sighed. "It is the most supreme duty soldiers such as the lieutenant and I have, to die in glorious battle for our countries. I salute him."

"I'm sure the general would have appreciated your thoughts," MacLeod said, remembering some of the comments Pike had made about Melgares and his self-serving manner.

MacLeod shuffled his feet while he waited, figuring there had to be another reason for him to be brought there other than to talk about General Pike. At least Griego wasn't around to add his lies to the conversation.

"I have been brought these," Governor Melgares said, pointing to a pair of beaver pelts lying beside the desk. "Is it possible they are yours?"

MacLeod had wondered what had become of the two packs of furs. He picked one up and studied it. "Can't say for sure."

"I thought once more of your story," the governor continued. "Perhaps you are not spies after all. Señor Griego could be mistaken. Perhaps you are what you claim to be, I say to myself. Not all of your story, of course, but a part of it. It is in your favor that I was given these by Señor Griego, although I can see no use for such small furs."

MacLeod felt it would be useless to argue the point.

Governor Melgares sat back, pushed the furs to one side of his desk and clasped his hands together over his immense belly.

"What part ain't true?" MacLeod said, stalling for time. Did the Governor have both packs of furs or just the two pelts?

"Oh, I do not believe this story of some Indians stealing these things from you. Perhaps you and this other one who came with you stole them from your other friends, and then killed them, and not like you say that some Indians did this thing. There are many such possibilities."

MacLeod couldn't help laughing at the absurd accusations. "Everything I've told you so far is the truth." Well, almost everything, he thought, at least the important parts.

"So you say, but I have other thoughts about this. Here is my final offer to you. Turn over your furs to me that I believe you have hidden somewhere, and I will reconsider your confinement. I may even forget the atrocities you have committed here in our peaceful country. I will even forget that you might have been looking for a place to build a fort in Spanish territory, perhaps on the Rio Animas. I will forget this also."

Here was his chance to get out of this miserable place. If only he knew for sure that Charbonneau was all right. "You said we would speak about my friend later. I want to know about him now."

"Your friend is doing well. I had him taken to a more comfortable place, where he will be cared for. Now," Melgares continued, "you accept my offer and turn these furs over to me so that I might see that you are speaking the truth. You can be assured that they will be returned to you when you are set free, or most of them. Some may be used to help pay for your keep while you are here. So, where are they?"

And beavers fly like eagles, MacLeod thought, remembering the stories of the other parties picked up in New Mexico and stripped of their goods. No one had ever received compensation for the stolen property.

"I can't give you them, governor. "Like I said, the Utes took them and if you want I'll take you to where I buried my friends, if it'll do any good. And what about the atrocities your Señor Griego committed? Or does it only count one way?"

"Señor Griego is an officer in the *urbanos* and is trusted fully," Governor Melgares shrieked, causing Lieutenant Zavalda to step forward and signal the guards. They seized MacLeod's arms and held him fast.

"The governor warns you that time is short and his offer will not last long. He says the furs will prove your innocence. Otherwise, it is obvious you are a spy."

MacLeod couldn't resist one more comment as they dragged him toward the door. "Who runs this place anyway, you or these Griegos?"

Somewhere North of Santa Fe

Miguel Griego watched them gather. They sat on their horses and waited for him to approach. This is good, he thought, they are afraid.

A man slouched on his horse off to one side, his face swollen and purple. Griego kept his eyes on the man who sold the information about his exploits to Don Antonio. It took time, but he had found out who had money to spend. Then he beat a confession out of him. He beckoned to the man. "Do you remember the place of trees on the river last year?"

"Where the Comanche gathered?"

"That is the place," Griego said. "You will go there and find them." Griego took a small pack off the back of his saddle and gave it to the man. "Show these to the Comanche and find out what they will give for them." Griego watched as the man wheeled his horse and rode out of the arroyo toward the south. He thought about the rest of the furs Don Cordero had turned over to him. If what the *Americano* had said was true about trapping these animals, perhaps there were many more of them someplace. But who would want them? He hoped he would soon know.

The anger rose again, forcing him to ride off by himself. Everything he wanted had suddenly disappeared like smoke in a windstorm when the man came to him and told him of Maria's visit to the jail. The man had become curious and waited through the night and watched her slip away at dawn. Griego knew they now laughed at him behind his back. "I will kill them both," he swore. "But not the way they would wish to be killed. They will die again and again."

A man stationed on the ridge above waved and pointed to the south. Griego nodded. Soon the news of Maria's sin would reach the ears of his father, and Miguel did not wish to be present when it did. He knew he would be blamed. He also knew Don Griego's hatred for Maria's father would be even greater, and that was where his salvation lay.

Miguel Griego's plan would please his father. Don Griego lusted for the land and money the marriage would bring. However, he could never live with the fact he married his son off to a woman who had given herself to another first. *Why did she not waited until after the marriage, as many women do?*

"How long?" Griego called up to a man on the rim of the arroyo.

"Not long," the man answered, edging his horse back a few steps to remain out of sight.

Griego surveyed the men serving him. He knew they watched or a sign of weakness. They were vultures. For their silence, Griego had offered riches beyond their greatest dreams, and for betrayal, only death. He knew much depended on his handling of Romero, and possibly these furs would give him the silver he needed to pay off the debts his father knew nothing about.

A word came from above, and Griego knew it was time. He ordered everyone to move to their prearranged places.

Sometime that night he would be in a bed in Santa Fe with a woman. Others would not be so lucky, but that was the price they must pay for what they had done to him.

The early day promised a warm ride back to the hacienda of her father's friend, where Maria planned to spend the night. In the distance, the towering peaks of the Sangre de Cristo Mountains stood out against a sky too blue for the eyes to rest on. Deep-green junipers sprouted from the red earth in contrast to the black of the mountain mass and the blue of the sky. Maria thought that part of the trip held the most beauty. Someone told her Francisco Vasquez Coronado had camped there two hundred years before.

Ahead, the two men sent by her father to escort her back to the Cordero hacienda halted to let her catch up. She did not want to catch up. She wanted to return to Santa Fe, where she could see him, or at least know he was near. She smiled, remembering how clumsy each of them were and how tender and how wanting, and how much she wished she could lie with him each night. "Oh, please, William Wallace MacLeod," she whispered. "Please come for me before it is too late."

Peche grunted, pointing toward a group of riders who suddenly appeared from the depths of an arroyo.

"Who are they, I wonder?" Maria said.

The two out-riders halted and waited.

"*Urbanos*," Peche growled.

"How do you know?"

"We must ride away," Peche said, wheeling her horse around and reaching for the bridle of Maria's mare.

"Why? They can mean no harm to us."

"They are the ones who took me and Sebastian."

The approaching riders fanned out and encircled the group before Peche and Maria could respond. Others pulled Maria's guards from their horses and held them at gunpoint.

"What are you doing?" Maria said. "I am Maria de Cordero. Do you know what will happen to you when the governor learns of this?"

Miguel Griego pushed through the ring of men. "Will you be the one to tell him?"

Maria gasped, feeling a tremor of uncertainty. "Miguel, what is the meaning of this?"

"Shut up," he growled. He spoke to his men, and they moved as a group back to the hidden depths of the arroyo.

She knew she must be as strong as possible. Miguel Griego wanted to scare her. He wanted to punish her for the way she had treated him. What other reason could there be, she wondered. After all, wouldn't their marriage be punishment enough?

They followed the dry riverbed for an hour and emerged in an area far from the traveled road to Taos. Griego had not spoken since he had led the two women away.

Maria tore the reins from the hands of the man assigned to lead her horse and rode over to Griego. "Miguel, if all of this is to frighten me, I demand to know the reason?"

"S

Her eyes flared at the insult. Her father would kill this man if he had heard such words. But the shadow of doubt cooled her reply. "How dare you call me such a name?"

"I will call you a whore because you have proved to be one. Do not deny this. I have proof of it."

An icy chill flowed through her body. Someone knew of her visit to MacLeod's cell. Someone had seen her entering or leaving, even though she made every attempt to hide her identity. Could the guard have recognized her?

"And this proof, someone has told you of this thing you accuse me of?"

"Someone has told me, *si*."

"This person, you would believe him before you would believe me?"

Griego made no effort to soften his words. "He has no reason to lie, and he is too stupid to make up such a story."

Maria sensed that Griego could barely control his rage.

He edged his horse alongside hers. "You have made a fool of me and the name of Griego. You have given yourself to another man when everyone knows you were promised to me. I should kill you for it."

The truth stung. She had not thought it would hurt so much, but what else had she expected. "Do you not lie with whores every night? See how you scratch. Is your body not covered with the lice they have given you?"

"It is different with men and not something a woman should speak of," he said.

"And what is the difference?" she said, raising a gloved hand to point her finger at him. "Is it because you pay these women for your pleasure? Is that why it is different?"

"We will not talk of this. There is much difference, but it no longer matters what you think."

Maria couldn't stop herself from one last taunt. She laughed at him. "Yes, I did not pay for the pleasure he gave to me."

Miguel Griego struck her, knocking her from her horse.

When her head cleared enough for her to push herself into a sitting position, she ran her hand over the swelling on the side of her face. As she rose to her feet, Maria realized Miguel Griego had crossed a line he could never wipe away. No man in New Mexico could get away with attacking a woman of her stature. Surely he knew this. So why did he think himself safe?

Griego dismounted and gripped her upper arm, dragging her to where the others had gathered.

Two *urbanos*, dressed in short, leather jackets and beaded pants, held Peche. Cordero's two riders stood under guard a few paces away.

"Your moment of pleasure is going to be of great cost. I want you to watch this and think about what it is you have done by giving yourself away to this man.

"These people," Griego continued, indicating her father's men, "they are only doing what your father ordered them to do. They have women and they have children, I am sure, and now what will their families do?"

What are you going to do, Miguel? They have done nothing to you."

"I am going to have them shot."

"No, please," Maria cried.

Miguel Griego nodded. Two men stepped forward and fired their muskets. Maria's guards slumped to the ground.

She turned away. She had known those men and their families since she could remember. Griego grabbed her shoulders and forced her to look at the bodies. She tore herself loose and fell to her knees.

"I have not finished with you yet, whore." Griego seized her hair and forced her head back. "You will watch this."

Grinning, two others wrestled Peche to the ground and held her arms and legs while a third tore at her clothing. She fought back, but her strength was no match for the raw lust showing on their faces.

"No, leave her. It is me you want to hurt. She has done nothing to you."

"She helped you. You will watch everything."

They took their turns raping Peche, while Griego held Maria's head up to watch. Their lust spent, the men joked among themselves while keeping an eye on Griego.

Peche lay sprawled in the dirt with her knees drawn up to her chest. A trickle of blood ran down the back of her legs. She had not uttered a sound during the attack.

"What will happen to you will be much worse," Griego said.

"You are a pig. You kill two men and do this to another because you cannot have me. What kind of a man are you?"

"I am a man and that is all you need to know," Griego snarled.

Maria struck him across the face with her hand. "You are not a man; you are a stupid child in a man's body. I know a man and you are not one."

"Shut up, whore. I would have shown you what a real man is."

Maria ran the back of her hand across her eyes. She knew her words stung Griego, but she had more to say. "What have you ever done to earn the reputation of being a man? You drink yourself into oblivion every chance you get. You lie with every whore who will accept your money. You gamble away money that is your father's or money you have made selling children. You kill old men and women who have no way to protect themselves. This is what a man does? No, Miguel, this is what a coward does."

She knew of men he had killed for saying, less but she couldn't stop. "You wanted to marry me. Do you know how much I hated the idea of marrying you? What I did with this *Americano* was what I will never do with you. I gave myself to him," she cried. "He will always be the first man I lay with. I did this so I would not do it with you."

Unable to speak Griego, struck her again, knocking her to the ground.

Maria rolled unto her back and laughed through the pain.

He kicked her, and again and again, bellowing in his blood rage. "Whore! Whore!"

Griego's troops watched in silence. None dared interfere. Peche crawled toward Maria and fell across her body in an attempt to protect her from his kicks.

"Miguel!" The shout came from the lookout posted some distance away. The man pointed toward the south. "They come."

Miguel Griego climbed onto his horse and rode to where the lookout sat high above the temporary camp. For some time they watched together.

Her body screamed in pain, but Maria would not cry out. She tried to avert her gaze from the crumpled bodies that lay in the dirt and mouthed a silent prayer for their families.

Peche helped her to a sitting position, and they held each other while the late afternoon sun cast long shadows across the rocks and desert floor. The air cooled.

Griego rode back to the group. He looked nervous, Maria thought. She had wondered about what he would do next. He couldn't let them live. How could he explain the beatings and the killings? They were not disposable peons or Indians. He must kill us, she thought, but why is he waiting?

She felt Peche stiffen.

"What is it?" she asked.

"Apache."

Maria turned. They came in a single file, a line of ten, their bare legs hugging their horses, black hair chopped, and carrying lances loose in their hands.

The *urbanos* fingered their own lances and muskets. No one spoke.

The Indians fanned out in a half circle, facing Griego and his men. Maria and Peche sat on the ground between the two groups.

Griego barked an order and one of his men pulled the women to their feet. An Apache walked his horse forward and halted in front of Griego.

Maria had never seen anyone as menacing. The Apache's black eyes speared her soul as he looked down at her. She couldn't tell his age; his hair was longer than the others and showed streaks of grey. Scars showed white against the sienna skin on his muscular body. His hands were large and calloused. But it was the face that sent cold fear through her body. A face devoid of expression, colder than anything she could imagine, but lined with pain and suffering.

"Who is he?" Maria whispered.

"Romero."

"How do you know?"

"There is only one like him. Who else could it be?"

Maria's eyes shifted back to Griego. Very nervous, she thought, seeing the shadow of fear beneath the weak smile.

"You have come, that is good," Griego said.

A young warrior rode up beside Romero. He looked Spanish rather than Apache, and spoke for Romero. "You have something my father wants," he said.

Griego shifted in his saddle. "*Si*, he will like what I have for him."

"We do not see the one who killed my brother. Where is this strange one who kills from far away?"

"I have brought you his women. This is she." Griego pointed toward Maria. "Soon I will have the other."

Romero's voice cracked with guttural Apache words.

"My father says he will take the woman, but if he does not have the one who killed his son, you will take his place. He says your death will be described by your people for many years.

"Will you pay for this one? I must pay my men or they will not help me with the other one."

Maria knew the other one they talked about had to be MacLeod. How would he ever find her or remain alive long enough for her ever to see him again? Would it be better to die at this moment, than be sold to the Apaches? Stories abounded in New Mexico of women taken captive by them, but few stories were told about any who returned.

She heard her name spoken. Griego's eyes flickered between her and the Apache leader.

"This is better than killing you," he said and laughed. "You will suffer more this way, but who knows. Maybe you will like it."

"Why are you doing this, Miguel? My father will find out. Someone will speak of it, and he will know it was you. My father will not rest until I am found."

"Who is there to talk, your Indian friend? She will not say anything. She is going with you. So who is left?"

"You cannot keep it a secret."

"I think so." Griego chuckled. "The governor will send me to look for you. "Where do you think I should look?"

Before Maria could answer, two of Romero's men slid off their horses and pulled Peche and Maria apart. A third Apache brought two horses forward.

"What about the silver?" Griego asked. Sweat ran down his cheeks and soaked the front of his shirt.

The young Apache tossed a leather pouch in the sand. "My father says he will not wait long for the other."

As the two women were tied to their horses, Griego could not resist a parting remark.

"I wanted you to be my wife. You will be Romero's now."

"Think about me, Miguel," Maria hissed. "Think about what you wanted of me. Dream about what could have been, Miguel. You will have nothing but your fat whores."

"The whole village will have you."

An Apache picked up the reins of Maria's horse and started to lead her away.

"Do not sleep too much, Miguel. When the *Americano* finds you, he will kill you."

"I will kill him first. No, I will sell him to the Apache," Griego said, laughing. "Maybe you will see him again."

Romero wheeled his horse and led the others into the night.

Maria trembled at what she knew lay ahead.

SANTA FE

Toward midnight a chilling wind scoured the plaza. MacLeod huddled as far from the draughty door as possible, his back to the mud wall, and his knees clutched against his chest. His guard had sought shelter hours before.

MacLeod's head came up as his cell door swung open. Three shadowy figures entered and quickly pulled him to his feet. While two held his arms the other swung an awkward fist that cracked against the side of his face.

They took turns, but in the dark MacLeod managed to twist his body from side to side to deflect some of the blows. Eventually, the attackers let him slump to the floor. He lay with his arms covering his head while they drove their boots into his sides and arms. Through the daze he could hear the breaths of his attackers coming in gasps. They argued amongst themselves, and once he thought he heard one of them mention Griego. Finally only darkness remained.

The cold woke him. He tried to move and cried out in pain. No one came to investigate.

He passed out again.

When he came to, the light had faded and again the night chill crept into his cell. He forced himself into a sitting position and waited for the pain to ease. Very gently he explored his face and body, then moved his arms and legs, which brought on a sickening wave of nausea. He figured some of his ribs were cracked. He reached for the pail of water kept in the corner of his cell but saw it had been upended in the struggle. Summoning what strength he had left, he rolled over and pushed himself into a kneeling position, then crawled to the door and pulled himself to his feet. Every breath rewarded him with searing pain, forcing him to close his eyes and lean against the door until the spinning ceased. Through the barred window in the door he saw the guard slowly walking the short length of the cells. MacLeod waited until he was a few feet from the cell and called out to him.

The guard halted.

MacLeod motioned for him to come to the window. "Water," MacLeod mumbled.

The guard lit a cigarillo and resumed his pacing, then moved to the end of the row of cells and seated himself on the bench.

MacLeod lay on his straw-covered pallet, feeling the chill more than ever. His body begged for nourishment to help heal his injuries but used up what reserves it had left to combat the chilling cold.

The next morning, MacLeod watched the guards exchange the old musket they carried and share a cigarillo. They looked toward his cell and laughed. He wondered how long they intended to ignore him. Why not simply shoot him and be done with it? And what had happened to Zavalda?

He dozed and woke to the urgent scratching of rats looking for food around the overturned pail. His tongue felt swollen. He could think of nothing but his terrible thirst.

Voices outside of his cell sought his attention. He recognized the whining cadence of his day guard but not the other voice. A brief argument ceased and his cell door opened, revealing a tall, gaunt, figure wearing a rough, brown, woolen garment. The figure drew back involuntarily when assailed by the smell, then entered the cell and stood waiting for his eyes to adjust to the darkness.

So this must be the one Maria called Alvarez, MacLeod concluded. He picked up the empty water bucket and held it out to the priest, who immediately took it outside and returned a moment later with water sloshing over the side.

The man knelt beside MacLeod and gently held a water-soaked cloth to his lips. MacLeod sucked the delicious water into his mouth, gripping Alvarez's arm so he could not leave.

Much later MacLeod leaned against the wall and closed his eyes. "Thank you."

"You are welcome, my son," Alvarez said.

MacLeod's eyes opened wide. "You speak English."

"Yes."

"Are you Father Alvarez?"

"I am."

"Maria sent you?"

"Maria de Cordero asked me to look in on you on occasion. I have been away. I am sorry I could not come sooner."

"Have you seen her?"

"No," Alvarez said. He dipped the cloth in the water and began to wash MacLeod's face.

"That thing you did with your hand," MacLeod said.

"I was blessing you in the name of Christ."

"I don't believe in your church."

Father Alvarez smiled. "Do you believe in Christ?"

"Of course, but not the way you do."

"Perhaps we can finish this discussion at another time. I want you to try to stand so we may go out into the fresh air."

"Can you do that? What about the guards?"

"I told them their eternal souls were in my hands at this moment if they did not allow me to help you."

"They believed you?"

"It was the truth."

MacLeod's legs sagged as he stood and tried to take a step. Alvarez took his arm and placed it around his neck, and half carried him onto the street. Across from the jail, a wooden bench sat beneath a stick-and-earth-covered roof. MacLeod's guards often slept on the bench while on duty. Alvarez sat him down and placed the thin blanket around MacLeod's shoulders.

"Please," MacLeod begged. "Ask them for food. It's been days."

Father Alvarez nodded slightly and turned toward the guard, who still paced in front of the open door to the cell. They spoke for a moment and the guard scurried off.

"Why are you in this condition? Who did this to you?" Alvarez asked. He seated himself on the bench beside MacLeod.

"Three men, or maybe four, I can't be sure. I think it must have been three nights ago."

"And no one has come to see you since?"

MacLeod shook his head.

"You have made many enemies since you came to this country. Do you know this?"

MacLeod watched for the guard's return. "I didn't come here to do that. We only came to get help for my friend, and then to go home."

Alvarez nodded. "Nevertheless, your path has led to confrontations and trouble. We would be better off if you had not come."

"Well, I'll tell you something. I wish I hadn't come either. Since I've been here, I've been accused of everything you can think of and told so many lies I wonder if anyone here ever tells the truth. The only good thing about any of it is meeting Maria."

"Yes, Maria. It appears you have also caused her much trouble."

"I didn't mean to. I never met anyone like her before. I'd do anything if I could take it all back."

"But that is impossible," Alvarez said. "It is done and you will live with the consequences."

"What consequences?"

"There are always consequences when you sin," Alvarez said. He rose as the guard approached with a jug of water and a bowl. He took it and held it to MacLeod's lips and helped him drink.

For the next few minutes neither spoke as MacLeod consumed the gruel in the bowl. He wiped out the inside of the bowl with the one tortilla the guard brought.

"Where did you learn to speak English?" MacLeod asked.

"I studied in Madrid. At one time I had plans other than the Church."

They sat and spoke for some time while curious Santa Fe residents walked past, or watched silently from a distance. Occasionally, someone spoke to Alvarez and he blessed them as he had MacLeod.

"Do you believe me?" MacLeod wanted to know, after explaining how he and Charbonneau came to be in New Mexico.

"Yes, I believe it is as you say."

"Can you help me?"

Alvarez smiled. "I will see that you are treated properly and that you are fed as you should be, but there is little else that I can do."

"Can you speak to the governor?"

"There is little we agree on."

MacLeod began to feel he could trust Alvarez. "Can you find out where Mr. Charbonneau is? I can't get any news about him. He's like you, about the church."

"Then if he is of our Church he will need my blessing. The governor cannot refuse. I will go to see him as soon as our governor returns."

MacLeod studied Alvarez for a moment. He needed to know where the priest stood. "Do you believe that it was slave traders I saw?"

"I have no doubt what you have described to me was our notorious slave traders at work."

"Then they are real?"

"Unfortunately, yes. The Indians have been raiding each other from the beginning. It is their way of life. They also raid many of our outlying villages and steal the women and children. Many of our own important people buy these captives from the Indians and use them as slaves. This is what I was sent here to report on."

"But those I saw were not Indians trading with other Indians."

"No, what you may have seen were our own people selling captive Indians, and in some cases they even sell some of our own women and children to these Indians."

MacLeod had also heard stories of the Church enslaving Indians for the purpose of saving their souls, but he wasn't about to get into a discussion with Alvarez. "But this governor fellow says these stories are all false, why?"

"Certain people who allow this trade to continue reap part of the profits. It is a way of life for some." Alvarez sat down on the bench and placed his hands in his lap. "There are several who practice this trade in captives, the ones they call the Comanchero, of course, but others also. Our governor does not like to offend certain people."

"That sounds like this Griego," MacLeod said.

"Yes, he is the worst of all. He gambles heavily and owes much."

Across the street, the open door of MacLeod's cell beckoned. Alvarez noted his glance and called to the guard, who sullenly leaned his musket against the wall and, after words with Alvarez, proceeded to empty MacLeod's slop bucket and fill the water jug.

"I can't help thinking about Maria, and her marriage to this Griego. Isn't there anything you can do about it?"

"You have problems of your own you must address. You must forget Maria de Cordero."

"I can't do that, Father."

"You must."

"What did she say to you when she came to Santa Fe? She must have said something about us."

"What she said cannot be repeated. It was between us only. As her confessor, I can repeat nothing, although I do not expect you to understand."

Alvarez folded his arms into the heavy folds of his woolen robe and lowered his head.

"What is it?" MacLeod asked.

I will tell you this. It is only a matter of time before you hear of it from others. "Maria cannot be found. It is believed she has been taken captive."

MacLeod's cry of anguish brought the guards running until Alvarez sent them away. "No, Father, it can't be true. It must be a mistake."

"It is no mistake. The bodies of her guards were found two days ago. There were many tracks."

MacLeod stood and grasped Alvarez by the shoulders. "What are they doing about it? Are they searching for her?"

"Don Cordero has many people looking, but it is certain that Indians were involved, possibly the Apache Romero."

"No, if anybody is responsible it is Griego. If he is involved, Father, I swear to you I will kill him."

"Killing is not always the answer."

"Not always but in this case it's the only one. I swear I will get out of here and I will find her, and if anything has happened to her, I'm going after him. Tell him that, Father. Tell him for me." MacLeod sat on the bench and buried his head in his hands.

Father Alvarez laid a hand on MacLeod's shoulder. "I will speak with the governor. In the meantime, remember what I said about trust."

"Why did they take her Father?"

"You and Maria insulted one of the most powerful and dangerous families in New Mexico. I cannot condone what you have done. Nevertheless, I will pray for you both."

MacLeod reached up and grasped Alvarez by the front of his robe, his voice as cold as ice. "Pray for Maria, Father. Pray as hard as you can. Her indiscretions are nothing compared to what I will do to these people."

Alvarez leaned down and kissed MacLeod on the head. He signaled to the guard. "I must go now."

Hour upon hour and sleep would not come until exhaustion sapped the last strength from his body, and his head fell forward.

He woke with the tiny cross and chain Maria had secretly passed to him clutched in a hand. He held it out in front of him, letting the delicate chain slide through his fingers before pressing it to his lips.

Sometime later the sounds of laughter forced him to get up and go to the window of his cell. Governor Melgares, accompanied by Lieutenant Zavalda, stood talking with Father Alvarez. MacLeod could see that Alvarez was furious. When he heard Maria's name mentioned, the governor shrugged and walked toward the palace.

Two days later MacLeod, watched four armed militiamen approached his cell. One unlatched the door and stood back. *"Americano, pronto."*

His regular guards shifted about in the presence of the better-armed and equipped regular militia. They appeared happy to give MacLeod over to someone else.

With the point of his rusted bayonet, the one who appeared in charge indicated to MacLeod he would walk between the two rows of soldiers.

The distance from the jail to the Governor's Palace took less time to cover than it took to line up the militiamen and march across the dusty plaza.

Once again the smell of cooking and spices cleared MacLeod's head, and he momentarily forgot the squalid conditions of his cell.

The procession came to a halt at the door of the palace and the officer in charge entered, followed by MacLeod and two of the militiamen.

On the governor's desk lay a piece of paper with an official looking seal at the bottom. Each time Melgares' pacing took him past the desk, he uttered another curse.

MacLeod waited, unacknowledged, until Zavalda pointed to a chair and sent the guard away. Zavalda then began a long discussion with the governor, who appeared to agree. He sat behind his desk and picked up the offending paper.

"You are well?" Zavalda said, stepping closer to MacLeod as he spoke, then stepping back quickly. He lit a cigarillo.

"Guess I'm somewhat rank," MacLeod said.

Zavalda let it pass, moving a few feet away. "Some years ago a policy of trade was implemented by the Commandant General, in Mexico, His Excellency Nemesio Salcedo. This policy encouraged trade with the Indians to the east, the Comanche in particular. The thought being that if trade was encouraged between us, they would be less likely to attack our villages. What the Indians want, of course, are guns and powder, something we have so little of ourselves."

MacLeod spoke up. "The Pawnee seem to get all the powder they want by trading furs to renegade fur traders. It ain't legal, but it's done."

A smile creased Zavalda's face. "Yes, that is what we have heard."

It didn't take long for MacLeod to figure out why he was there and where the conversation was going, but he decided the best thing to do was play dumb.

"If our governor can satisfy the Comanche, it will be better for everyone. The Indians are happy, and hopefully they will use their powder against the cursed Apache."

All the while, Governor Melgares busied himself with flattening out the dispatch from Chihuahua.

Zavalda sat on the edge of the desk with his arms folded. "Governor Melgares feels that he would like to give you one last opportunity to secure your release, and at the same time help him and the people of Nuevo Mexico. That letter he has in front of him is also an answer to a plea he made on your behalf, and of course the other one. He does not wish to send you to Mexico unless he has to, so he asked the commandant general permission to release you if you had anything of value to pay the expenses of your capture and your imprisonment. I realize this is only a formality, since you have already said you have nothing." Zavalda turned and walked to the back of the room, giving MacLeod time to think about the offer.

While flies circled him in waves, MacLeod tossed about the offer. Alvarez had said that the governor couldn't release him without permission. There, apparently, was the permission, except for the fact that there was no way for a report to travel to Chihuahua and back in such a short time. The dispatch the governor held in his hands might well be about pacifying the Indians, but it didn't include information about MacLeod. Which meant it was all another lie. MacLeod figured he would play along and see what happened.

"I guess maybe there are a few furs the Utes didn't steal. Not many, but we figured we might need what we had left to trade for horses and supplies," MacLeod said, figuring Griego had not shared with Zavalda the information about the two packs of furs Don Cordero apparently gave to Griego when he returned to see Maria. Of course, it wasn't to Griego's benefit to acknowledge the possibility MacLeod's story was true about their being only trappers. So how did the governor get the two pelts?

Governor Melgares pushed himself to his feet and waited.

"The Governor would like to know what you mean by a few."

MacLeod figured that if the governor was really worried about his Indian Policy failure, and needed the furs that badly, maybe he would consider releasing them.

"I can't be sure what furs were left."

"Surely you have some idea," an exasperated Zavalda blurted.

"Must be a couple of packs."

A smile creased Governor Melgares' face. "Good, good, excellent in fact, I think. How many in a pack?"

MacLeod realized they knew nothing about trapping or beaver pelts. "Maybe fifty to seventy five, depending on their size."

"And what kind are these furs?"

"Beaver skins, like the two you showed me the last time you had me brought here."

Zavalda nodded. "I suppose these beaver are desired by the Indians, the same as the skin of the buffalo."

"If they trade them to the Pawnee, they're worth more," MacLeod said. He hadn't figured on educating them as well.

The governor beamed his pleasure and wrung his hands together. Zavalda lifted a quill pen and a piece of paper from the desk. "Please, you will draw us a map of where these furs can be found."

MacLeod pushed the paper away, realizing the next few moments might seal his fate. "No need to do that. They ain't there anymore, since your Señor Griego has them already." MacLeod knew he should leave it there, but he couldn't resist adding another comment. "Perhaps he'd be willing to help the people of New Mexico and give them to you."

"This is more of your lies," the governor said, pounding the desk and knocking over a cup of wine. "Señor Griego himself has told me you had nothing with you to prove you were only these trappers as you say you are, but I think he is mistaken. I think you might be what you say and have hidden them somewhere before you decided to come her without permission and kill two of my loyal followers."

Zavalda waited until the governor sat down and began wiping the spilt wine off the dispatch. "I do not understand why you do not take this offer and save yourself and your friend. The governor has said he will only ask for enough to pay for your confinement, and he may forget the other problems you have caused."

"Sorry, Lieutenant, but I know that letter on the governor's desk ain't about me. There's no way word gets back from Mexico this soon. Seems none of you here are worth a hoot when it comes to truth telling. If you need a straight answer you can tell the governor to shove his offer up his fat arse."

Before MacLeod had finished, Zavalda barked out orders to the guards. They sprang forward and wrestled MacLeod to the floor. Moments later someone appeared with shackles and chain, and in minutes MacLeod was led from the governor's office, dragging the heavy chains attached to the manacles on his arms and ankles.

Miguel Griego wanted to kill the *Americano*. He knew he couldn't; in fact, he had to make sure that nothing happened to him, otherwise Romero would come after him. Griego shivered at the prospect of death at the hands of that Apache. Nobody lived to describe it, but many had seen the results or spoke of the cries that lasted far into the night and the next day. Still, he envisioned a helpless MacLeod begging him to spare his life, while Maria de Cordero watched. Then the pure rush of pleasure he would get when he watch MacLeod die at his feet.

Across the dark room, four of his troopers sat on the dirt floor playing a game of monte, Griego's favorite, but unfortunately not his best game of chance.

One had drunk more than his young years could control. His comments centered on his time with Peche. When he grinned and mentioned Maria, the room fell silent. Griego moved across the room before anyone could react and grabbed the youngster by the throat, lifting him off the floor and hurling him against the mud wall of the cantina.

Sergeant Gomez stepped in front of Griego to shield his charge from further punishment.

"Out of my way," Griego snarled.

"No, Miguel, he is only a boy. He does not know better."

"He will know when I have finished with him."

"What good will it do to kill him? Find another way to punish him." The sergeant pulled the youngster to his feet and sent him sprawling out onto the dirt outside the cantina.

Griego sat down and poured himself another drink. He didn't need any reminders about Maria de Cordero. Her image burnt his memory like a hot iron. Miguel Griego emptied his glass and poured another drink.

Gomez took the chair opposite him. "Miguel, you must forget this woman."

"It is easy for you to say who do not know of her."

"The sergeant grinned. "She is only a woman. There are many women."

Griego grunted. He stared at the pockmarked face of his trusted sergeant. "But such a woman. Have you ever seen one like her anywhere?"

"But she is gone, Miguel. The Apache will use her and then kill her. She is probably dead already. Get drunk and forget her."

Yes, he might forget her, but how could he ever forget how close he came to the Cordero money and land, enough to free himself forever from his father's tentacles. With the land and power that came with the money, he could influence the next governor. His father had served too many terms as *alcalde mayore*. Perhaps it was his turn. But his dream had vanished like the smoke that swirled around the lamps in the room. The Cordero money would never be his.

"There is word that your father is looking for you, Miguel. How long do you think you can stay away from him?"

"He is an old man. Maybe he will die soon," Griego snarled.

"But maybe he finds you first."

"Are you afraid of what will happen to you?"

Gomez ran a rough hand across his unshaven face. "I have thought of many things lately."

Griego reached across the table and grabbed a handful of the sergeant's shirt. "What things? Are there things you do not approve?"

"Miguel, we have done many things together. We drink, we make love, we steal, but there are things we do maybe we should not do. You know of which things I speak," the sergeant said, looking into Griego's eyes.

"You do not think we should have sold her to Romero? But you took the silver I paid you."

"I know this, but I did not like it."

A man entered the cantina's back door unnoticed and slipped into the chair beside Griego. He poured himself a drink and looked around to be sure he would not be overheard.

"You found them?" Griego said impatiently.

The man nodded. "*Si*, they were near the Pecos."

The sergeant spoke up. "Do they know the value of these beaver skins?"

"I do not know, but they were very excited and the Comanche seldom show it. I think it has been a hard year and they have little to trade."

Griego smiled. "Good."

"You know something you have not told me?" the sergeant asked. "Do you know if these furs truly exist?"

"Soon I will find out for certain."

"How?"

"The other one, you know the one. Find him for me."

"Miguel," Gomez pleaded, "the Governor is already asking too many questions, and *Teniente* Zavalda says he thinks you are the one who took the Cordero woman. He is very nervous about Don Cordero's power."

"Melgares is a fat fool. He has no proof of anything."

Gomez laughed and said, "Since when does a governor need proof?"

"Never mind the governor, find out where the other one is," Griego said.

The noise in the cantina made it impossible for anyone to hear their words. Still, the sergeant lowered his voice to a whisper. "That is not all, Miguel. The governor also thinks you might already have these furs and if you do, where is his share."

"He thinks this?"

"Zavalda says he will want more than his share. He will want them all because he thinks you have been taking advantage of his position."

"The man needs to leave us alone. He wishes to become rich before his time is up like all the others before him."

"It is true, Miguel, but these things are what he asks. It is said that he will replace your father if he discovers you have lied to him like this."

Strip his father of his position? The idea put as much fear into Miguel Griego as Romero's threat. But those furs meant silver, and silver put distance between him and his father. He knew the next step was finding out when the *Americano* would be sent south and how many would escort him. Romero would want to know, and Griego wanted to be sure there would be no mistake.

The owner of the cantina beckoned to Gomez, who left the table and followed him outside. For the moment Griego sat alone with his thoughts. When Romero had the *Americano*, he could concentrate on getting the furs to the Comanche. Piss on the governor. Griego didn't care what he thought.

"Miguel," Sergeant Gomez said, leaning over the table. "They will leave for Chihuahua in six days."

"Good. Send three men to find Romero and arrange a meeting."

For the first time in weeks Griego smiled.

The guard woke MacLeod with his foot, then walked back outside the cell. Lieutenant Zavalda ducked his head and entered.

MacLeod loved to watch the reaction on his visitors when the smell hit them. He always wondered how long they could hold their breath.

"You should try it for a day. Maybe then you'd think about cleaning it out once in a while, like you promised."

Zavalda removed a heavily scented cloth from his nose. "I am sorry. It was supposed to be done." He shouted at the guard, who removed the slop pot and returned it empty moments later.

"Seems I hear that a lot," MacLeod muttered. The rusted chains and shackles on his wrists and ankles rattled as he pushed himself to his feet.

"There is little time," Zavalda said. "Please trust me and listen."

"What do you mean, little time?"

"We have received word from Chihuahua. You are to be sent south."

"How soon before I leave?"

"It will take some time to ready your escort party. As you can imagine, the trip is long and somewhat dangerous. Many men and supplies are needed for such a journey."

"All this for me. Seems a waste."

"There are others to be sent also. Their cases are not as important, but it is better to send them now. I think in about six or seven days."

As he left the cell, Zavalda turned. "I wish there was something you could give the governor to satisfy him. If you would trust me, I could go in your place. Think about it."

Three days later Father Alvarez stood in the open doorway of his cell.

"I'm glad you came, have you heard anything?"

"Only rumors, nothing more. Some say the Navajo took her, others say it was the Apache. But I have seen your friend. He is well."

"Are they sending him to Chihuahua?"

"No. It is possible they believe he can tell them something you would not. They will only say it is because you are responsible for the two who were killed."

They sat for some time without speaking. "Am I keeping you, Father? It's all right if you have to leave."

Alvarez smiled and MacLeod thought he had never seen a sadder smile.

"No, I will stay as long as you want."

"It's been so long since I spoke with anyone. Before, when you came to see me, I never asked. Who are you anyway?"

"If you mean with the Church, we are called Franciscans. Our order was founded six hundred years ago by Saint Francis of Assisi. They said there was much work to be done here and in Mexico, and many of the Indians to be taught about Christ and our Church."

"Have you been happy here?"

"At times. The people are poor but happy, but there is so much evil. The Indians, when you are able to gain their trust, will show you that they live better lives than many of our ruling citizens. My own people are more in need of the teachings of our Church than the savage Indians."

MacLeod scratched at the scabs on his legs where the shackles cut through the skin.

"Now it is your turn," Alvarez said. "Tell me something about yourself."

For the next hour MacLeod related the events that brought him to New Mexico. Alvarez listened without comment.

"In this place you call New England. Tell me how it is different from here. I have no knowledge of your country."

MacLeod leaned against the mud wall and closed his eyes. How could he explain such differences to someone who had never stood in a field of clover, full of fat milking cows, or knelt beside the road to smell the delicate aroma of wild roses growing alongside the fence? "The rivers, Father. They're clear and cold and taste sweet on a hot summer day, and if you sit awhile you can sometimes see the trout holding below a riffle."

Alvarez smiled. "There are trout in Spain; I have eaten them."

"What will they do with her?"

"We must forget Maria, my son. She will not come back to us."

"Why? She might not be dead. They might still find her. Didn't you say Don Cordero was still looking for her?"

Alvarez shook his head. "No, she is gone from us now. You have other worries. Do not hurt yourself more with thoughts of Maria."

"You didn't answer my question, Father. What will they do with her?"

Nothing prepared MacLeod for the pain on Alvarez's face. He sat tight-lipped and shook his head. Finally he spoke. "We can only hope that they will kill her quickly. Otherwise, they will use her until they are tired of her, and then trade her to some other tribe."

Visions of Maria lying dead beside an Indian village, her body torn and filthy from abuse, reopened the wounds that MacLeod had tried to forget. Across his cell a silent Alvarez sat with tears streaking his gaunt cheeks.

"You love her, too, don't you, Father?"

"I love all my children. It is not only Maria," he said.

"But you love her more than the others," MacLeod said.

With the slightest nod of his head, Father Alvarez acknowledged MacLeod. "She made me see the truth in many things."

Dark shadows crept into the corners of the cell and the air cooled noticeably. "I'm afraid I've been thinking of myself lately. It's kinda hard not to. What will happen to me in Chihuahua?"

"It is in God's hands; I cannot answer. Much depends on who our governor's enemies and friends are, and how much influence they have. If his enemies are more powerful, they will try to discredit the official reports and believe your story," Alvarez said.

"Yeah, but what about the other way, if his friends have more say. What happens then?"

Outside the cell the guards changed. Alvarez rose. "It is in His hands, my son. I will send word to my bishop. It is all I can do, and perhaps he will have time to see you. If he believes your story, he can help. It would have been easier if you were of our Church."

For a time neither spoke. The sounds of a disgruntled wooden cart being dragged down the street blended with a barking dog. A loud curse, then the painful howl of the dog, and all became quiet again.

"I guess if you see Charbonneau, you could tell him I kept my promise."

"I will do that," Alvarez said.

"Father, I don't know what you could do, but if I don't come back . . . you know, if something happens to me in Mexico. I guess my mother would like to know what happened. Her name's Mary MacLeod, and she lives in Boston."

"That would not be easy but I would try," Alvarez said as he moved toward the door and spoke to the guard. The door swung open on sagging hinges.

"I never asked you," MacLeod said, "but why are you doing all this for me?"

The slightest of smiles creased Alvarez's face. "For the same reason you will not give up the skins of these animals. I made a promise."

MacLeod nodded and lowered his head to rest on his crossed arms. "I'm afraid."

"Fear is with all of us. I will pray for you."

APACHE RANCHERIA

The water that trickled over the rocks and formed a pool came from the snowmelt that ran clear and clean from the high mountains. An old woman watched as they always watched her whenever she left the camp, a camp that consisted of a dozen low shelters built from branches and thatched with matted grass and mud. A hole in the roof let out the smoke from the cooking fires. Since her arrival in the camp, she had lived in the *wickiup* of Romero and his wife.

How long had it been, Maria wondered? A month, two months? She couldn't tell. The first days had been a constant round of kicks and beatings by the women, never the men. The men squatted on their haunches with their tanned loin clothes tucked between their legs and watched. They made no comment, or showed any change in their expressions. It was as if they were watching water run over the pebbles in a creek.

The old woman who watched Maria removed a pipe from a fold in her moccasins. Maria watched her go through the ritual of packing the pipe before placing it between toothless gums. During the first couple of weeks, the woman had led the daily punishment. A series of sharp kicks aimed at her most sensitive areas chased Maria outside into the numbing cold of a mountain morning. There she would hope to find an ember or two still glowing beneath the thick layer of grey ash. If her luck held, she would lay dry moss and twigs over the ember and blow gently until a tiny flame appeared. When the fire burned by itself, Maria walked the short distance to the stream to find a spot where the water had not frozen clear to the bottom.

Later she learned that one of the women spoke Spanish. She was taken in an Apache raid on their village years before and would never return. Life with the Apache, to some, was better than they could expect in the village where they had lived.

Maria spread a pouch of tubers on the ground and began cleaning them while she thought about MacLeod. Even if he managed to escape, could he ever find her? She wanted to believe so, yet she had no idea where she was. After they left Griego's camp, they moved day and night, stopping only for brief periods to rest the horses and sleep for short periods of time. Sometimes she rode and at other times they forced her to run alongside one of the horses until she could run no farther. Then they placed her on a horse and continued on until the horse faltered.

On the fourth night, as she lay on the ground, her hands and feet tied, Romero appeared. He slit the leather thongs that bound her legs and rolled her onto her stomach. He made no sound as he pulled her to her knees and lifted her skirt up over her back. Maria felt him push her legs apart and thrust himself into her. She bit down against the sudden pain until her lips bled, but she had refused to scream or cry. In the days it took them to reach the *rancheria*, Romero took her three times. He had not touched her since.

Maria completed the task of cleaning herself and waited for the old woman to finish packing her pipe. The remainder of the day would be spent gathering wood. If she was lucky, she might eat whatever was left in the cook pot after the others finished. The bags of dried roots and jerky were dwindling and often the cook pot contained little more than once-boiled bones and a few roots.

A week earlier, from Margarita, the woman who spoke Spanish, she learned that the *rancheria* would be abandoned soon and the spring gathering would begin. Narrow-leafed yucca, roasted in a pit and sun-dried, followed by the important spring gathering of mescal, acorns, and sumac berries. The food stuffs would be readied for instant consumption or stored in favorite hiding spots for emergencies. The Apache always prepared for sudden changes in living quarters.

Without warning, the old woman struck Maria with her stick and pointed toward the camp. Maria glared at her and shook her fist. The old woman grinned a toothless warning but backed up slowly and followed Maria at a safe distance. To emphasize her new independence, Maria reached down and picked up a stick of her own.

The next morning she returned from the stream as Romero emerged from his shelter and issued orders summoning the warriors in camp. Maria found Margarita, hoping she would explain what was happening.

"They will leave soon," the woman said, indicating the men gathered around Romero.

"We will go or stay behind?"

"We will stay."

The chosen warriors began to inspect their equipment and weapons, sharpening lances and arrow tips. Bags of rations, robes, and water were assembled and laid aside for packing. Each man secreted his own amulet or medicine bag among his gear.

Romero pointed at Maria. Whatever he said made the other men laugh.

"What did he say?" asked Maria.

"He says he is going to kill your man. He says I should tell you that when he returns, he will bring his head to show you and while you are waiting for his return you must decide which of his warriors you will have for a husband."

"But how can they do that? He is in jail in Santa Fe?" Maria said in disbelief.

"He says they are sending your man to Mexico, but he will never arrive. When the death of Romero's son is avenged, he will return and make you an Apache."

"Ask him how he knows this."

"The same way he knew about you, he says. Do you know what he means?"

"Yes, a skunk named Griego. But he does nothing unless it is for money. Ask him how much he paid for this information."

When the woman finished translating, Romero palmed a small skin bag. Maria heard the sounds of coins. It was obvious that Miguel Griego was making the most of his failed engagement. Both she and MacLeod would be gone and Griego would profit on both ends.

Watching the Apache, Maria knew MacLeod stood no chance against them. The Mexicans would march right into the ambush and the man who had been a part of her life for such a short time would die. Why? she asked herself again as she had done every night and every day. What had they done to deserve this? He would die and she would live the life of a wandering Apache wife, good for cooking and mothering new Apache warriors, and preparing mescal, or chewing deer skins until they were soft enough to satisfy a husband. All this because they had found love together. Real love, not the manufactured love of her mother or her friends.

Maria looked at the women in the camp and tried to picture herself in a year or two. For a moment her eyes met Romero's. But she felt no fear, only unquenchable hatred. She grabbed the arm of the Mexican woman. "Tell him my man will strip him naked and let the dogs eat his manhood. Tell him he will cower like a frightened bitch. If he is lucky, he may crawl back here in the dark for his wife to hide him in her *wickiup*."

For an instant Maria saw her hatred mirrored in the Apache's eyes. His hand went to the handle of his knife as Maria felt the blow on her back. She started to turn, but the old woman rained blows on her head and back until Maria fell to the ground and covered her head with her hands and arms.

SOUTH OF SANTA FE

MacLeod stumbled along behind the carts, slipping and stumbling in the thick mud, his hands shackled. The soldiers had placed a rope around his neck and laughed when he had to struggle to run to catch up.

The escort of twenty soldiers and one lieutenant had left Santa Fe in half a dozen *carrettas l*oaded with food and supplies. Each cart was pulled by a pair of mules. Everyone walked except a lieutenant, who rode a thin-hipped sorrel. He slept while he rode, but no one cared.

Despite the foul weather, the prisoners laughed and joked with the soldiers. Most agreed the food in prison could not be worse than what their wives fed them, and they wouldn't have to listen to their wives. Half a dozen of the prisoners were women, half-breeds or Indian accused of various crimes. If they made it to Chihuahua, their fates were uncertain. After five days and nights of repeated rapes no one expected any of them to live long enough to hear their fate.

Day after day the slow moving caravan worked its way south. The rain of the first week gave way to clear, brilliant skies, although the temperature still fell to near freezing at night. The rutted roads slashed the feet of those who failed to pick their steps carefully.

By the second week the ritual was set. The morning fires were made early by one of the younger soldiers, and the others gathered around for warmth while they ate. The prisoners ate the same meal twice a day—a mush they called *el café de Los Mexicanos*. MacLeod heard it referred to in Santa Fe as Indian mush called *atole*. It didn't matter what they called it; it tasted bitted and gritty, but it would be the only food they received.

The procession began its day early and continued until camp was made for the night, when the fires were again lit, and the night rituals began. No prisoners were shackled except MacLeod, and only one guard was assigned each night. He fell asleep early and no one seemed particularly concerned that anyone would attempt to escape, except for MacLeod. Each night they wrapped his chain around the base of a tree or drove a stake deep into the ground and attached the chain to it.

During the third week, one of the prisoners moved to the side of the rode and waited for MacLeod to catch up. He was an old man, thin, with one eye socket empty and a nose pushed to one side of his face. They walked together for some time before the old man spoke. He pointed to his chest. "Juan," he said, "You *Americano?*"

"I guess so. Why they sending you south?"

Juan grinned. "I steal from the governor, he say. He say I owe him ten sheep. I say no, no. He say if I don't give him sheep, it's same as stealing."

"Why don't you give him the sheep?" MacLeod figured it would be better than going to Chihuahua.

"I would, but the Navajo steal my sheep, and the governor say I hide them. So now I go to Chihuahua."

"Seems a big penalty for a few sheep. What will they do to you?"

Juan shrugged. "Who knows? But first we must get there."

The clean air had dried out the axles and hubs of the cottonwood wheels. At times it seemed that all of the wheels in the convoy protested in chorus, shrieking together in a high-pitched squeal that made talk impossible.

The land ahead appeared as a loosely thrown blanket of ups and downs with an occasional deep arroyo the train skirted. On either side empty mountains of rock and dirt served as barriers forcing them south, toward Mexico. For MacLeod, each step took him farther from St. Louis and farther from home. Maria's face dimmed in the endless land of scrub trees and cactus and dry ruts in the desert floor. The night before, MacLeod had cut strips from his blanket to wrap around his feet. The strips had become heavy with the dung and urine of the mules.

Each day Juan would drop back and walk with MacLeod. "This rain we had will be good."

MacLeod wondered about the relevance of the remark. "It sure makes walking hard."

"*Si*, but the waterholes in *el Jornada del Muerto* will be full and that is good."

"The *Jornada?*"

"The Journey of Death. Sometimes they say it is the Dead Man's Journey. We will be there soon. You will see for yourself. Most of the time there is no water. That is why it is good we have rain, but even then there is the Apache."

"How come you know so much about this part of the country?"

Juan sighed. "Many years ago I was a sailor, then we were sunk and the *Americanos* found me, then I come back to Mexico and become a soldier. Once, when I was a soldier, I come this way, but the Apache got me, and then I get some sheep and a wife. I should have asked the *Americanos* to keep me."

"That what happened to your eye?"

"*Si*, the Apache took it, and the governor say I cannot see so I cannot be soldier."

MacLeod looked around at the escort and wondered how they would fare against an Indian attack. Most of them carried weapons of dubious vintage. Poor care and the lack of spare parts, or a qualified gunsmith, made it appear as if the weapons would be of little help if they were attacked. He had seen Indians attacking, and he had also witnessed the personality of the Apache.

"You think we might be attacked?"

Juan shrugged. "Everyone knows the Apache want you, but maybe because we are so many they will not attack."

"You think this group will fight?"

"If they do not fight they will die. Their horses are too slow to escape."

MacLeod wondered what his chances were under the circumstances, figuring the lieutenant in charge might choose to use him as a sacrificial lamb offered up to Romero.

The caravan halted while the lieutenant got off his horse to relieve himself. Half a dozen mud and stick huts—Juan referred to as *jacales*—stood under the shade of a pair of cottonwood trees.

"These little places are sure strung out," MacLeod said. "Seems it might be easy picking for any party of Indians that might happen by."

"Oh, yes," Juan agreed. "Every week there are some killed, but others they still come. Sometimes the Indians only steal some of the sheep and leave enough for the next time they come. Sometimes they leave enough of the food for the people to get by so they will not leave. If they leave, who will be here to grow food for the Indians to steal?"

"Is there any way for the people to defend themselves? They don't have any weapons do they?"

Juan shook his head. "No, no weapons, but they pray a lot."

"Yeah, well, it doesn't appear to be working," MacLeod said.

The caravan followed the tracks, never far from the river and the line of cottonwoods. People living in the tiny hamlets stood silently watching, leaning on wooden tree limbs hacked into rudimentary digging sticks. An occasional dog barked its warning or drove wandering sheep back to the flock, then the village fell behind and the endless monotony continued.

Two days later, MacLeod watched the old man step to the side of the road and shake out one of his shoes.

"We will be there soon and then we will rest for a couple of days."

"This *Jornada* you talked about, you mean?"

"Oh, no, that is farther away. We will camp at *Fray Cristobal*. It is a good place to let the horses rest and fill the water barrels."

"And after that, what town will we come to?"

"El Paso, but that is still many days," said Juan.

"And Chihuahua?"

"Very, very many miles."

"I asked you before, but we got off the trail a bit. What happens to you once we get where it is we're going?"

Juan shrugged. "Who knows? Maybe they will let me go or maybe they put me in the calaboose, or maybe they will shoot me like they will shoot you. But it is far away and maybe we never get there."

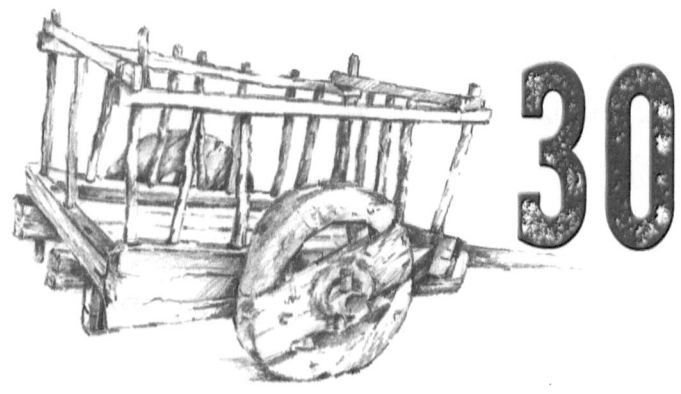

SANTA FE

Miguel Griego fingered the small stack of silver coins Romero paid him for the information. He didn't need to be told what would happen to him if the information proved false. That was three weeks earlier, and Griego felt certain the *Americano* was dead and Romero satisfied. Perhaps they could even start to do business again.

"They are coming in now, Miguel," Gomez said from the far side of a narrow clearing.

"Bring him to me and see that the guards are paid."

Two men dismounted, pulled Charbonneau from his horse and brought him forward.

"Do you know this man?" Gomez said, pointing to Griego.

Charbonneau rubbed his hand over his bearded face. He nodded.

"This man wants you to tell him about the furs that you claim you trapped. That is what you told the governor, is it not? That you are only innocent trappers."

"*Oui*, but why do you bring me here to ask these things?" Charbonneau shifted from one foot to the other while Griego grew impatient. "The Utes, they stole them. Your governor, he knows of this."

Griego seized Gomez's arm. "Tell him we know the Indians did not take these furs. The other one told us different."

Charbonneau raised his head when he heard Griego refer to MacLeod.

Gomez looked to Griego who nodded. "Señor MacLeod was killed by the Apache when he was being taken to Mexico."

"*Il mort*, it is a mistake, no?"

"There is no mistake. He is dead," Gomez said. "Now you must decide if you wish to remain in the *calaboose*, or follow your friend to Mexico. But Señor Griego wishes to offer you another opportunity," Gomez said, grinning broadly. "He wishes to offer you a chance to go home. Would you not like that?"

It took some time for Charbonneau to grasp what he was being told. "What is it you want of me, eh?"

"It is simply a trade. Señor Griego will trade you your freedom for the furs. He will even give you a couple of horses and supplies for your trip. You can leave soon. Is this not a good offer?"

Charbonneau wrung his hands. "I do not know about any of this. My head, it keeps things from me."

"Tell this old man he has no more time to think," Griego said. "I want to know where these furs are. Now!"

"I will ask him again, Miguel, but his mind is a little weak I think."

The sergeant put his arm around Charbonneau's shoulders. "Señor *Americano*, before your friend was taken south to Chihuahua, he told us about the furs that you have hidden because he thought you would want to go home. He was going to draw us a map, but they took him before he could do so."

"He would not do this," Charbonneau said, shaking his head. "He would not tell you where the furs are cached."

Griego grinned when Gomez related this to him. "So, then he admits they are hidden."

Griego barked out instructions, and two of his men seized Charbonneau by the arms while another stirred up the embers of the fire and placed the tip of his lance in the hot coals.

Gomez took a rough map from his pocket and placed it before Charbonneau. "We know this is the canyon where your friends were killed," he said, pointing to an area on the map. And this is the lake where your friend attacked us. Show us where these furs are hidden."

"I–I don't remember," Charbonneau stuttered. "I was too much hurt to remember." He tried pulling free from his captors.

"It would be much easier for you if you tell us," Gomez said.

Without warning, Griego picked up the red-hot lance and laid it across the side of Charbonneau's neck.

The sounds of his screams ripped the silence of the night. Both Griego and Gomez turned away from the smell of burning flesh. Griego dropped the lance into the fire as the two holding Charbonneau struggled to pull him to his feet.

"Do it again," Griego ordered Gomez.

"It will kill him."

"Again!"

Gomez reached for the shaft of the lance, but hesitated when Charbonneau cried out.

"I have no time to wait. Do it again," said Griego.

"*Non, mon dieu*, no more. I will tell you."

They dragged Charbonneau close to the firelight and showed him the map. While he pointed out the location of the furs, Miguel Griego examined the greedy expressions on the faces of his handpicked men.

"I think he has told us all we need to know, Miguel," Gomez said. "Do you want him returned to his guards? They will be very nervous."

For a time no one spoke. Griego stared at the moaning figure of Charbonneau and felt his anger return. This old *Americano,* and the other one, had deprived him of the woman and the Cordero land and power. If they had not stumbled upon him at the mountain lake, everything would have been different. It would be as it should be, not like this.

"You are sure you can find this place?" Griego questioned.

With his finger, Gomez traced the line he had drawn on the map. "I have been there before."

"What about him? Do you want to take him with you to be certain?"

"It is not necessary."

Griego pushed Gomez aside. "Hold him," he shouted, pointing at the limp body they held between them. He picked up the lance from the fire.

"No, Miguel, he has told you what you wanted to know," Gomez pleaded.

"Shut up. I do whatever pleases me," Griego said and pressed the head of the lance against Charbonneau's cheek.

Again, the Frenchman's scream pierced the quiet of the night, and the smell of seared flesh permeated the air. Those holding him dropped Charbonneau to the ground and turned away from the horror.

"Your pitiful friend is dead at the hands of the Apache and you will die like him," Griego said. "You will cause me no more trouble."

Griego drove the lance into Charbonneau's prostrate body. He jerked it free and handed it back to one of the men. "Take him back to where you got him."

"But what will his guards tell the governor?"

"That is their problem. They have the rest of the night to figure out what they will say. Be sure they understand they will say nothing about us."

Gomez shook his head slowly, "Miguel, it will be hard for the governor to look elsewhere. He has much explaining to do to the commandant general already, and he will not hesitate to point his finger at us."

"His time is soon up and we will have a new governor.

"And your father?"

"I will deal with him soon. But you, Gomez, what are you now going to do? Do I have to deal with you also?" Griego asked, then smiled.

Gomez shrugged. "What else is there for me to do? I have no other choice. I will go with you, Miguel. To hell, for sure."

JORNADO DE MUERTA

Consuela, banished from the cart and the other women, walked beside MacLeod. At *Fray Cristobal,* where the caravan had rested for three days, the girl, not much more than sixteen or so as far as MacLeod could figure, angered one of the soldiers. When MacLeod had asked Juan why they beat her, he had raised his eyebrows and said she had the curse. MacLeod had shared his food and water with her. Since then she had followed him, sitting beside him whenever they rested.

"They appear somewhat edgier than usual," said MacLeod, nodding toward the lead riders.

"*Si*, we are entering the land of the Apache. They could be anywhere, but probably ahead, at *Laguna del Muerto*."

"Where's that?"

"It is ahead, maybe. It is a favorite place of the Apache."

MacLeod pointed at the nearby mountain range. "They can't be there. Doesn't look like anyone could live there."

"The Apache can live where no one else can, or wants to, but no, those are the Fray Cristobal Mountains. Up ahead, over there." Juan pointed to the southeast. "Those are the San Andres, and behind them are the ones they call the Sacramentos. That is the home of the Mescalero Apache. Romero is Mescalero."

"So it's this Romero they're afraid of."

"They are afraid of all Apache, but more afraid of Romero."

MacLeod stumbled. The rope around his neck pulled taught and he grunted as the scabs on his neck broke away. He felt Consuela steady him again.

"She like you," Juan said with a grin.

"What did she do that made them send her to Chihuahua?"

"Like you, she kill a man."

"Her?" MacLeod exclaimed. "This little thing? Shucks, she ain't much more than a child."

"She is young in the years but very much old in life. She is Navajo but was taken by the Apache when she was a child. They killed her mother and her brother. Then, the soldiers come and raid a *rancheria*. It was a long journey back to Santa Fe, and a soldier offered her a ride on his horse, but all he wanted was her. After he raped her and beat her, he got drunk and fell asleep. She cut his throat."

"Can't say as I blame her. What will they do to her?"

Juan shrugged. "It is a long way to Chihuahua."

Each step south took MacLeod closer to whatever they had in store for him. He felt his strength and will seeping out of his body. Two promises made, and yet he staggered along, following the ruts of the squealing carts and the dung piles of the animals. The thoughts brought back the words of his father who had asked him why he had to leave the farm and follow General Pike. MacLeod said, "A man has to do what he believes in, especially if you made a promise to do so. I gave my word to the general and now I'm going to keep it." MacLeod recalled his father leaning over to kiss the top of his head when he left. He never saw his father again.

In the distance, the rays of the sun reflected off of a body of water. Lush grass grew in abundance around the edges of the calm water.

"It is the *Laguna del Muerto*," Juan informed him.

"We staying there tonight, by that lake?"

It brought a thin grin to Juan's thin face. "No lake, only so deep," he said holding his hands a few inches apart.

Six hours later the lieutenant arranged the carts in a circle and picketed the horses inside. The others gathered dry dung for a fire while some sat with their weapons between their legs. The few who had muskets were stationed under the carts, looking out toward the San Andres Mountains.

They lashed MacLeod to the wheel of one of the carts. No one sang or spoke. Consuela sat beside him and gently unwrapped the cloths on his feet. She washed off the dried blood and rewrapped them with a clean cloth she had stolen from one of the other women.

After most of the travelers had found spots to lie down and wrap themselves in their blankets, the lieutenant rose from the fire and stumbled over to the wagon where MacLeod sat. His right hand rested on the butt of his pistol, his left held a small jug from which he drank. He leaned down until his pock-marked face was inches from MacLeod's.

MacLeod turned his head from the lieutenant's foul, alcohol-laced breath. "You stupid bastard," MacLeod said, knowing the man couldn't understand a word but not caring if he did.

"*Si*," the lieutenant said and giggled. He tried pulling his pistol from his belt, but it snagged on his shirt. He gave up and pointed a finger at MacLeod instead, making believe it was a gun.

"Save that for the Apache," MacLeod said. "If they come tonight, none of us will be alive by morning."

The lieutenant grinned again and wandered back to the fire. He spoke to two of his men, who left the fire and went to MacLeod. They untied his arms from the wooden wheel and dragged him to the other side of the cart, facing out, toward the open desert. Again they tied him to the cart, as if an offering to Romero. One of the soldiers grabbed Consuela, who bit his hand. He howled in pain and knocked her to the ground, kicking her in the side while he nursed the deep bite in the fleshy part of his palm. She crawled under the wagon and lay behind MacLeod.

A full moon washed the desert with its pale light, outlining the shrubs and stunted trees that grew along the edge of the shallow water. The San Andres Mountains stood barren, inhospitable and cold below the moon. If the Apaches came, Juan had said it would be from those mountains. He had also told MacLeod he would not see or hear them.

The fire soon consumed the little amount of combustible materials on hand and went out. Looking over his shoulder, MacLeod could see most of the prisoners huddled together for warmth, while two of the guards walked the interior of the enclosure, searching for movement in the vast openness beyond the carts.

A three-quarter moon worked its way across the night sky, allowing MacLeod to make out the shape of everything within a hundred yards. He watched.

Nothing moved.

Hours passed.

He slept.

When he woke, the moon had begun its descent. MacLeod had only his thoughts to keep him warm. They raced about his head like a bird caught in a barn until he put them all away and thought only about Maria.

One of the night guards eased between the carts and walked out a few yards to relieve himself. He stopped beside a bush and squatted.

In the first warmth of the morning light, MacLeod watched the man stand and pull up his pants. Suddenly, he staggered and spun around, three arrows protruding from his chest.

Like flitting shadows, the Apache overran the camp. From behind him, MacLeod could hear the twang of bowstrings and the sounds of death. A cry of pain silenced as a throat was slit, or a stream of deadly arrows brought death before a body slumped to the ground.

MacLeod struggled to pull himself free from his bonds before the impact of arrows struck him. He twisted his arm and tried scratching at the knots that held him, but he could not reach far enough behind his back. Two women howled as troopers were pulled to their feet and slain. Consuela growled a question at an Apache who was dragging one of the soldiers out from his hiding place beneath the carts. The Indian rolled the whimpering man onto his back and plunged his knife into his body. The Apache turned back toward Consuela and pointed to a short, squatty figure holding a bloody lance in his hands. She moved to MacLeod's side.

"Romero," she said pointing at the figure with the lance.

MacLeod knew his only hope lay in the confusion that still seized the encampment. He jammed his heels into the ground and forced his back up the solid wooden wheel of the cart. Consuela began picking at the knots.

He saw Romero knock down one of the soldiers who was frantically attempting to fire his musket. The Apache drove his lance into the stomach of the soldier, then calmly placed his foot alongside the lance and jerked it out.

The rope binding MacLeod's wrists fell away. He dropped to his knees and crawled under the back end of the tilted cart. He looked around for a weapon.

For the moment, all of the fighting centered on the lieutenant and the last of the troopers still alive. They had made their stand behind the bodies of two slain mules. A shower of arrows silenced one, the other stood up and ran toward MacLeod, dropping his spent musket in the sand in his attempt to flee.

An Apache rose from the ground and drove his knife into the belly of the fleeing soldier.

MacLeod crawled toward the musket, knowing it was probably not loaded but at least it would serve as a club. He reached it as the Apache finished pulling his knife from the soldier's body and turned to face MacLeod.

MacLeod's attack caught the Apache off guard. He had only enough time to throw his hands up to ward off the blow from the musket. Without hesitating MacLeod brought the musket back again and crushed the Apache's head. Another Indian charged toward MacLeod, his knife held above his shoulder ready to strike. MacLeod dropped to his knees and found the hilt of the dead Apache's knife. He rose to his feet, the knife held low, waiting for the attacker's initial move.

The Apache lunged as MacLeod expected him to do and pulled away in surprise as MacLeod sidestepped the thrust and whipped his own knife across the attackers arm. Belanger had taught him well, and after the first few wild thrusts MacLeod knew the Apache was not equal to his mentor's training. He also knew he must kill quickly before his strength gave out. He couldn't afford to get in close and grapple with the Indian. He let the Apache move to his left and waited for an opening, knowing others would join the fight if he didn't finish it soon.

The Apache was not ready for MacLeod's feint and attack. MacLeod drove the knife deep and cut upward as hard as his strength allowed, the Indian shuddering as the knife sliced his stomach open.

The fight within the circle of wagons appeared to be over. Cries from the women were silenced by stiff threats from the Apache. Others calmly slit the throats of the wounded, while one of the dead mules was butchered.

MacLeod backed away from the encampment as the sun's rays broke over the ridges of the Sacramento Mountains. He looked for a place to hide, hoping the attackers might believe they had killed him in the fight.

Keeping the wagons between him and those ransacking the camp, he began to run, desperately searching for a place to conceal himself to wait until the Apaches left with their spoils. It dawned on him that Romero didn't know what he looked like, or what any American would look like. There was a chance the Indian would believe his son had been avenged.

Ahead, a pair of jagged rock formations jutted out of the desert floor. MacLeod's breath came in ragged gasps while he ran, and he expected the sudden jolt as lances drove through his back, or arrows knocked him to the ground.

The rocks ahead loomed like beacons of hope. Could it actually be possible? MacLeod wondered.

He did not see the two Apaches until they stood, their weapons ready, only a few feet from where he stopped. Although he still held the knife, it seemed useless against the seven-foot lances. He circled to his left, hoping to spot an opening, but found himself cornered. The pair moved forward, forcing him against the rocks. One made a motion toward the knife in MacLeod's hand. There had to be a reason they hadn't killed him already, MacLeod thought as he dropped the knife on the ground.

They marched him back to where Romero waited. The squat figure who had terrorized much of New Mexico stood among the bodies of the mutilated escort soldiers. MacLeod watched as the lieutenant's body was hacked into pieces. The governor would have a difficult time finding any military officers anxious to lead their men in pursuit of Romero.

A shudder passed over MacLeod as he looked into the man's black eyes. Romero's chest was thick and crisscrossed with scars white against the dark skin. The man's belly protruded slightly under the garment he wore around his waist, and his arms were longer than any man of his size MacLeod had seen. The deep lines in his face only served to enforce the look of terror his name produced in those who feared him. He spoke in a deep, guttural language MacLeod could not understand.

"He says you are the man who killed his son. He says now it is your turn to die."

MacLeod had not seen Juan until that moment. He wondered why he was still alive. "Why hasn't he killed me?"

Juan listened to Romero for a moment. "He says your death will take as long as the grass to grow. He says your screams will drive the birds from the sky, and you will know each hour it was he who did this to you."

MacLeod sensed Juan was holding something back. "Anything else?"

Juan shuffled his feet in the dirt. "He say your woman is now his woman, and that he will bring her your heart and eat it before her."

For a moment the anger in MacLeod flooded over him like a fever. Then he realized Romero had admitted Maria was alive. "Tell him he should not have sent a boy out to kill. He should have sent a man."

Romero's hand leapt to the knife at his waist. He held it at MacLeod's throat, the tip slicing the skin and drawing droplets of blood.

MacLeod filed the reaction away in his mind. Belanger had taught him to taunt his opponent whenever he could. Anger often clouded good judgment. If he lived through the next few minutes, he might have the opportunity to see if it worked.

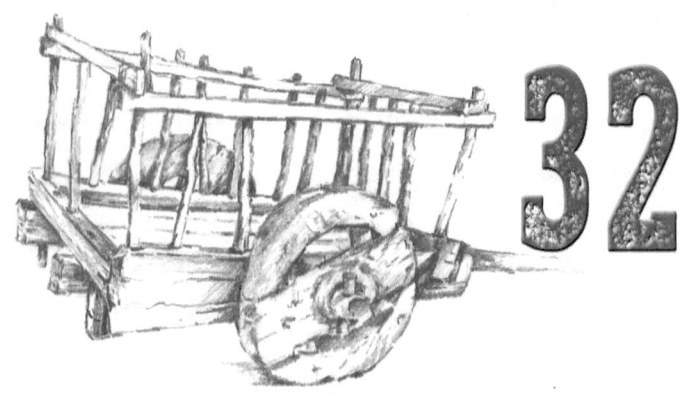

SACRAMENTO MOUNTAINS

R omero led the way, his thick powerful legs eating away at the miles of sand and sparse vegetation. The captives, their heads bowed and their breath coming in gasps, followed, prodded on by the guttural commands of the Apache. With his hands bound, MacLeod struggled to stay on his feet and keep up with the rest of the captives.

As the party rounded a tiny spur, MacLeod looked back to the far off line of trees that marked the Rio Bravo del Norte. He could still see the camp and the bodies of the escort. Romero had had his men strip the bodies, taking anything of value and leaving everything else scattered across the killing area. As a final warning to those who might follow, he had chopped off the lieutenant's head and placed it on the end of a lance buried in the sand.

At noon the party stopped briefly among the jagged rocks of the San Andres. MacLeod fell to his knees immediately but struggled back to his feet when he saw Romero squatting on a rock nearby, watching him.

An hour later MacLeod, realized the treachery of the clear air in that strange land. A vast plain of desert stretched for miles before the climb into the mountains began.

Romero jogged on, seldom turning to see if anyone followed. Behind him, two of his warriors kept the women bunched and moving. Twice MacLeod had seen Consuela step to the side of the trail, each time she was quickly pushed back into line behind the others. MacLeod and Juan followed with their own guards, and some distance back two more Apache herded the mules and horses with the loot from the governor's militia.

Juan moved up alongside MacLeod. "I think he will not stop until we are there," he said, indicating the still far-off mass of mountains.

A look of concern crossed MacLeod's face. "I doubt the women can make it that far.

"They know Romero will not let them stay behind. He will kill them first."

"Why bother? They can't hurt him."

"A life means nothing to an Apache. If you are not one of them, you are the enemy. A dead enemy is a good thing. A dead woman cannot have children who will be Apache enemies."

MacLeod had to admit it made sense, if you thought like an Indian. But Juan was wrong. At dusk the Apache herded everyone together in a tight group for the night. They passed out strips of the mule meat cooked earlier. MacLeod did his best to chew and shallow small portions of the tough flesh. All day he had felt his strength slowly ebbing away, and the next day they would begin the climb into the mountains. He thought about rewrapping the cloth strips around his feet but knew it would only break open the scabs if he did. He left them alone.

MacLeod woke to a still night, no sounds, only the breathing and occasional snort of the captives and the squat figure of Romero sitting on his heels watching him. Didn't he ever sleep? Here was the man who had Maria. Was he taking MacLeod to her, to have her watch his death? All of this was because his son was killed in a fight that shouldn't have happened. Why not kill him and be done with it? Why did he need to take Maria? MacLeod remembered something Juan said earlier, that Romero's private war with MacLeod was unlike the Apache. There was too much risk for too little reward. The tribe gained little.

MacLeod sat up and stared back at Romero. His own hatred blew on the smoldering ember in his gut, and he felt a strength return. "You think you've won and I'm as good as dead, don't you, you bastard," MacLeod muttered. "But that's where you're wrong, and that's your second mistake. Your first was not killing me back at the camp when you killed the others."

For the first time since his captivity began, MacLeod's face broke into a grin.

Romero shifted his feet and changed position. Had he felt something? MacLeod laid his head in his arms and went back to sleep.

At daybreak Romero led them out of a dry watercourse and into the first line of stunted trees. Above rose the dusty-green slopes of the Sacramento Mountains, the home of the Mescalero Apache, and somewhere in the canyons and high alpine meadows of those mountains was a rancheria where Maria waited.

MacLeod lowered his head, time enough to lose himself in thought. At that moment, he needed to concentrate on each step he took, to place his feet on the flattest rocks or on the padded earth between them.

The line of travelers wormed its way up the steep slopes and across narrow ledges of rock, following an old trail. At midday the party intersected a main trail and turned to follow it alongside a stream. They paused to drink from the coldest and clearest water MacLeod had tasted since he arrived in New Mexico.

Juan sank down beside the stream and drank. For the first time, MacLeod saw the dullness in Juan's eyes and knew he also wondered why Romero kept him alive.

The air thinned as they climbed, the trail dipping down to cross-trickling streams, then climbing back up again, around heavily wooded ridges. In the shaded areas, MacLeod felt the chill in the air and recognized the feel of the altitude. His breathing became more labored, and he noticed the others felt it also. Some of the women were bent over, climbing the steep trail with their hands on their thighs, constantly prodded by the Apaches who followed

An old woman dropped to her knees, her head hanging down to her chest, gasping for breath. An Apache jabbed her with his lance as everyone watched, thankful for the momentary pause. Romero growled an order and the guard prodded the woman again. She cried out but refused to move. The lance rose above the Apache's shoulder and flashed downward, piercing the woman between the shoulder blades. From where he knelt MacLeod, saw the head of the lance protruding from the woman's chest. With a heave the Apache freed his lance. The woman's body toppled over, leaving one less enemy for the Apache to worry about.

High into the pine forests they climbed. Two young women faltered and fell to their knees. At a word from Romero, two mules were brought forward for the women to ride and the group resumed its climb. An old woman was simply another mouth to feed, but these young women would be carrying Apache babies by winter.

MacLeod focused on putting his feet one ahead of the other until he reached the next rock or the next clump of bushes, whatever goal he had set for himself. The trail passed through willows growing in the moist soil next to a shallow creek. Romero knelt and scooped a handful of water into his mouth.

MacLeod fell to his knees and plunged his hands into the cold water while the others found space by the creek among the stomping hooves of the horses and mules.

Romero stood and signaled for two warriors to go forward. They loped across a wide meadow, disappearing among the rocks on the far side and reappearing a few moments later high up on a rocky ledge. From there they waved the group forward.

"I think we will stop here," said Juan.

MacLeod followed his guard through a narrow gap between two large boulders and into an area two or three acres square, flat like a parade ground and enclosed by a wall of rocks, some thirty or forty feet high. The two Apaches Romero had sent ahead sat watching from the height of the rocks. Nothing could approach from any direction without being seen.

MacLeod watched as Indians herded the stock toward the lush grass in the eastern end of the square. No need to watch them too closely as the stock had plenty to eat and would stay put for the night.

In the center of the enclosure stood a lone tree, its leafy branches spreading a canopy of shade over the remnants of an old fire. A dozen yards off, a fallen pine lay on its side supported by its broken branches.

The women lay where they had fallen, opposite the pine log. A pair of Indians seized Juan and dragged him toward the sentinel tree. They lashed his feet together and stood him up against the tree, running the rope around the trunk until he was secured.

While MacLeod's guard stood nearby, others moved out into the surrounding trees beyond the wall of rocks and returned with armloads of twigs and dead branches. Soon a fire burned on the bare ground beneath the lone tree.

For a time everything in the camp appeared normal. One Apache fed the fire while others sat and watched. Across the clearing the women began to move as they regained their strength. Consuela sat apart from the others, talking occasionally with the Apache who stood guard nearby.

Romero barked a guttural command and two Apaches pulled MacLeod to his feet. They moved as a group toward the bound figure of Juan, whose head hung down to his chest. Romero grabbed Juan by the hair and held his head up.

Juan's eyes lifted until they came to rest on MacLeod.

Romero pointed to MacLeod and spoke to Juan, who translated.

"He says I am to tell you everything he says. He says if I do my death will not take as long as yours."

"How will he know what you're saying to me?"

Juan's eyes shifted. "It does not matter what we say. Nothing will change what will happen to us. We die soon."

MacLeod nodded. "Ask him about Maria. Ask him if she's alive."

For an instant it looked as if Romero smiled as Juan translated, but the face hardened again when he spoke.

"He says she is alive," Juan said. "He says she will take the place of his son who you killed. He says she will be Apache and bear many Apache children."

It gave him comfort to know she was alive, but it also meant she would be waiting for him to come for her.

At a word from Romero, MacLeod was dragged back toward the fallen log. He struggled but had little strength left in him. His captors ripped off his shirt and placed his back against the log, and bound his hand behind his back. They then lifted his hands over the log and the rope dropped down, which they wrapped around his ankles. Without warning, one of the Indians jerked MacLeod's feet out from under him, and he hung from the log by his arms. He screamed out with the sudden surge of pain as his shoulders felt as if his arms were being ripped from his body. The flesh of his back tore on the log's rough surface as his weight pulled him down toward the ground. He felt warm blood dripping down his sides and could no longer think of anything but the pain.

He watched Romero jog over to the pile of loot from the escort and rummage through it until he found the leather wrapped canteen that had belonged to the lieutenant. He drank. The others reached for their own secreted supply of stolen liquor.

MacLeod realized the Apaches knew he would not die for days, that this was only the beginning of the death ritual. Through the fog of pain, MacLeod heard screams and knew they were not his. Long wailing, moaning screams, of someone who knows death had come to pay a visit. MacLeod opened his eyes and watched as Juan's body was lowered head first over the bed of red-hot coals from the fire. They had removed his shirt and hacked off his hair so it would not catch fire and bring his death too quickly. His arms hung down, giving him the option of attempting to ward off the heat by holding his hands over his head, or letting his brains cook within his skull. Cries of compassion rose from the huddled group of women, who wondered if they would suffer a similar fate. But MacLeod knew the exhibition was for him.

While the Apaches drank the stolen liquor, Juan's hands and fingers roasted until he could no longer protect his head, and his hands fell away and hung down into the coals. The night breeze brought the smell of burning flesh to MacLeod. He wondered why the Apaches did not cut Juan's body down as it rotated slowly, no longer recognizable.

The coals turned to ash and only the sentries posted outside the encampment remained awake.

Sometime during the night, between the snores of the Apaches and the whimpering of the women, MacLeod's mind shut down and his own moans ceased.

In the hours before dawn, a figure rose from the ground and crawled toward a sleeping Indian. It slipped off the high moccasins and eased a knife from its sheath, then made its way toward the fallen log and the suspended body.

The feeling had left MacLeod's arms and legs hours before, and he was unaware of the squat figure who sawed away at his bindings. Suddenly he fell forward, slamming face first into the dirt beneath the log, a hand clamping over his mouth instantly to cut short his cry. Being free from his bindings intensified the pain, bringing it to new heights. He felt himself being rolled onto his back and his lifeless arms placed across his chest, then dragged through the grass and away from the still camp. A voice within him told him to stifle his cries no matter what increase in suffering it brought.

When the dragging stopped, he opened his eyes and saw the shadowy form of Consuela hovering over him. She began massaging his feet and legs, then his arms, until feeling began to creep back into his limbs. As quickly as she had appeared, she vanished into the thinning darkness for a moment, returning with water from the creek. She lifted him into a sitting position so he could drink.

Sated, he fell back into the soothing coolness of the wet grass. From somewhere close by he could hear the stamping of the animals and the smell of fresh dung, and fought his own battle against hope that pushed its way through the pain. Overhead the stars blinked out as heavy clouds enveloped the high mountains.

By the time Consuela returned a second time, he had managed to fight his way through the fire in his body and push himself onto his side. She helped him sit up and slipped a pair of moccasins over his feet. Two horses munched grass nearby, one of them he recognized as Romero's, the other the thick-bodied mare the lieutenant had ridden.

Consuella helped him to his feet and pushed him onto the back of the mare, wrapping his fingers in the mare' mane. As she led the horses through the opening in the rocks, he remembered the guards and recalled seeing them being changed once. He wondered if they had taken part in the previous night's festivities. Romero hadn't appeared to be that careless.

Consuela halted and indicated to him to remain quiet. He saw the flash of a blade as she disappeared through the opening.

Moments later she returned and led the horses through the opening and across the area leading to the main trail. They passed the body of the guard slouched among the rocks a few feet from where they rode. He shivered at the coldness of the act but knew it had been necessary. Still, what woman did he know who could slice a man's throat with such ease?

The rain beat cold on his back, numbing the ache. He clung to the mare's mane and followed the Indian girl into the dimming darkness.

The crack of thunder broke simultaneously with a bolt of lightning. MacLeod felt the spark in the air and his head jerked up. He saw a figure poised to leap onto Consuela.

Without thinking, MacLeod kicked the mare and felt her lunge forward, knocking Consuela aside. The Apache's leap carried him over the mare's head. He landed on his shoulder and rolled over onto his stomach, a knife clutched in his hand. MacLeod threw himself onto the back of the Apache, driving him to the ground and momentarily winding him. The Apache heaved himself up and rolled over, tossing MacLeod off his back. Out of the corner of his eye, MacLeod saw Consuela, her knife raised, running toward them, but he knew she wouldn't make it in time. He tried to grasp the arm of the Apache, but his own arms hung almost lifeless by his side. He could barely make them function. Instinctively, he did what Belanger had done to him in one of their less-than-friendly brawls. As the Apache rose to his knees with his knife extended, MacLeod

E. Paul Bergeron

launched himself forward, smashing the Apache's nose with his head. The Apache's hand went to his face, giving Consuela time to sink her knife into the side of his throat.

Hot blood coursed up, covering MacLeod's face and chest. He rolled off the body and felt a searing stab of pain in his side. He touched the spot where the Apache's knife had sliced through his shirt, and his hand came away covered with his own blood. Consuela lifted the shirt and probed the cut with her fingers, then took his hand and placed it over the wound, pressing it with her own until he understood what she wanted him to do.

She helped him back onto the mare and trotted on, leading the two horses. A hundred yards ahead she located the main trail and swung onto the stallion's back.

The rain continued through the night. Twice MacLeod slid off the mare and had to be helped to mount again, both times causing the wound in his side to reopen. But stopping to rest wasn't an option. They followed the dim path that had brought them into the mountains the previous day, each minute MacLeod wondering how long it would take Romero to discover their escape. Maybe the rain would help blot their tracks, but MacLeod doubted it would fool the Apaches for any length of time.

As if she had read his mind, Consuela led the stallion past two fallen pine trees that MacLeod remembered from the day before. The trail continued along a rock wall on the right. She swung up onto the ledge and let the stallion go. As he approached, MacLeod saw that she wanted him to follow. He eased his leg over the mare's neck and stepped onto the rock, with Consuela grabbing his hands and pulling him toward her. The two horses continued on down the trail.

He stood for a moment, his legs trembling with the effort. She had chosen well—a long, flat outcropping of rock that led north, along the flank of the Sacramento Mountains, and away from the main trail.

They followed it for a quarter mile, then left the rock ledge and dropped down to a stream. Consuela pulled weeds from the streamside and made a poultice of mud, which she placed on his wound. He drank from the stream while she rearranged rocks over the spot where she had pulled the weeds.

With the first indication of dawn, she pushed him harder, continually looking back to see if anyone followed. Each time he slowed, she pulled him by the arm and forced him to move faster. Finally, he could go no farther. He sat on the nearest rock and dropped his head into his arms.

Motioning him to get up, she pointed to a line of thick bushes. He nodded and pulled himself to his feet using the branch of a small tree for support. Consuela growled and inspected the branch, making sure he hadn't left any broken twigs on the ground.

They made their way along the flat surface of a ledge to the bushes, where MacLeod rested as she inspected the area. The head-high brush backed up against a slanted rocky ridge. Above the ridge, the pine-studded mountain rose abruptly.

A forbidding sense of aloneness swept over him when she disappeared from view. For a moment he wondered if thoughts of her own safety surpassed her desire to help him. He glanced back the way they had come and saw that anyone following would naturally take the route below where he sat and follow it down into a narrow canyon that ran toward the open plains below. She had chosen well; too well, in fact. That spot, along with the place where they left the trail, caused MacLeod to wonder how she had known about it.

A fresh rain shower increased the heavy scent of the forest and rotting pine needles. It also brought Consuela trotting back to where he sat.

"I sure wish you could talk some," he said as she took his hand and led him slowly along the face of the bushes.

She stopped and parted the brush. Without a word she dropped to her knees and crawled through the opening. Grimacing in pain, MacLeod knelt and followed her. After going about ten feet, the bushes opened into the mouth of a small cave in the rock wall. MacLeod continued into the blackness of the cave and collapsed.

He had no idea how long he had slept. When he woke, he was alone, wrapped in a musty robe, about ten feet from the mouth of the cave. He tried pushing himself into a sitting position but gave up when the bolts of pain in his arms and shoulders made him sick. Instead he rolled over onto his side and used the rough wall of the cave to push himself up into a sitting position. He sat holding his elbows in his hands, trying to ease the terrible ache in his joints, needing water but unable to move about to find any. He needed food, but could do nothing about that either. He was helpless without her.

As he sat, he wondered how Consuela had known about the cave. And if she knew of it, wouldn't Romero know of it as well?

He drifted off, then woke with a jolt, hearing voices, then the stomp of horses. Using his feet, he pushed himself along the floor of the cave toward the entrance until he lay within the dense thicket of brush. Only six inches or so of twigs and leaves hid him. Carefully, he parted the last few remaining branches and held his breath. Romero sat on the same rock MacLeod had used, his back to the line of bushes; four of the Apache's warriors lounged close by. They appeared to argue.

MacLeod recognized the one who pointed toward the bushes where MacLeod lay. He was the one with a long scar along the right leg who had helped tie Juan to the tree. He kicked the ground in front of Romero and pointed again toward the line of bushes. Romero stood and turned to see where the Apache was pointing.

MacLeod held his breath. A line of ants bearing the carcasses of their prey changed their course, crawled up MacLeod's finger and down his arm to his elbow. Others followed as the moments passed and still Romero stared at the spot where MacLeod hid. Finally, seeming to make up his mind, he walked toward the bushes.

MacLeod held his breath as Romero bent down to inspect the brush half a dozen yards away. The Apache pushed a branch aside with his foot and studied the ground, then turned and jogged back to where the others waited. As quickly as they had appeared, the small band moved down into the canyon.

The sun slowly settled itself far to the west, its warmth following its rays as they raced down the side of the mountain.

Without a sound, Consuela crawled through the brush and into the cave.

That night MacLeod slept like a contented child, his stomach full of roasted rabbit.

For the next three days, MacLeod would see her only in the late afternoon when she returned with food, a rabbit or a grouse, sometimes a quail or two, but MacLeod ate whatever she cooked. It became apparent that she knew Romero would not be back, so MacLeod figured some of her time away must have been in following his trail.

From the depths of the cave, she retrieved leather packets of jerky and tanned hides, obviously stored as emergency rations. While Consuela set about cutting and sewing the hides into clothing and moccasins for him, MacLeod tried his few words of Spanish on her. The language she responded with was nothing MacLeod could recall hearing. He gave up any further attempts to communicate.

Feeling stronger each day, MacLeod grew restless and began to explore the cave. He had watched her take a fire brand and disappear into its depths for a time, emerging with whatever she sought from its apparently well-stocked interior.

One morning after she left, he wrapped some twigs and moss around a branch and lit it with the hot embers of the fire. He crawled down the tunnel-like corridor until it opened into a large cavern. He found the storage area in a small alcove. Stacks of leather packets containing enough dried food to keep a number of families for months. The alcove also contained hides for clothing and moccasins, pottery, half a dozen lance shafts, reeds for arrows, and half-carved bows.

MacLeod searched the interior of the cavern and found another narrow opening that led to a smaller room. As he crawled inside, a hand touched a round object, too light for a rock. He raised the object to the light of his torch and looked into the vacant eye sockets of a skull. He dropped the skull like a hot iron and pushed it aside, his torch revealing the bones of the remainder of the skeleton. At the rear of the room, MacLeod's found a small stack of oblong objects. He brushed away the thick coating of dust and picked one up. It was too uniform to be a rock. He turned it over, amazed at the weight of what appeared to be a small bar of metal. No telling how many of them were in the stack, but it appeared considerable. He needed a closer look at one of them in a better light.

MacLeod returned the entrance to the cave, the thin bar in his hand. He was pretty certain it was silver, but he couldn't be sure. Suddenly the little cave took on a far greater significance, but posed a lot more questions than he could think of answers for. Did whoever put the foodstuffs in the cave know about the bars?

MacLeod decided not to show Consuela what he had found. If it was silver, it might help buy his and Charbonneau's freedom, along with the governor's protection from Griego until they got out of the country. But what about Maria?

The nights grew cold and Consuela had taken to sleeping next to him. The first night she slipped between the robes and pressed her naked back against him. When he failed to respond, she had grunted once and immediately fell into a deep, snore-filled sleep.

Two mornings later, Consuela shook him awake at first light. She wrapped their few belongings in a hide and placed the packet over her shoulders. He gathered from her actions the time had come to leave their sanctuary.

While Consuela did her best to cover their tracks, and carefully arranged the branches over the entrance to the cave, MacLeod took the time to place the spot in his mind, the same way he had when caching the furs. He made note of the rocky ledge and the nearby stream that ran into the canyon. He guessed they were about halfway up the mountain, judging by the height of the trees. As she led them down into the canyon, MacLeod turned often to view their back trail and memorize the features of the land. Not that he ever figured to come back, but he couldn't help thinking about the pile of ingots in the back of the cave.

By dark they had dropped down from the mountain into a series of low foothills and spent the night huddled in a dry arroyo.

Before daybreak Consuela woke him and they walked onto a dry mesa cut deeply by arroyos and shallow runoffs. MacLeod realized where they were when he turned around and saw the same snow-covered peaks he had seen days before. He had a rough idea of where the big river lay that led to Santa Fe—and Don Cordero. He knew he could find his own way from there. A faint breeze fanned a spark of hope.

Hours passed as MacLeod followed closely on Consuela's heels. Twice he had seen her turn to look behind. He followed her gaze and saw the distant puffs of smoke rising from the mountains. Could

Romero have given up? He had doubts the Apache would ever give up as long as he thought MacLeod was still alive.

When darkness forced her to look for a place to spend the night, he felt he couldn't walk another step. She knelt in the bottom of a dry streambed and scooped out the dirt from beneath the roots of a dying pinion tree, creating a small space. He crawled inside and curled up into a ball without eating the strip of jerky she tried feeding him. He needed sleep more than food.

As the sun's rays crept down the far side of the arroyo, Consuela rolled out of their den and scrambled to her feet. Moments later she grabbed him by the arm and pulled him to his feet, pointing over the rim of the arroyo. A mile and a half away, maybe two, he saw them. Four horses in single file line, heading toward the arroyo.

He felt the ray of hope wither. His stomach knotted with agonizing frustration. When he turned back, Consuela was gone. For a moment he saw her head bobbing above the edge of the arroyo before she disappeared again.

MacLeod watched them approach until he could make out their features. Definitely Romero. He felt a deep sense of loss. She had risked her life to help him escape, making all the decisions for the past week, yet she appeared to have abandoned him and run for her life. It puzzled him, but he couldn't blame her.

The floor of the dry streambed was covered in loose rock and pebbles. He knew the Apaches would find his tracks as soon as they reached it, but he didn't care. He broke into a jog, following her footprints down the streambed. The walls rose on both sides and the floor narrowed, gravel gradually giving way to a sandy bottom.

MacLeod scrambled over the ankle deep sand as fast as he could, knowing the Indians would soon cross his tracks. Then only minutes would be left of his life. Romero would not postpone his death a second time.

So why run? His left wrist had swollen to twice its size from a fall, his feet throbbed with pain, and the sand behind was spotted with his blood. Still, he staggered down the channel.

The streambed widened and the arroyo became shallower as he approached a broad plain. He would no longer be hidden. He crouched down and moved to the low bank, raising his head to look over the rim. Less than fifty yards away the line of Apaches walked their horses toward him as if they knew where he had run and had angled their horse toward the place where he knelt. He began to crawl along the edge of the arroyo wall, looking for a place to hide. He searched for something to use as a weapon, picking up a rock, then dropping it when he saw a small dead tree stripped of its branches by time and the intensity of the water passing over it. He pulled it from the sand and hefted it. Not much against their lances but better than his bare hands.

For a moment he sat with his back to the sandy wall, counting the seconds and playing it out in his mind. He looked around, choosing his battleground. A number of large boulders lay embedded in the sand on his left. They might impede the Apaches' horses for a moment. Then he spotted a knee-high shrub growing on the edge of the arroyo wall above him that offered itself as a screen. He crawled toward it and peered through its exposed roots, freezing at the sound of the hooves of a horse striking rock. He pulled his head down quickly. Romero was less than thirty feet away and moving toward the lip of the arroyo, but the other warriors were further back. He had a chance. He would wait until he figured Romero would be directly above him. If he could surprise the Apache, he might be able to knock him off his horse, then mount and make a run for it. There was a good chance Romero had the best horse of the bunch, and MacLeod would have a head start.

MacLeod lowered his head below the rim and inched his way to his right, to a spot where the sandy wall had crumbled. He went over it again. Only a few steps up the crumbling dirt and over the top, then a quick left, and he would be a step or two from the Apache.

The seconds ticked away. MacLeod wiped his hands on his shirt and gripped the branch. He mouthed a silent prayer. Everything depended on surprise. He began to count.

He vaulted up the side of the arroyo, the branch poised to strike and heard a cry.

The cry distracted Romero, causing him to turn. MacLeod stood exposed, the raised branch in his hand, as Romero urged his horse into a lope back toward the others.

A mile away a figure ran, arms flailing, as the Apache warriors closed at a hard run. The figure fell, rose, and ran again.

Even at that distance MacLeod knew it was Consuela. He fell to his knees with his heart pounding and his breath coming in gasps. Lifting his head, he watched as they surrounded her and knocked her to the ground. One of the Apache raised his lance to strike but stopped as Romero shouted an order. The warrior lowered his lance and stood over the prone figure.

MacLeod dropped back into the arroyo. Only raw luck had kept Romero from cutting across their earlier tracks.

He continued to watch as they appeared to argue. Romero kept pointing back toward the arroyo, but the others wanted no part in a further search. One of the Apaches helped Consuela onto his horse and the three turned toward the Sacramento Mountains. For a moment Romero sat searching the land where MacLeod hid, then wheeled his horse around and rode after the others.

MacLeod sat at the bottom of the arroyo as the blazing sun beat down on him. The waters that had formed the arroyo had found other avenues of escape, spreading out across the desert floor. A hundred yards below the arroyo ended. If he tried following it toward the river, they could easily spot him once he was in the open. Thirst soon took the place of fear, but he sat with his back against steam bank and waited.

The sun fell slowly in the west. It would be in the Apaches' eyes if they turned and looked back. He rose and the branch, the only weapon he had, became a cane to help him stay on his feet. He began walking toward the falling sun, and the river.

By day he found refuge in whatever shade made itself available, shifting his body as the sun crept across a brilliant, endless sky. In the late afternoon he rose and walked west, a step at a time, looking over his shoulder, always fearful of what, or who, may be following. Two days, or maybe three, he figured since Romero captured Consuela. The land rose and fell, always cut with strength-sapping jagged arroyos, always bone dry. On top of the last rise he thought he saw the dark shadow of the tree-lined Rio Bravo del Norte before darkness overtook it, but he couldn't be sure. Again he stumbled and fell.

He lay sprawled in the sand. All thoughts of Maria and his promise to her, or Charbonneau, or fear of Romero, had vanished from his mind. The terrible hunger no longer gnawed at his insides. Only the need for water occupied his thoughts.

Somewhere he lost his shirt. His feet were swollen to twice their normal size, but the sand, mixed with the blood, served to stop further bleeding. He no longer cared about that either.

A tiny shrew poked its head from its hole to investigate the strange object lying across its path. Satisfied that no danger existed, it scampered around the body and sat on a nearby rock, eyeing the strange creature.

MacLeod watched the shrew's movements. He took a great interest in it, but he didn't know why. He tried to rise. He had to keep moving, but he couldn't remember where he meant to go. He began crawling, not aware of his direction until exhaustion carried him down into the shallow grave of unconsciousness.

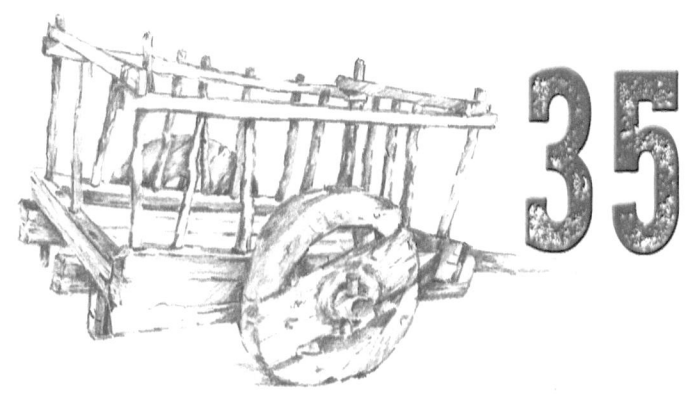

APACHE RANCHERIA

A restless feeling enveloped the camp. Maria dropped her load of firewood by the cooking fire and stretched her back. The smell of the cook pots brought a momentary wave of nausea. A group of young boys raced past her with sticks in their hands, one stopping for a moment to pretend to shoot an arrow at her. She leaped at him, sending him racing after the others. The older boys had left camp much earlier with their bows bent and whatever arrows they had clutched in their hands. With luck they might return with a rabbit or two, or even a quail. Lately they had supplied the only fresh meat for the pots.

Maria glanced over the group of old men who gathered each morning in front of Walking Like a Dog's wickiup. Her friend, Margarita, moved over to her side.

"They tell their stories again," Maria said.

"Some have more than others."

"When our men gather they all talk at once. It is not important what the others are saying."

"Yes, I remember, but this way they will all tell their stories and no one will question them. It will take all day."

Two men struggled to their feet and went to relieve the lookouts. Both moved with a sprightliness shown only when the younger warriors left the camp in the charge of the old people. For a few days they acted as young men again.

Maria smiled, watching Walking Like a Dog tell one of his tales. His knurled hands, despite the pain and stiffness she knew he suffered, flew about as he described his feats in some long-ago encounter. For weeks Maria had tended the old man's fire and slept in his wickiup. One night, seeing the agony his crippled hands caused him, she picked up a glob of grease from the edge of the cooking pot and began to massage his fingers and hands. From his reaction, she realized no one had done that for him before, and it became a nightly routine. Sometimes, while she rubbed away the pain, he spoke to her in his battered Spanish. He told her how he had killed many of his enemies, including many of her people, but he hoped that none where from her family.

She liked the old man, and he appeared to like her, maybe because she didn't show the perpetual sullenness that other captives displayed. Maria spoke to him about MacLeod. Walking Like a Dog said he had heard of this great warrior with the pale look. He said whoever killed him would have a great story to tell and everyone would listen. He only wished he was many years younger that he might go in search of him.

Maria turned to Margarita again. "When will the others return?"

The woman shrugged. "It is already late. The early food will die soon. We will need to hurry."

"Where will we move the village to?"

"Toward the early sun, but it may be too late for gathering the yucca."

The question that plagued Maria returned. What news would Romero bring, or would he return with MacLeod? Romero's long absence gave Maria hope. Possibly the troops beat off the attack, maybe even killed him. They might be marching south toward Chihuahua with MacLeod. Who knows what would happen in Mexico? She tried remembering how he looked the last time she saw him, the look in his eyes when he promised to find her and take her with him. Such a foolish promise. But that's what made him so different. He believed he could do these things he promised. A sad smile softened her face for a brief moment. This strange lone man, from so far way, had brought such turmoil to her and her country, yet she lived on the hope of those promises. Maria shook her head. I must find another way if I am to live, she told herself.

The old woman watcher waved a stick at her and pointed toward the pile of wood. Maria took a step toward her, making her scurry to a safer distance.

Two days later, word reached the camp of Romero's return. A nervous excitement swept over the people. Maria knelt by the fire as the women gathered to meet the returning warriors and claim their share of the spoils. This was the moment she dreaded, the moment of impending doom. Would they bring his tortured body back with them? Romero would do it, to show her what he had done.

From the edge of the camp they watched the train of warriors and captives approach. Romero led, with the captives struggling along in front of the loose stock. The first moments of excitement and relief gave way to a growing nervousness. Maria sidled up to Margarita. She could feel the change in the camp.

"What is it?" asked Maria.

"They have not all returned."

"Maybe the others follow."

"No, they would all come together."

Maria searched for MacLeod among the captives. She heard the voices of the women, uncertain, questioning. She moved toward the others, her own anxiety growing.

Two women suddenly cried out, realizing their men were missing. The mother of a young warrior, on his first raid, fell to her knees beside her wickiup. His horse had returned without him.

Romero rode through the camp and dismounted. Others turned their horses over to the young boys and sought the shelter of their *wickiups*.

A high-pitched wail rose from the throats of the women who would be forced to eke out a living on their own, nor would they receive a share of the plunder.

Maria searched for the captives. They would know what had happened. She ran to the group of women huddled in a circle and guarded by the older boys. Most of the women lay where they had fallen, others begged for water. An Indian captive sat sullen-faced by herself, marks of a recent beating on her face and arms.

Maria approached one of the captives. "Please, tell me what happened."

The woman raised her head, her split lips moving but making no sound. Maria held a jug of water to her lips.

"Tell me," Maria begged.

"He came at night. He killed all the soldiers and only the one they call the *Americano*, and another, did he not kill."

Maria's heart leaped. "Tell me about the *Americano*."

"He killed two of the Apaches, but they captured him, but then they took us all into the mountains, and he and that one ran away one night," she said, indicating the squat figure who sat off to one side.

"He escaped?"

"*Si*, they killed two more, but now he is dead."

Maria stifled a cry. "How do you know he is dead?"

"That is what she says. It is all I know."

Maria knelt beside Consuela, offering her the water jug. "You were with him. Tell me what happened."

Consuela's black eyes glared back at Maria. In battered Spanish she muttered, "He is dead."

"Please tell me about him."

Consuela sat motionless as if she had not heard.

"She will tell you nothing," the young Mexican captive said.

"Do you know? Did Romero kill the *Americano*?"

Between drinking the water Maria provided, and eating a piece of meat Maria had stolen for herself, the young woman told her as much of the story as she could. She told of MacLeod's treatment at the mountain camp and of Juan's death and how they all awoke the next morning to find two Apaches dead and Romero gone in pursuit. From one of the other women who understood a little Apache, she learned of the chase and Consuela's capture. Romero had returned to the camp in a rage when the other warriors refused to continue the search for MacLeod.

Maria felt her heart skip a beat. "You mean no one saw his body?"

"Only the Indian woman, no one else. She says he died the third day, because of his injuries."

After more questioning, Maria realized the woman knew no more about MacLeod's escape. Only the one they called Consuela knew, and she would not talk. It would take time to gain her confidence, and Maria had nothing but time. She dropped the last of her stolen meal in Consuela's lap and rose as voices in the camp increased in anger.

Margarita stood among the other camp women who gathered in front of Romero's wickiup demanding answers. Why had four warriors died for a few horses and mules, some broken weapons and a number of captives who meant more mouths to feed? And who was this pale-faced demon who killed so many Apache?

In spite of his reported death, Maria felt a tremendous surge of pride at his single-handed fight for his life. She was also aware of the eyes of the women watching her. MacLeod's battle to save his life would bring the women down on her. They had accepted her as another captive, but knowing of Maria's feelings for the man, they would attempt to drive her from the camp. Maria knew she must bide her time until she chose to be driven away, and it would not be until she found out from Consuela what had happened to MacLeod. Romero might have other ideas, but Romero dared not overrule the women too often. If they became too belligerent, he might take a few warriors and leave for a while.

A woman whose husband died turned from Romero and saw Maria.

"Be careful," Margarita warned.

The woman picked up a stick of firewood and ran toward her. Maria knew the Apache reverence for courage. Her one hope of surviving was to show that she had courage and would pass it along to her Apache children. Her role in the tribe as a producer of children made her a valuable asset, if she lived.

A grim determination swept over her as she reached down and picked up her own weapon. The camp turned to watch, expecting her to run from the attack. As her attacker swung her club, Maria dodged, holding her own ready. The woman pursued Maria, swinging wildly while screaming out her rage. The rest of the village spread out giving them room. Soon the woman's wild attempts began to sap her strength. Maria bided her time. She understood the woman's anger, but she knew she had to show the others no weakness. It hurt her to do it, but after another uncontrolled lunge, Maria swung her club and drove the exhausted woman to the ground.

An angry cry rose from the surrounding women. Maria circled the prostrate attacker, daring another to take her place. The crowd backed away from her until she found herself face to face with Romero. Neither moved, while the rest of the camp watched the confrontation. Finally Romero spoke in his mixture of Apache and Spanish.

"The strange one is dead and will kill no more Apaches. I have done this thing."

She smiled but it was not her nature to remain silent. "Can you be sure he is dead? How many less is in your *rancheria* because of him? If he still lives, your people will be only women. He will kill all of your men. Look what this one man has done to you."

Most of the women did not understand Maria's words but they joined her in chastising Romero for his costly war party to avenge his son's death.

Without waiting for a reply Maria returned to Walking Like a Dog's fire and sat down. She would need time to gain the confidence of the Navajo girl they called Consuela. She stirred the pot hanging over the fire. Surely they would kill a mule or one of the horses and share the meat.

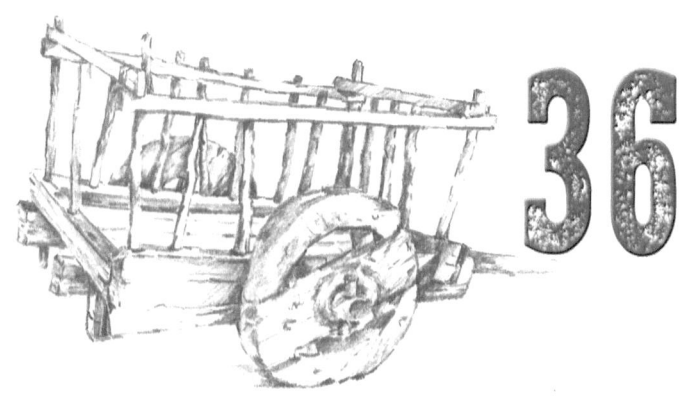

SANTA FE

Santa Fe basked in the warm, summer-like weather. Snow still clung to the north-facing slopes of the Sangre de Cristo Mountains, but in the valley of the Rio Bravo del Norte the warmth of early summer brought new life to the land.

Miguel Griego breathed in the fresh, clean air blowing through the canyons to sweep Santa Fe clean of its choking human smells. Even with his usual morning hangover, he felt a new sense of life to go along with nature's cycle.

With the governor watching his movements carefully, Griego had not accompanied Gomez to the north to look for the furs. Instead he remained in the vicinity of Santa Fe with most of his *urbanos*. His absence from the search party had not mattered. Gomez had returned with the news that the furs had been found, more furs than he had hoped for.

A rider entered the courtyard and dismounted.

"Where is Zavalda?" Griego demanded.

"The governor has instructed him to stay in Santa Fe while he is away, but *Teniente* Zavalda says he must see you also, and very soon. He says he has orders from the governor for you."

"What orders?"

The messenger shrugged.

Griego nodded. He knew it had to be important for Zavalda to send such a message. He ordered his horse to be saddled.

Three hours later, Griego found Zavalda pacing the floor in the governor's office much the same way the governor did. "You have heard?" Zavalda blurted before Griego had time to greet him.

"I have heard many things. Which do you speak of?"

"What do you think I speak of? The escort taking the prisoners to Chihuahua, what else?"

"Such fools," Griego muttered. "What were they doing to be caught off guard like that?"

Zavalda ignored Griego's question. "Did you have an agreement with this Apache?"

Griego bristled. "What do you mean by this agreement? You were the one who gave me the information on when they were to leave. What did you expect me to do with it?"

Zavalda wrung his hands. "I did not expect all of them to die, and such deaths. Their bodies were scattered all over the desert. In pieces."

A shudder shook Griego. That could have been him lying out there instead of the militia.

"The governor has instructed me to do something about this," Zavalda continued. "I will need your help."

Griego scratched himself, wondering just what kind of help Zavalda had in mind. "Gomez returned last night."

Zavalda caught the implication immediately. "Was he successful?"

Griego grinned. "You would not believe what he found. In fact, he will have to return for what is left."

"That is another thing," Zavalda said as he flopped into the governor's chair and put his head between his hands. "He has ordered me to investigate the death of the other *Americano*. Why did you have to kill him? It is making everything more difficult."

"The governor has many problems; he will soon forget this one."

"You may distract the governor, but this Father Alvarez will never let him forget. He is demanding answers."

"He is always asking questions," Griego muttered. "It is too bad he was not going to Chihuahua with the others. Then we would be rid of him." Griego understood how Zavalda felt.

"At one time did you not speak of orders the governor received from Chihuahua about furs?" Griego asked.

"It is here somewhere," Zavalda said. While Griego lit a cigarillo, the governor's aide rummaged through the assorted papers on the desk until he found what he wanted. "Yes, it this policy our commandant general wishes to put into action. We have very little use for these animal skins and no knowledge of acquiring them, but it appears the Indians use them in trade with the *Americanos*. It is thought that we might buy a little peace if we help supply the Indians with furs. That is why the governor wanted to believe the story they told him."

Griego grinned. "How much will the governor pay for furs? Enough to satisfy Chihuahua?"

"I do not know," Zavalda said. "There is very little money in the treasury for such things. Our commandant general might wish to see certain plans put into action, but he does not provide us with the funds to do so. Why do you ask?"

Griego had not thought of that. If the governor had no money to buy the furs, Griego figured he should keep the idea to himself for the time being. "Nothing, but we have not spoken yet about why you have asked me here."

"It is this thing with the Apaches. The Governor has ordered me to take some troops and find Romero. You and your *urbanos* are to go with me."

Griego's quickly forgot his earlier headache. "You do not find Romero, he finds you, if it is what he wants."

"But the governor has ordered it."

"And you could not change his mind?"

"He would not listen," Zavalda said. "He will need to inform the commandant general on what progress he has made."

Griego had no intentions of riding out in search of Romero, at least not if there was a chance of finding him. "Where is our governor now?"

Zavalda smiled. "Taos."

"Yes, of course, that would be the safest place to be."

"It would seem so," Zavalda said, rising from the chair to sit on the edge of the governor's desk. "But our problem is still unresolved. What do you suggest?"

"I think it will take us some time to gather supplies and prepare the troops. By then Romero should have left the mountains, and we will have little chance of finding him."

"See that you are back before the governor returns. We must be gone by then," Zavalda said, returning to the chair and reaching for the stack of papers on his desk.

A week later Miguel Griego rode into Santa Fe at the head of his troops and found the governor's aide in a near panic. With Governor Melgares said to be on his way back to the capital, Zavalda wanted to be out of reach when he returned. Instead he was standing beneath the overhang in front of the Presidential Palace talking with two men. He beckoned to Griego.

"I think you should hear this. It is probably nothing but it is odd."

"What is it?" Griego asked.

"These men arrived from Vera Cruz only yesterday with dispatches for the governor. They say they found a man in the desert, near Fray Cristobal."

"That is not so difficult. I find men all over Nuevo Mexico," Griego said and laughed.

"Yes, but they say this one is different. These men said his hair is like the sand, and his eyes are blue. They say he does not speak like us."

The news sobered Griego. "Where is this man?"

The two traders explained to Griego where they found the man and their decision to leave him at Isleta.

"It could be nothing, but it could be him. The man will not die. If it is him, we must find him before the governor does." With the death of the Frenchman to go along with the other questions the governor had about Maria de Cordero, and how the Apache knew about the escort taking the prisoners to Chihuahua, Griego did not want the *Americano* returned. He needed time for these questions to die their slow death.

"He cannot go anywhere; he has no papers. I will issue orders that he be brought to me if he is found."

A fleeting thought struck Griego. Could he sell this one to Romero twice? He chuckled. "I think we will find him in Isleta."

"Do you think Romero will be looking for him also? We may be searching for Romero as the governor has ordered, but do we really want to find him?"

"How many men do you have?" Griego questioned.

"I have thirty available and equipped with what the governor left. He took much of the weapons on his trip."

"Good. Romero will not attack such a force. When will you be ready to leave?"

Zavalda indicated the saddled horses within the enclosed part of the presidio. "We have been waiting for you."

ISLETA MISSION

The gentle caress of warm, scented air washed over MacLeod like a summer shower. The sound of voices, soft and gentle and unhurried, with no anger, made him think he was dreaming. He dozed again.

When he woke he stretched cautiously and leaned back against the warm adobe wall of the mission church, savoring the delicious smell of the late blossoms. He sat on a narrow, hewn-log bench, shaded by the fruit trees growing alongside the mission, and watched the Indians go about their chores. Often a child, its black eyes staring, would come and stand under the tree to watch him until scooted away by one of the padres. Seldom did anyone speak to him after the vain attempts to communicate the first few days. They left him to hobble about using the makeshift canes he had fashioned. Twice a day someone took him to the room where everyone ate. They dished out bowls of a thin stew, a little meat, a few vegetables, and hard bread, always the same but never enough. The meals were a short affair, a few muttered prayers, the serving of food but no conversation. When they finished, everyone rinsed their bowls and left MacLeod to sit by himself.

Each day he asked himself the same questions. Were they still looking for him? Did the governor believe he was dead?

He closed his eyes and ran through his limited options. Who could blame him if he tried to get out of the country? Maybe next year he could return to see if the furs were still in the cache, but that still left his promise to Maria. Whatever he decided, he would first need to make it back to the Cordero hacienda. Don Cordero had offered them horses and supplies, and their guns were at the hacienda, if they hadn't been turned over to Griego. He had no idea how Don Cordero would treat him, and he would have to travel through the very country where the governor's and Griego's forces moved freely, and do so unarmed.

Which left one option. Do nothing. It was the one lesson that had been the hardest to learn: Let your enemies make the first move.

MacLeod dozed again and woke to the sound of voices.

"You look well."

MacLeod jolted upright. He pushed himself to his feet and turned to see the hollowed cheeks of Father Alvarez.

"Father, how did you find me?"

Alvarez seemed to sense his fears. "No one suspects. They all speak of your death, but word will eventually reach them."

"Then how did you find out?"

He took MacLeod's arm. "Can you walk on those?" he said, indicating the two sticks MacLeod had carved into canes.

"Well enough."

"Then we will walk a little."

"Have you heard anything about Maria?"

"Only the same repeated rumors, and they are like the sands of the desert, there are so many."

"But I know where she is." MacLeod related everything that had happened since he left the prison in Santa Fe. Long before he finished they found a spot by the river and sat down to rest.

"Our Blessed Mother looks over you," Alvarez said.

"I guess it's got to be more than luck."

"Some of what you have told me we knew. The bodies of the escort were found. At first the governor tried to blame it on those coming to rescue you, but too many people witnessed the rampage of the Apache to believe otherwise.

"And Griego?" MacLeod wanted to know.

"Yes, Señor Griego. He is seldom seen. His father is saying that Don Cordero sent Maria away to Mexico secretly, to avoid the marriage, and Miguel has somehow paid off his debts and continues to gamble."

"It tells me Romero paid him for both of us."

"Of course, but who would believe you?"

They rose and walked slowly past the women washing clothing in the river.

"What is this place, Father?"

"It is the Mission of Isleta. Is it not a beautiful place?"

"It sure is a lot more peaceful than some places I've been lately."

"When he returned to New Mexico, Don Diego de Vargas used this town as his headquarters and restored the mission."

"Do you come here often?"

"Whenever I have the opportunity. Father Ramirez and I share the same concerns on many things."

"You mean like the slave trade," MacLeod said.

"Yes, but you ask about the mission, and I must tell you a story. When Francisco Vasquez de Coronado returned to Mexico in the year of our Lord 1542, two of our brothers chose to remain and continue their work among the Indians. Fathers Juan de Padilla and Luis de Escalona were left alone near Quivira. It is believed they were slain soon after Coronado left. The people believe that when this mission was built the body of Padre Padilla was buried beneath the alter, and once a year his body rises to the surface and can be seen by the true believers."

MacLeod stopped walking and sat down to rest his feet. "Right here in this mission?"

Alvarez nodded.

"Do you believe the story?"

"It is not important. The people believe it."

"Have you ever seen it happen?"

Alvarez shook his head. "It has not been my fortune to be here at the right time, but now I will try to answer some of your questions. You were found by soldiers bringing dispatches from Chihuahua for the governor. It was easier to leave you here than bring you to Santa Fe, and they do not know of you. I was in Santa Fe at the time and heard the story. I came at once."

"What about the governor, does he know?"

"No, he was called away on official business and has not heard yet. It may be some time before he is told."

"What do you think he will do when he hears?"

"He will probably assign the task of bringing you back to Miguel Griego. Our governor thought he was rid of you, but now he must again decide what to do. And Miguel Griego cannot have you brought back. You would bring too many questions that cannot be answered."

"Sounds like you're saying I wouldn't make it back to Santa Fe alive if Griego finds me here, is that it?"

Alvarez clasped his thin hands behind his back and walked a few paces off. "This country and this government have been a test of my faith since I arrived. I have begun to wonder if I can make a difference. But now there is something that brings a great amount of sadness to my heart. I must tell you that your friend is dead."

MacLeod's head shot up. "Mr. Charbonneau's dead?"

Alvarez nodded.

"How did you know?"

"I was called to hear his confession, but it was too late."

The news sent MacLeod reeling. Even though it had been months since he last saw Charbonneau, his death left him feeling lost and alone. *They are all dead. Belanger and Stewart in the canyon, and now Charbonneau. Who will tell his family?*

"But Maria is still alive," MacLeod said.

"There is nothing you can do for her. If what you say is so, it is too late."

"No, it's never too late, now that I can tell them where she is. Won't they go after her?"

"No."

"Why not?"

The pain in Alvarez's face made MacLeod wince. "What would they do with her if they found her?" he said softly.

MacLeod drew his knees up to his chest and wrapped his arms around them. He nodded but didn't speak.

"Father Ramirez and I have things we must speak of while I am here, but I will see you again before I leave," Alvarez said.

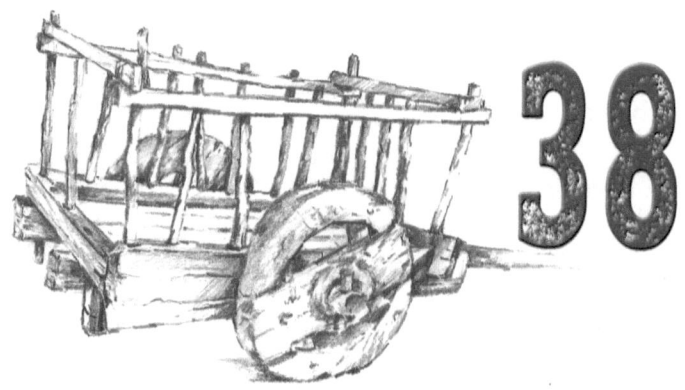

38

Rain clouds gathered over the mountains to the west of Isleta. MacLeod walked hesitantly across the plaza, drawn once again to the waters of the river. The early morning smells of the village mingled with the sharp freshness of a new day. He eased himself to the ground beside an abandoned ox cart and watched the gates of the mission, hoping to see Alvarez after morning prayers.

The morning passed like all mornings. Men trudged out to tend the spring crops, crude wooden implements balanced on their shoulders. Women carried water from the river, and fruit and vegetables to the kitchen cooking pots, while the children raced dogs and goats through the dusty lanes, seldom catching them.

An hour later Alvarez appeared.

MacLeod waited to speak until the priest halted in front of him. "How did Charbonneau die?"

"What does it matter how?" Alvarez said.

"I need to know. Was it from his wounds?"

Alvarez shook his head

"Then somebody killed him because they couldn't get the information out of me about where the furs are. Do you know who did it?"

"There is no way to tell. It is better to put it from your mind as we all must do at times."

There it was again. MacLeod saw it in Alvarez's face. What was it, resignation? Using the crude wooden wheel of the cart, MacLeod pulled himself to his feet. "They killed Charbonneau for the furs, they took Maria because they couldn't have their way with her, and they've been trying to kill me. My other friends are lying in the ground where I buried them. I ain't blaming the Indians, but the others here are supposed to be responsible and civilized people. I can't understand it."

"You were not born here. You cannot understand."

"I suppose you're right," MacLeod acknowledged, "but it's still not right. I don't care who you are. If I'd known different, I'd have shot Griego when I had the chance, and taken Maria and Charbonneau and left your damned country."

Although Father Alvarez hadn't spoken, MacLeod could see the man was troubled. "What is it, Father?"

"As you cannot understand the way things are here, I cannot understand the ease with which you speak of killing. Does it not trouble you?"

MacLeod took a moment before responding. "Sometimes . . . the young Indian . . . he was just a kid. I think about him."

A peal of far-off thunder rumbled across the mountains from the west but still the rain remained absent.

"Does it become easier, this taking of life?" Alvarez questioned.

"That's hard to say. I guess I'd have to say I don't stop to question myself at the time because I know if I did, they'd kill me."

"And you will do so again, I imagine." Alvarez's voice struck that tone of resignation again, as if he knew it couldn't be stopped.

MacLeod decided not to answer. Other things needed to be talked over before Alvarez returned to Santa Fe. "Father, I'm not leaving. I guess I've made up my mind now. I'm going to find her."

All the troubles of New Mexico appeared to fall on Father Alvarez's shoulders. "You must know they will come looking for you. It will be against the law for anyone to help you. Have you thought of this?"

"For weeks I've been asking myself the same question and I kept getting the same answers. If I don't look for her, who will?"

MacLeod witnessed the pain on Father Alvarez's face.

"Do you think that you are the only one who wishes to find Maria, that you are undertaking this mission, this search, with no help from anyone?"

"It sure seems that way."

The thin, robbed figure stood with his back to MacLeod. "I must ask you a question first."

"What question?"

"Have you prayed for Maria?"

MacLeod wasn't prepared for Alvarez's question and thought about his response. "I've thought about her every day, sometimes most of the day and night."

"That is not prayer, my son. Have you asked the Lord to watch over her, to protect her from her doubts and give her strength?"

"I guess I haven't done that, have you?"

Moments passed as Alvarez stood and gazed across the plaza to the thick mud structure of the mission church. The sun appeared briefly between gaps in the fast-moving clouds, bringing momentary warmth. MacLeod wondered if their conversation was over.

"Yes," Alvarez said, breaking the silence. "Every day and night I have knelt and prayed for her return, and I will do so until she is found."

MacLeod remembered earlier conversations about her acceptance if she returned. "What would they do with her, Father?"

"I have thought of this also. I would bring her here, to Isleta. She could help teach the children. If that were not possible, then I would try to send her to a place in California, the Mission San Gabriel Arcangel. I have a friend there, Father Sanchez, who is also of the Franciscan order."

MacLeod remembered the same faith in prayer in his mother, yet his own frustrations surfaced. "It's been a long time since they took her," he whispered. "Do you think maybe it's not working? I mean, we can't always get what we pray for, can we?"

Father Alvarez eased the heavy cross he wore from beneath his robe and touched it to his lips. "We must never question His decisions. Sometimes He seems to move too slowly for our liking, but that is His way. In a way my prayers have been answered. You are again free to look for Maria, are you not? It is not what I would have wished for, but it is not for me to question how my prayers are answered."

"But why me? I thought you wanted me to go back to St. Louis."

"Yes, but I knew you would not. Now we must join together in our search for Maria. I will provide what you need and whatever else I can do."

"Father, what about the governor, and Griego? How long do I have before they come?"

"They will certainly come looking for you if they suspect you are alive," Alvarez said with the faint hint of a smile. "But nothing moves quickly here in this land, even when they are in a hurry. You have time to strengthen your body and prepare yourself for this task you have chosen."

"And if they should come, will Father Ramirez be in danger?"

"There is an ancient custom that anyone fleeing the law may seek the protection of the Church, and no one may enter to arrest him. Father Ramirez is in no danger, other than igniting the outrage of our governor, which he has already done."

MacLeod had a hard time picturing the innocent-looking figure of Father Ramirez standing up to the forces who would be looking for him. "If they are not in the mountains, the Apache I mean, do you have any ideas where they might go?"

"Sooner or later they will show up at the villages where they rid themselves of captives and looted goods. These towns are visited regularly by many of the tribes. They have agreed among themselves to a temporary truce while trading."

MacLeod remembered the gathering of captives that Griego had arranged. "Do you know where any of these places are?"

"Yes, I have tried to get the governor to close down these fairs but he refuses," Alvarez said. "One is in Cunero and others are held in Abiquiu and Cebolleta, and there is one at a place they call Bosque Redondo. They are known for being places to buy and sell slaves. Even our own people will sometimes go to these places to purchase slaves for their daughters. If this Romero has too many captives, he may go to one of these places to get rid of them."

"I need my guns that I had to leave with Don Cordero. I can't fight these people bare handed. As long as I get them before Griego shows up, I won't let him off again. You understand, Father?"

Alvarez bowed his head. "This killing, I cannot condone it. It is for our Lord to decide who dies. For all his sins it is not for us to punish Miguel Griego."

"Father, if you had said this to me before it all got started it might have meant something, but now my friend is dead, and the woman I love was taken and sold to Indians. All because this man, Griego, couldn't have what he wanted. I'm sorry, but I can't wait for someone else to punish him. If you ask me, I would think the Lord has too many other things to do. He may not get around to Griego for a while. You said your prayers were answered now that I was free to look for Maria. Maybe the Lord doesn't want to dirty his hands with Griego so he's decided to use me to do it."

Alvarez nodded his head. "We will see what He has in mind. In the meantime I must leave and hurry back to Santa Fe. There is much to be done."

MacLeod and Alvarez walked back to the mission in silence. Father Ramirez stood beside the hammerhead mule that would take Alvarez back to Santa Fe.

MacLeod put his hand on Father Alvarez's arm. "There is one other thing to ask. Could you ask for some paper, and a quill and ink? I would like to write some things down."

"I will talk to Father Ramirez and see what he can spare."

Alvarez mounted the sullen mule. "Stay close to the mission and heal quickly, because once you leave they will not rest until you are caught."

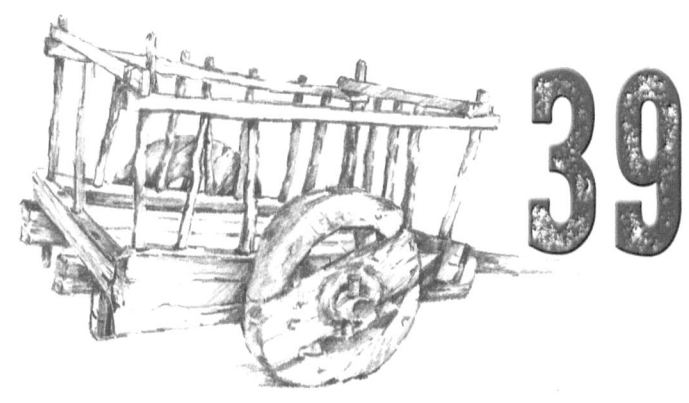

APACHE RANCHERIA

Maria and Margarita walked back to the camp with the rocks they had gathered to line the cooking pit. Others would fill it with the wood and dried stalks needed for the fire. Soon Maria and her friend would begin gathering the cabbage-like mescal cactus plant. Once the fire had burnt down, the pit would be filled with the cactus and yucca plants and covered with grass soaked in the nearby stream.

For a moment Maria paused as another wave of nausea passed over her. She saw the knowing look in Margarita's eyes. Other indications from her body told Maria what was happening and it brought a wave of conflicting emotions. Was this her new mission in life, to breed Apache children who would grow to manhood and kill more of her people? Would this life growing inside her look like her, or Romero, or would it be fair and maybe have eyes the color of the sky? The thought sent a chill through her. What would Romero do if the child was not his?

Margarita stood and stretched her back. "They will be leaving us soon," she said, pointing her chin toward the far end of the encampment where the men gathered.

"Is that why they danced last night?"

"It may be so, I don't know. You need to be an Apache to understand why they dance."

Maria remembered the shadows circling the fires and the masked figures beating the ground with their feet while the women stood and swayed with the chants. She couldn't remember seeing Romero take part in any of the activities.

"Will they be gone long?"

"It is hard to say. They may go to the buffalo grounds, which is many days away."

Maria watched the women prepare food and pack it for the hunters. Weapons were inspected and sharpened while a sullen Romero stalked the camp issuing orders. On several occasions Maria had seen the old warrior, Walking Like a Dog, speak with Romero and watched the disgruntled leader stalk off in anger.

"It is a good thing he is leaving. Maybe the hunt will be good and everyone will forget what has happened," Margarita said.

"Will we stay here long?"

"For a while, then we will move to a place where we can find the wild onions."

"Why is he always so angry?" Maria said, pointing toward Romero. "Is this the way it is always?"

Margarita filled her arms with rocks while she spoke. "Since his son was killed by the *Americano*. Before that there was always food, and horses taken from the villages he raided, and many captives to help in the camp. But he has not raided the towns since."

Romero emerged from his shelter and watched the women work, while the children chased each other in their mock battles, keeping out of Romero's sight. Maria could sense the uneasiness in the camp.

"He needs to raid again or battle his enemies. If they go after the buffalo, they will be in the land of the Comanche and the Kiowa," Margarita said.

"If the *Americano* is dead, why is he still so angry?"

"Only the Navajo woman saw him dead. Romero only believes what he sees himself."

"Have you spoken to this woman?"

Margarita shook her head. "No, she does not speak of it. It seems she spent much time with this man before they were taken. The other women said he shared his food and water with her when she was being punished by the soldiers."

Maria had not heard that. Every attempt to communicate with the Navajo woman had met with silence.

Romero stepped into Maria's path, causing both women to stop. He pointed at Maria to leave no doubt his words were meant for her. When he finished speaking, he strode back to his stick shelter where his wife readied his needs for the morning departure.

Maria shook Margarita's arm. "What did he say?"

"He said none of the men want you as a wife. He said when the hunting and food gathering is done, he is going to trade you to the Comanche."

Maria had a thought. "Will he still do it when he knows about the child?"

Margarita paused before she answered. "He will trade you, but he will wait until the child is born and give it to a woman of the camp to raise as an Apache. I have seen it done."

She knew she would never allow them to take her baby if it was MacLeod's, but what if Romero was the father? What would she do then?"

ISLETA MISSION

MacLeod continued to regain his strength and the wounds on his body healed as the days drifted past. Time seemed to stand still, with no one to talk to and little to do but eat and sleep. Each day he watched as the men left to tend the sheep and the few horses and goats belonging to the mission. Often he walked with them as far as the river, where they watered the animals. As his strength returned, he began helping with the feeding of the animals and working alongside the mission Indians in the fields, carrying water from the river for the crops.

He glanced overhead. The cloudless sky promised an unrelenting sun that left him wishing for the days spent high in the far off mountains, where cool shade and even cooler water made life a daily adventure. These thoughts brought a momentary smile to his bearded face as he dipped water from the river and washed some of the dirt from his hair. He knew he should shave before he left the mission. Far easier to go unrecognized if he wasn't wearing that golden-hued beard in a land of dark-haired people.

One day he passed through the gardens and found a faint game trail leading into the dry hills beyond. Soon the trail entered a narrow canyon, and MacLeod left it to work his way up a steep slope. Loose rock rolled from under his feet to tumble down the hillside, sending up tiny puffs of dust. Ten feet above him he saw the practiced response of a desert rattlesnake reacting to his approach, and he eased his way out of the rocks and back onto the sandy part of the hillside. By the time he reached the top, he could do little except gasp for breath. Below him the mission and its gardens stretched out along the banks of the river, and the tiny figures of the Indians moved slowly through the courtyard, carrying goods and water to the kitchen area.

From his vantage point, MacLeod could see for miles along the river in either direction. He found himself climbing the hill often, carrying water and a couple of tortillas from the breakfast table. His eyes rarely looked in any direction but north, knowing it would be from there the troops would come, and it was also from the north that anyone sent by Father Alvarez would come.

The days turned into weeks, and doubts began to cloud MacLeod's thoughts. Perhaps Father Alvarez had not found anyone to send, and MacLeod wondered what he would do if no one came soon. Alvarez had mentioned that late fall was the time when the Indians met in the slave trading towns to sell their captives. Every day that passed with MacLeod sitting on his hill meant a day lost in finding Maria. He held the tiny silver cross and chain in his hand, then from inside his shirt he pulled the pieces of paper Father Ramirez had given him to start his journal. He reread what he had written, including what he could remember about the location of the cave where Consuela had taken him.

A week later he saw a plume of dust rising far to the north. He sat through the morning and into the late afternoon, watching the cloud creep closer, figuring it would be well past dark before the riders reached the mission.

The long shadows cooled the sun's rays and dusk crept across the valley. MacLeod could make out the line of riders and wagons slowly closing the distance between them. Alvarez had said the mission was a sanctuary, but a sanctuary was only as good as the fear of the penalty if it was violated, and the resolve of those in charge. How much fear would the meek figure of Father Ramirez strike into the heart of someone like Miguel Griego?

With no horse and nowhere to run, MacLeod knew his fate was in the hands of the little padre. He rose from his perch on the hill and made his way back to the mission.

The gentle smile on the face of the young Franciscan disappeared when he understood that troops were approaching. He immediately dispatched a rider to find out the size of the party and when it would arrive.

Ramirez ordered the night meal served at once and beckoned to MacLeod to follow him inside. He led the *Americano* to the back of the church and pointed to the wooden ladder leading up to the bell tower. MacLeod didn't need any explanation.

High above the rough planks serving as pews, MacLeod crawled into one of the slits in the tower. Even at that height, the walls of the church were four feet thick. He watched as the priest sealed the other entrances to the mission grounds and returned to stand at the only entrance still open.

From a quarter mile off, the squealing wheels of the supply carts announced their imminent arrival, then MacLeod heard the stomping of horses and the jangling of spurs and halter chains, along with the squeak of many saddles.

The two Franciscans stood shoulder to shoulder, looking like uniformed servants in their sack-like gowns and wooden sandals. Each clutched a large, wooden cross in his hands as Miguel Griego and Lieutenant Zavalda halted their horses at the gate. Four-dozen troopers watched nervously, some crossing themselves in the presence of the priests.

Words were exchanged. At first they appeared to be words of greeting, spiritual words, with Ramirez issuing a blessing on the gathered men. Then Griego pointed to the interior of the mission compound and urged his horse forward.

Father Ramirez's voice rose, not in anger but with the tone of authority.

Griego jabbed a finger at the church, looking up to where MacLeod lay hidden, and again attempted to push past the priests.

Neither stepped aside. Ramirez held up his wooden cross with one hand and turned the head of Griego's horse away with the other.

MacLeod watch Griego and Zavalda argue over their next move until Zavalda wheeled his horse and led his troops toward the supply carts. After another volley of angry words directed at Father Ramirez, Griego swung his horse away and followed the others. The priest ordered the heavy gate closed and dropped the locking bar in place. No one would enter or leave without permission, but for how long? MacLeod wondered.

Before descending, MacLeod watched the troops as they surrounded the mission and set up their shelters. Soon the flicker of fires lit to cook their meals and drive away the darkness marked their positions. He wondered if Griego or Zavalda would post sentries to prevent his escape.

41

Four nights later MacLeod woke to someone gently shaking him. The soft light of a flickering candle lit Father Ramirez's face. The priest touched his lips and motioned for him to follow.

They made their way through the supply rooms to the eating area, where another candle flickered in its dish, outlining the profile of an old man eating from a bowl. MacLeod moved to the far side of the table, curious as to why he had been brought there in the middle of the night. The old man cleaned the last of his food from the bowl with a piece of bread and looked up as MacLeod sat down.

MacLeod recognized him immediately. "Sebastian!" The old man nodded. "Who sent you?"

"Father Alvarez says come."

"Does Don Cordero know?"

Sebastian nodded.

"I didn't figure he'd give up hoping the way all the others did, so I guess there are some we can still count on."

During the awkward conversation, implemented by hand gestures, Father Ramirez slipped from the room, returning moments later with an armload of dark clothing for MacLeod.

He changed quickly, knowing it would be useless to ask any questions, and followed Father Ramirez through a narrow hall toward the storeroom.

Sebastian handed MacLeod a piece of charcoal and motioned for him to blacken his hands and face while Father Ramirez pulled aside large bags of grain to reveal a small door built low on the mission wall. Sebastian slid it open and MacLeod recognized the narrow ditch leading to the dry watercourse the mission used at one time to bring in water. It wasn't deep, but the ground on either side was rough and rocky, and the guards chose to set up their shelters on dry, flat areas some distance off.

Father Ramirez muttered a prayer and blew out the candle. MacLeod wondered if he was included in the prayer. He followed Sebastian through the opening and into the bushes growing along the outside wall.

When his eyes had adjusted to the thin moonlight, MacLeod searched the surrounding darkness for the fires marking the campsites. Either Zavalda or Griego had positioned their night sentries at fifty yard intervals, which meant the guards would pace halfway to the next camp before retracing their steps.

Sebastian moved out, hunched over and duck walking across the rocks. MacLeod's knees wouldn't allow him to do the same. He bent over as far as he could and followed.

The narrow watercourse led though the crop fields toward the distant rise of low foothills that MacLeod had climbed each morning. A campfire glowed close to the streambed, giving off enough light for them to be seen by the pacing sentry. Sebastian froze until a slow-moving cloud put them back in its covering shadow. MacLeod heard low voices coming from the direction of the fire. Sebastian moved up another five yards and halted again when the talking stopped. MacLeod heard the awkward sound of boots crunching unsteadily on loose rocks, indicating the sentry had crossed the stream bed above where they lay.

The cloud moved off, uncovering the quarter crescent of the moon, forcing them again to drop into the rocks and remain motionless. MacLeod could hear the footsteps approach, scuffling the rocks and pebbles. The guard appeared to stumble, voicing his complaint in a series of whispered curses and MacLeod could smell the chili he had eaten. He raised his head, wishing he had a weapon, anything, to use if he had to. His hand edged toward a rock. It would do if the guard spotted them. But getting past this one guard wouldn't mean they were safe.

The muttering stopped but so did the footsteps. From the camp below, laughter and occasionally the high-pitched squeal of a woman split the night silence. Apparently, Griego, or Zavalda, had let their men bring along their pleasures. More likely it was Griego.

MacLeod held his breath anticipating the sound of the alarm. Seconds crept into minutes and still the guard did not move. Then MacLeod caught the sound, then the smell, of urine as the sentry relieved himself. MacLeod felt the hot sensation as the warm liquid splashed off a rock and struck his hand. The sentry grunted in satisfaction and bent to search for his musket at his feet. MacLeod prayed that the cloud blotting out the moon wouldn't pass on before the sentry renewed his pacing.

A shout from the sentry on the left brought a muffled response from above. Shuffling feet on loose rock indicated the man was crossing the watercourse to meet with his counterpart. MacLeod felt Sebastian's feet move away and continue crawling quickly toward the upper end of the dry streambed.

MacLeod's knees ached from the rocks and pebbles. Then, as if in answer to his pain, the rocks gave way to the softness of sand. Sebastian rose to a low crouch and MacLeod followed as the moonlight reappeared and showed them the way into the canyon, but left them exposed to the sentries for the next fifty yards.

They needed only a minute or so until they would reach the protection of the narrow canyon. Sebastian sprinted ahead, leaving MacLeod to limp behind until they rounded a low hill and found themselves hidden from anyone who might turn and look in their direction. MacLeod knew from his own exploring that the canyon led through the hills to what he thought was a high plateau. They climbed steadily until dawn began to creep down the canyon walls.

MacLeod knew the plateau was only a short distance above them, but he had never gone that far before. The canyon continued to narrow, the walls rising on either side. They reached the spot where the canyon opened up onto a dry plain as the sun broke free of the night.

Sebastian trotted out onto the plateau, moved toward a grove of trees on the far side and disappeared. MacLeod caught up with him and came to a halt. He felt like laughing. The big black mule stood watching them, its ears turned to catch the sound, and the little bay mare MacLeod used for packing stood beside his own mare and Sebastian's grey mule. He whipped a blanket off the pile of goods lying beside his saddle and saw his rifle, with a strip of cotton wrapped around the flintlock and pan, lying beside Stewart's musket and the pair of pistols. It brought a mile-wide grin to MacLeod's face. For the first times in months he saw a glimmer of hope, somewhat dampened by the forty or so troopers who would be making an appearance very soon.

Sebastian climbed up the side of a low rock formation and sat cross-legged, watching the canyon for the first signs of movement. MacLeod saw the concern on his face.

"How long do you think we have?"

The old Indian shook his head.

MacLeod went back to the equipment and found his powder horn and the deer-skin bag containing his lead and the mold for the balls, and the one thing he needed most, the worm to pull the balls. There was no way he would ever take a chance that his rifle would fire after all these months.

As he worked at drawing the balls from the guns, MacLeod realized they had not talked about what they would do if they did get away. For a while, however, their plans would depend on Griego and Lieutenant Zavalda.

Sebastian slid through the rocks and squatted by the equipment. "They come," he said in a matter of fact tone.

"Damn, I didn't think anyone would pick up our tracks with all the others around. My guess one of the Indians from the mission passed the word. "How long we got?"

Sebastian shrugged.

"That long, huh? They coming the way we came, up the canyon?"

This time he received a nod.

"Well, there's no way they can come out of that canyon if we don't want them to. 'Course we can't leave either. I think maybe we better take a look around while we still can."

He rammed new balls onto fresh powder and changed the flints. Then he struck his forehead with the palm of his hand.

"I'm getting stupid. How did you get up here with the animals? You sure didn't come up that narrow canyon."

Sebastian pointed toward the northern end of the plateau.

"Well, we can get out of here that way, can't we?"

"But it will take us to Señor Griego."

"That may be better than being stuck up here, and maybe we can make a run for it. Let's get the equipment packed and I'll take a look around." MacLeod wasn't about to try to pack Belanger's black devil until he had to. The mule had been eying him ever since he arrived. He eased around it and walked out onto the plateau.

It ran about a quarter of a mile in length and looked to be fifty yards or so wide. He jogged to the other side to take a look. Rocks from his feet rolled over the edge and bounced out into open space. Far below the red earth stood out in stark contrast to the green of the junipers and pinion pines. Unfortunately, what separated them and the valley looked to be a two hundred-foot drop. He pushed another rock over the side and watched it strike shale-like rock fifteen feet down, starting a small avalanche that carried all the way to the floor below. He turned and jogged back to the animals.

"No way but the way you came it seems, unless you got another idea."

Sebastian shook his head.

"Then we better be doing it now."

While Sebastian led the big black mule and the bay mare out from the rocks, MacLeod saddled his mare and checked the rifle and musket. He slid the musket under the waterproof canvas and carried his rifle. He swore he would never be far from it again.

With Sebastian in the lead, they moved across the plateau toward the far end. MacLeod let the old Indian find his way while he kept an eye on the mouth of the canyon. He wanted to be long gone before anyone appeared.

A shot rang out from Sebastian's end of the plateau. MacLeod kneed the mare into a run.

"They must have known about this end and split up," MacLeod said. "I didn't think they had that much sense."

He moved behind a sandstone outcropping, listening to the voices drifting up from below. He knew his advantage lay in the fact that they didn't know he had his rifle.

Two figures worked their way up a shallow incline toward MacLeod's position. He could see half a dozen others about two hundred yards farther down. They sat on their horses, waiting for the advancing troops to find out what they could. MacLeod ran across a sandy stretch to a large, tabletop rock that looked down on the group. They saw him at once and fired their muskets. MacLeod saw a puff of dirt kick up about fifty yards in front of the shooters. He remembered hearing that most of the troops had little powder and were probably using half loads. He pulled himself up onto the rock and lay on its flat top. The two shooters sat on the ground, about seventy-five yards below him, reloading their muskets.

He eased the rifle up to his shoulder and took a bead on a large boulder behind them, not wanting to kill anyone, simply frighten them enough to drive them back.

He fired, and the ball slammed into the rock face a few feet from the two men. It took a moment for them to realize what had happened. Then they both reacted as one, dropping their muskets and scampering for cover.

The others below milled about in confusion. MacLeod watched a heavy-set man on a white horse move to the center of the group. "Griego, you son of a bitch. I've been waiting for this chance for a long time," MacLeod said.

 He poured powder down the barrel and seated a ball, then tapped a few grains of powder into the pan and snapped down the frizzen. He rolled over and cradled the rifle in his arms, laying his cheek on the walnut stock and sighting head-high on the unsuspecting figure. He had no reservation about shooting him. The man gave up his rights when he sold Maria into slavery. MacLeod took a deep breath and applied pressure to the trigger. The rifle barked, but a sudden gust of wind pushed the ball off to the side. It plowed a furrow across Griego's chest, sending the heavy figure tumbling to the ground.

MacLeod swore and quickly reloaded, but by that time the group had run another hundred yards farther down the slope.

He watched as the original attackers, minus their weapons, joined the others. A half dozen muskets were fired in his direction, the balls hitting the ground far short of his location. To convince them his first shot was no fluke, MacLeod rang a ball off the rocks close to where they all milled about.

After reloading, MacLeod mounted the mare and rode to the other end of the plateau. He could hear the scuffing of boots on the rocks below as Zavalda's men moved up the canyon. MacLeod fired another shot to drive them back and returned to where Sebastian held the animals.

"They'll stay where they are for a spell, but we can't hold them off forever."

Twice in the next couple of hours MacLeod checked both approaches to the plateau. Griego and his men had set up camp a quarter mile away. MacLeod figured the troops under Zavalda posed the real threat. As soon as the sun went down, they could move up undetected and trap them between the two forces. There was no way to get past the troops in the narrow canyon and, despite Griego's faults, he, or his next in command, had chosen an excellent position. MacLeod and Sebastian could never make it past them no matter how much they might surprise them.

"I'm about out of ideas. If you got some I'd be glad to listen," said MacLeod. "No way out, unless we walk, and I done my share of walking. Besides they'd catch us as soon as they figured out what we'd done."

MacLeod rode across the plateau again to look over the side that fell away into the sloping valley. The mare hopped about as he forced her close to the edge, acting as if she wanted no part of what she couldn't see. He rode along the rim as far as he could before riding back, inspecting the ground below the drop-off. In spots the crumbling sandstone had broken away, creating narrow chutes. MacLeod stepped down and knelt at the mouth of one chute. He tossed a handful of small rocks over the side and watched them come to rest on a ledge about ten feet below. From the ledge his eye traced a route that zigzagged down the side of the canyon. He called Sebastian over and showed him what he had in mind.

"Once we go over there's no turning back."

The look MacLeod got was all the answer he would get. He grinned and said, "I don't suppose you want to go first?"

They rechecked their equipment and the pack loads. He knew that once they committed, they couldn't stop until they reached the bottom. If any of them went down, it would be a long tumble.

"We better do it now if we're going to—"

A shot startled him. It had come from the mouth of the canyon, where one of Zavalda's men had made his way to the top. The rest would be right behind as soon as they discovered no one was there to stop them.

Without waiting for a reply, MacLeod pointed the mare at the narrow chute and kicked her hard. She went into the slide and sat back on her haunches, with MacLeod leaning as far back as he could and hoping the big black mule wouldn't roll over the top of them. They slid the short distance to the end of the slide, and MacLeod forced the mare off to the left along a thin ledge of stunted junipers that managed to survive on the side of the mountain. Somehow she understood what had to be done and kept her feet moving. Her momentum carried them down on an angle toward a deep cleft. MacLeod could see the valley floor below through the tops of the pines, and it looked a long way down. Dirt and rocks from the mare's sliding hooves fell and bounced into space in a continual stream. He felt the presence of the black mule behind him. He had no idea if Sebastian followed.

The ledge ended in a steep gulley. MacLeod saw it coming and pivoted the mare in a half circle that sent her sliding down the dirt slope to another ledge fifty feet below. He took a quick glance over his shoulder and saw Sebastian following, throwing up his arm to ward off the storm of rocks and pebbles knocked loose by the hooves of the stock above him.

The mare trembled under him as she labored to keep her feet. MacLeod could see cuts from the rocks on her legs. Twice they were forced to switch back before they reached the level of the treetops. The mare sensed a dim trail beneath her feet and quickly followed it.

He heard the popping of muskets from above and risked a quick glance. Zavalda's troops lined the edge of the plateau, firing in a futile effort at MacLeod and Sebastian, but no one followed.

MacLeod and Sebastian made their way down to the valley, where they found a shaded area to rest the animals and check the loads.

"Do you have any idea where we are?" MacLeod asked.

The old Indian trembled and shook his head.

"I didn't think so. Let's work our way back to the river and see about getting to the other side, then maybe we can figure out what we're going to do. I got a feeling those fellows back there won't give up." MacLeod handed the lead rope of the black mule to Sebastian and moved ahead.

GOVERNOR'S PALACE- SANTA FE

"He does not ask me to come, he demands I attend him. He sends these idiots to bring me before him. Does he not remember who I am?" Miguel Griego made no effort to hide his rage.

The tired and dusty militia who accompanied him from Bernalillo to Santa Fe sat on their horses and waited patiently for Lieutenant Zavalda to dismiss them.

"There is a misunderstanding, I am sure," Zavalda said. "The governor has been under much pressure lately, and it is almost certain his words were misunderstood."

Griego whipped his hat against his pant legs in an attempt to beat off as much dust as possible. They had not allowed him to stop for a moment and change his clothing. "This man will live to regret this insult," he fumed.

Zavalda nodded his head in agreement. "I'm sure he does not mean to insult you. Let me go and tell him you are here."

Thirty minutes later Miguel Griego entered the office of Governor Fecunda Melgares, who sat at his desk with an official-looking paper held in place by his drinking cup and the edge of his dinner plate. His dinner appeared untouched.

Miguel Griego looked around for the chairs that were usually placed in front of the desk. They sat against the far wall, both occupied by minor officials, forcing Griego to stand in front of the desk and wait. He knew he must control his anger, but this impertinent government jackass was attempting to humiliate him. He was tired, he was hungry, and most of all he needed a drink after such a long ride. He thought about turning on his heel and marching out of the office immediately. But where would he go? His father's position no longer gave him the power and immunity it once had. Don Antonio Griego had made it obvious to everyone that his son now looked after himself. And all of this disrespect and humiliation came about because of this *Americano*. Griego's hand instinctively massaged his chest where the ball from the *Americano's* rifle had left its mark. Miguel Griego knew his life would never be the same until he had killed the man.

Finally, Zavalda leaned over and whispered in Melgares' ear. The governor looked up.

"Señor Griego, it is about time you have come."

"I would have been here sooner, Your Excellency, if I knew of its importance. Your troops were not necessary, but I thank you for your concern for my safety."

Governor Melgares appeared taken back by the use of his proper title. He sat up straighter in his chair. Griego bowed his head a fraction, knowing he had taken the first step.

"Why don't you begin by telling me about your failure in the search for this *Americano*," Melgares said, waving a hand in the air.

Griego glanced over his shoulder at the two officials who occupied the chairs and thought about walking across the office and taking one. No, not yet, now is not the time, he decided.

"Well, Your Excellency," Griego began, "As I am sure the good Lieutenant has already informed you, we have spent many weeks searching for him. When he escaped from us near the Mission of Isleta, I believed he would try to leave our country, so we moved quickly to the east to prevent it, but he did not go in that direction. Then we began our search along the river, but he still eluded all of our efforts. I would like to mention the help he received from these priests in the missions in helping him evade capture. I would hope you could someday control the actions of these men." He saw Governor Melgares flinch with his last remark.

While Griego related the efforts made in searching for MacLeod, the governor pushed his plate aside and picked up the paper on his desk. Griego realized the governor wasn't as interested in MacLeod's capture as he was in the contents of the letter. He quickly ended his story.

"So, you have found nothing of him after all this time?" Melgares chided. "And you are positive he has not left and gone back to his own country?"

"I am sure he is still here."

"And why is that? What proof do you have?"

"When we searched for him in the south, the people said they did know of him, but I am certain they knew something they would not tell us."

Zavalda nodded. "It is true. Before you recalled me to Santa Fe, I sensed the people were not telling us everything."

Governor Melgares spread his hands. "But why would they not tell you?"

Zavalda appeared to struggle with his answer. "This man has become something of a legend to these people because he defies the authority of the government."

"Very well," Governor Melgares said. "We will come back to him later if there is time. Now we must deal with more important issues. Let me begin by saying I am not happy with you, Captain Griego. In deference to your father, I have overlooked many of your, how shall I say it, indiscretions."

The governor continued, still holding the letter in his hand. "I cannot prove this, but I believe you had something to do with the abduction of Señorita Cordero, and also this mysterious death of the other *Americano* in my jail. If I could prove this, I would have you arrested. There are other things of which I do not approve which we will deal with later."

Griego seethed. "Your Excellency, what are these things of which you speak? I wish to know now what I am being accused of?"

The governor rose and slammed his hands on his desk. "Have you any idea how much pressure I receive from the Church for things they are not happy with? This Father Alvarez spends as much time in this office as all the others together. With him it is this trade in Indian captives. I ask him, how does he expect me to stop the Indians from trading their captives when I can't stop them from raiding my villages? Do you know what he says to me? He speaks of you, and accuses you of not only selling Indian captives, but also stealing some of our own people and selling them to the Indians."

"This is absurd," Griego blurted. "I will make him apologize for this insult."

"Let us leave time for that later, also. Alvarez has gathered much information that says otherwise." Governor Melgares seated himself and picked up the letter from his desk. "This is what I have called you to Santa Fe to discuss. This dispatch from our commandant general demands that I do something about this Apache menace who is killing so many of our people. He even tells me what I should do about it. He asks why I have not put into work his plan of paying the other tribes to seek out and destroy this Apache. He even tells me how I should pay these savages. Furs, he tells me again. He has heard that these Indians can trade furs for the things they want and we cannot give them, and he has the nerve to accuse me of not following his previous directions of obtaining these things to pacify these bloodthirsty savages." Melgares' voice rose to a near scream. He could not remain seated. "Of course, like all of these orders I receive from Mexico, he does not provide me with any additional funds or tell me how to get these furs. So now that you have heard what I have to say I ask you, what is your answer?"

"Your Excellency?"

"I have asked you what you believe I should do about this letter?" The governor pinned the letter to his desk with a food-stained finger.

Griego saw his opening. The governor was giving him the opportunity to present his plan without admitting his involvement.

"Your Excellency, the commandant general obviously has no idea how difficult it is to govern this country and how hard you work in attempting to do so." Griego shifted his heavy bulk from one foot to the other, not accustomed to being on his feet for any length of time. He noted a softening in the governor's manner. He took a chance. "Do you mind if I sit? I have been traveled many hours to be here today and I am very tired."

"Of course, of course, how thoughtless of me," Melgares crooned, motioning to one of the seated men to bring his chair forward for Griego.

Griego eased his thick body onto the narrow seat and held his breath. The chair sagged noticeably but remained upright. "Thank you. Now, our commandant general has mentioned this Apache, Romero. Has he also mentioned the *Americano*?"

"No, he was never told the *Americano* did not die in the attack. We were never sure of his escape."

"I see, and the other one, the Frenchman?"

"I reported that he died in prison, as is true," said Melgares impatiently.

"Then the commandant general is concerned only with the Apache raids?"

"It appears this Romero is also responsible for many raids in the northern parts of Mexico, some all the way to Chihuahua. I do not believe this same savage could do so much damage, or be in so many places at one time, but to the commandant general all these Apache are the same. And the *Americano*?" Melgares said, waving his hands in the air in a gesture of insignificance. "Who is to say he is not dead already. As your governor I must say it would be better for Nuevo Mexico if he simply did not appear again, then I can go about the business of governing. In fact it might be difficult to explain to the commandant general his sudden appearance."

Griego sensed the governor was thinking along the same lines as he was. "I can see your position, and I may be of some service."

"Good, good, that is very good. Tell me," Melgares chanted.

"These furs you are in need of. I have heard that some might be found."

"Tell me about them. I suppose they were found only recently? I keep hearing of their possible existence but have not witnessed any of them yet besides these two small skins I have here on my desk."

"Yes, very recently," Griego said, accepting the offered peace. If the governor was willing to forget where, and how, the furs were obtained, their relationship might return to normal.

"This is what I would like to suggest, which may help His Excellency with our commandant general," Griego said, mentally calculating how many of the furs would pacify the governor. "These furs that we discovered could be brought to Santa Fe for you to use in purchasing the help of whatever Indians would be willing to fight the Apaches. These Indians might even buy a few weapons, which would greatly increase their confidence."

A smile began to form on the governor's face. "I believe that would go very far in helping with our problem."

"There is also this other problem. I am also willing to put myself at your disposal to find this *Americano* and make him, as you put it, disappear before word reaches the commandant general's ears of his still living. However, our strength is not enough for so large an area. If Your Excellency will put under my command a sufficient number of your own troops, I will personally chase this man until he is captured."

"You wish me to leave Santa Fe undefended while you chase this man all over Nuevo Mexico? You have not been able to catch him before and now you want me to help you?"

An additional reward would be necessary and Griego knew it.

"I will also bring you Romero's head."

The governor's eyes and mouth opened wide in astonishment. "How do you propose to do what I have been unable to do?"

"I have received information that Romero has the woman Maria de Cordero. Also, and I do not know if you are aware of this, the *Americano* is responsible for the death of the Apache's son. That is the reason he attacked your troops taking the prisoners to Mexico. Since it is impossible to chase both at once, it will be necessary to have them come to me. To do this I plan to send out the word that Romero will take the woman to one of these places where the Indians are known to trade their captives."

"But how will you get the Apache to go there?"

"It is simple," Griego said with a smile. "If this Apache thinks the *Americano* is going there to find the woman, he will go there himself. He wants him and he will use the woman to get him."

"It may work," Melgares said. He rose from his desk and began to pace, his hands behind his back. "Forgive me, Miguel, I did not know you were capable of such intrigue. Perhaps there will be something else I may reward you with when this is done."

"Maybe I should go also," the governor said. "If I am there to lead my troops, they will have much more confidence. Do you think the Apache will fight?"

The governor's proposal stunned Griego into silence. That would ruin his plan to take the furs with him when he met with the Comanche.

"Your Excellency, your presence would most certainly inspire the men," Griego said," but it is such a long way to this place, and there will most certainly be a fight. You would be better here in Santa Fe to look after the affairs of our land."

Governor Melgares stood as tall as he could and stroked his chin. "You may be right, and I have so much work to do here. Where is this place that you speak of where they trade their captives?"

"There are a number of such places," Griego said, knowing the governor was familiar with every one of them but also knowing he had to play along with the game. "It is on the Pecos River, at a place they call Bosque Redondo."

Griego waited while he knew the governor considered the proposal. He had little to lose and much to gain, since the troops spent most of their time getting drunk and sleeping. The governor seemed to be living for the moment he would dispatch a fast messenger to the Commandant General of his capture of the Apache and the procuring of the furs for future use.

Finally, Zavalda stepped to the governor's side and whispered in his ear.

The governor nodded and looked at Griego. "I believe I will approve your plan. I think I will have Lieutenant Zavalda accompany you. When do you plan to leave?"

"This meeting of the Indians is held in the fall of the year. We are not yet certain of when."

"In the later months? It is a shame it is so far off, but the furs, when will you deliver them to me?"

"I will send men as soon as possible. It is far off in the mountains. It will take time."

"Make it quick. I would like to have them in my possession so I might send word to the commandant general."

But not too quickly Griego thought. With his plan approved, he could turn his attention to the satisfaction of capturing and killing the *Americano,* and with luck seeing the whore again, and see what being ravaged by the Apaches had done to her precious beauty. And Romero, why kill him? They had much trading still to do.

ON THE RIO BRAVO DEL NORTE

From afar the clutter of mud huts resembled little more than bumps on the flat plain that ran to the river's edge. MacLeod shielded his eyes and squinted, trying to control the dancing images that played in the sand before him.

"Doesn't look like anybody but locals. Don't see any horses. Place have a name?"

Sebastian shrugged.

"Hell, what's a name anyway? They all sound the same to me. Appears they're all named after some dead guy who's supposed to protect them. Don't see how much good it's doing." He urged the tired mare forward and dug a grain of sand out of the corner of his eye. He lifted his canteen and dribbled a few drops of water onto his tongue. "Shoot, this water's as hot as morning coffee, but I'm thinking that river up ahead is going to be a lot cooler."

Sebastian grunted, but MacLeod still could not distinguish between a yes grunt and a no grunt. He had taken to talking to himself to pass the time. "I ain't never seen it this hot before, never in all my years. You sweat all the water out of you and then the dust rises up and sticks to you like pine gum. I ain't never been this thirsty before either. I can feel that cool water down there creeping up my legs all the way to my belly. Soon as I get there I'm going to slide off this here horse and go all the way to the bottom and stay down for a spell, just as soon as we get to that river."

The sun hovered over them as they plodded toward the strip of muddy water in the distance. A mutual truce seemed to be in effect between him and the black mule. It had followed behind for the last few days without causing a serious confrontation. He figured the heat had got to it also.

They reached the river by late afternoon and MacLeod rode in as he had said. He and the mare stood ankle deep on the rocky riverbed, in midstream.

"Well, at least it's cool, although it's awful scarce." MacLeod lowered himself into the water and dug away at the gravel around him, trying to form a shallow pool. Finally he gave up and lay on his back, letting the tepid water flow over him.

Children's voices brought him back to reality. Sebastian was already mounted and moving toward the tiny village. MacLeod sat up and splashed his head and beard with the water until it ran clear. Then he felt his stomach toss and realized they hadn't eaten since the night before. He walked to the river's edge, where a number of children had gathered to watch and picked up two of them, placing them on the back of the mare. He then followed Sebastian toward the group of people gathered in the dirt track running between the houses.

Sebastian seemed busy talking with some of the men as MacLeod approached. He hoped they were discussing food.

The village appeared to have risen out of the dirt. The houses varied in size depending on how many children in the family. Some houses sprouted extra rooms that resembled temporary lean-tos, some with two or three such additions. Without any access to timber, the length of available sticks for roof poles limited the size of the house. A few chickens scratched away in the dirt. MacLeod eyed their movements, hoping there might be one or two fewer chickens in the morning, while two barefooted young women dressed in low-necked blouses flirted with him. He turned away, doubting that even the heavy beard could hide the blush on his cheeks.

While he waited for Sebastian to finish talking to the men of the village, he wondered how this tiny place had escaped the wrath of the Apache. For weeks he and Sebastian had ridden through the remains of a dozen such villages until MacLeod began referring to them as Apache fodder. This one seemed to have escaped the fate of the others.

"Señor Griego pass many days ago," Sebastian said as MacLeod approached the group.

"Which way?"

Sebastian pointed upriver. "That way. Santa Fe."

"They ask about us?"

"*Si*, but they only stop to water. Some talked to the young women."

MacLeod nodded. "Same story we've been hearing. I think we can cross the river right here and bypass the road to Santa Fe by tomorrow night."

"It will be good to be there." Sebastian grinned and scratched himself.

Their luck held and they crossed over the river once they felt safe. The Cordero hacienda lay some miles ahead but their welcome was still uncertain.

Word had reached the hacienda before them. Don Cordero stood at the gate waiting and came forward as MacLeod dismounted. "Welcome, Don MacLeod. I see Sebastian was successful in his efforts. I am glad."

MacLeod handed the reins and the lead rope to a young Indian boy who stood waiting to take possession of the stock. "Couldn't have done it without your help, sir. I'm much obliged."

"It was so little after the mistake I made by not believing Sebastian, and letting Miguel Griego take you. I also have heard about your friend. I am sorry."

"I know you're wanting to know about Maria."

Don Cordero tilted his head and smiled. "Yes, but by not asking questions sometimes the answer is avoided."

"Well, sir, I believe she's still alive. Didn't Father Alvarez tell you?"

"Yes, it was more than we could have hoped for, but the uncertainty is difficult to live with."

Don Cordero then held up his arms in a welcoming gesture. "Please forgive me, I would like to hear everything, but first you must eat and drink. Later time will be available to talk."

MacLeod bathed and shaved off the months of accumulated whiskers. He found clean clothing lying across the chair by his bed, and Don Cordero waiting for him in the eating room. Sebastian had not reappeared.

Don Cordero rose. "Come. If you are not too tired, we can talk while we walk around the garden. I know it is of no help now, but I have sent word to people of importance I know in Mexico of our governor's response to your escape, and of his lack of initiative when Maria was taken. Now, please tell me everything you know. My wife is waiting to hear."

MacLeod picked up the story with Romero's attack and told of his own capture and escape. He thanked Don Cordero again for sending Sebastian and the weapons, and he told of how the two of them had traveled south through the tiny villages always a day or two ahead of Griego and the governor's troops.

"And you have heard nothing of her?" Don Cordero asked.

"Only vague stories, but I know Romero has her. He told me so, but I don't think he'll harm her."

"Why not?"

MacLeod walked ahead of Don Cordero and turned around. "Because he wants me, and she will be the bait."

"What did you do to him?"

"I shot his son."

"So my daughter is the one to suffer. Why is this so?"

"Don Cordero, please try to understand. I love Maria. Who could guess what would happen because of what we did? I'd tell you how sorry I am but I don't think the words would help. But we're standing here talking about this Apache when we should be talking about Miguel Griego. He's the one who's to blame and now he and your governor are looking for me instead of your daughter. What kind of place is this anyway?"

"We have many ancient rules and customs in our country," Don Cordero said. "You would not know of these types of things. We had heard rumors about Miguel's indiscretions, but since he was a young man without a wife, I did not view them as a reason not to make the marriage. The Griegos have been here in Nuevo Mexico for many generations, and it would have been a good marriage for any worthy woman, but not for Maria. I'm afraid I failed to understand what lengths she would go to in order to avoid their betrothal."

"But you loved her anyway, even with all her different ideas, didn't you?"

That brought a thin smile to Don Cordero's face. "Yes, like a son, whose place she took when her brother died. If he had possessed her spirit and strength, perhaps he would be alive today. Now all I have are these wild rumors. She is here, she is there, she has gone to Mexico. This time someone on the way to Taos mentioned the name of a priest he met in Bernalillo who is said to have more recent information about a Spanish woman the Indians have."

"What kind of information?"

"He did not say. The priest was on his way to Acoma," Don Cordero said.

"Acoma, how far is that?"

"It is a few days, I believe, but it is only another rumor. You must think about leaving this place while you can. I would feel a great sorrow if you were captured."

"I think it's worth a few days to check out. If there's nothing to it I guess it's finished. I can't see going back into those mountains alone to look for her."

"You have done everything it is possible to do and you have paid the price." Don Cordero put his hand on MacLeod's shoulder. "I would hope that my own son would have done as much."

"I'm sure he would have, Don Cordero. I think I'd like to check this last one out before I go."

"Very well, but take a couple of days to rest yourself and your horses, the priest will travel very slowly."

ACOMA PUEBLO

They rode through a long, wide valley surrounded by mesas, the red earth dotted with stunted trees, each separated by its own space as if someone had placed them by hand. On his left a towering wall of rock rose from the desert floor, circular in shape, and topped with tinges of green vegetation. Similar towers rose miles ahead.

"Ever wonder what's on top of these things?" MacLeod said.

Sebastian's voice startled MacLeod since the old man had scarcely spoken since they left the hacienda. "I have seen."

"How? There isn't any way up that I can see, unless you can fly."

The old man did not answer, leaving MacLeod to his thoughts. He was struck with the clean beauty of the land, with its endless blue sky and air as pure as he had ever known. For hours they rode across the flat-bottomed valley with only the sounds of the horse's hooves striking the desert sand and the squeak of dry leather of his saddle. He spoke to himself only to hear the sound of a voice.

"I don't think I've ever been so alone before. Everything is so far away."

"Not alone," Sebastian said, pointing toward the north, where MacLeod saw a thin column of dust rise and hang in the air before being drifted away by the gentle breeze.

"How long have they been there?"

"Long time."

"And you didn't bother to tell me."

"What you do?"

"I don't know, but I'd like to know what we're up against. You think its Griego?"

"No, he does not come this way."

"Who then?"

"Soon we know." The old man edged his horse toward a long, sloping rise, where they would get a better look at whoever was slowly cutting them off.

MacLeod could see the fast-moving column of riders heading toward them. He pulled his rifle from beneath his leg and laid it across his saddle. "Any idea?"

"Navajo."

MacLeod counted fifteen riders with extra horses. At the front rode a man who appeared larger than the others, and rode with a definite look of command. "You think they're looking for trouble?"

"Soon we know."

The Navajo quickly circled MacLeod and Sebastian, with the big warrior coming to a halt in front of them. He appeared to be sizing them up before he spoke.

Sebastian shook his head and began conversing in a combination of words and signs. The Navajo seemed disappointed, then pointed at MacLeod.

"What's he want to know?"

"He wants to know if you are the one they talk about who killed the Apache. He says the Apache are his enemy too, and he hopes you will kill many more of them."

Sebastian spoke at length with the Navajo before they wheeled their horses around and rode off.

"They also look for someone," Sebastian said. "His woman and children and others were taken from his village when he and most of his warriors were gone to hunt."

The dust from the retreating party rose lazily in the air and drifted off in a thin cloud. MacLeod watched them ride toward the river and was struck by their similar fates, both in search of information of people lost. Perhaps the Navajo had information to go on, but probably they were doing the same thing MacLeod was doing, chasing the ghost of rumors.

The rocky pillar protruding from the desert floor appeared fluted, its base covered with loose shale. MacLeod watched Sebastian ride toward it and dismount at the base of a deep cleft that ran down from the top of the mesa. No village could be seen—no horses, no dogs, no scampering children—nothing but the weathered mound pushing its way high above their heads.

"Where do we go now?" MacLeod asked.

Sebastian pointed to a footpath that disappeared among the rocks at the base of the mesa.

"Up there. You telling me we're going up there?"

The old man's face broke into a slow grin. He led his horse to a nearby stream and began stripping his saddle.

MacLeod grumbled out loud but followed Sebastian to the creek. He wasn't sure how they were going to make it to the top, but he knew his horse was staying behind.

A half hour later, MacLeod stood panting atop the three hundred-foot mesa. The mud huts of the village of Acoma lay sprawling before him, with the looming bulk of the mission church on the far side. A few men greeted Sebastian while two small children took his gnarled hands and led him toward the church.

They found the recently arrived priest dozing in the shade of the church wall. Sebastian woke him.

APACHE RANCHERIA

"Maria, come quickly," Margarita called out excitedly.

Maria de Cordero heaved herself up from the ground where she had spent all morning pounding dried berries for winter storage. "You hurry. I am not hurrying for anyone."

She waddled past the *wickiup* of Walking Like a Dog and smiled at the old warrior. Without his support she would have had no place to live while the child grew in her belly.

The new camp was located along both sides of a stream on the eastern edge of the Sacramento Mountains. With summer at its end, the food gathering centered on the collection of berries and chokecherries, and the fruit of the prickly pear cactus. Maria's job involved mixing dry berries with jerked venison and fat to make the pemmican that would feed the tribe during the cold winter months.

"And where will I be this winter?" she asked herself. The child would come soon and then what would happen? She had confided in no one, not even Margarita, that the child might not be Romero's. Everyone assumed it was his, including Romero's barren wife, who made it known she would take the child away from her.

"Let her think what she wants," Maria muttered. "The old hag will rot in the ground before she touches my baby."

People rushed past her and ran toward the upper end of the camp where a band of riders approached. Maria saw Romero emerge from his shelter and squat by the fire with the new arrivals.

"Oh, God, what now," Maria groaned. She stopped for a moment to stretch her back and rest. She wondered if they would move again before winter or remain there, then shook her head and laughed bitterly.

Margarita hurried toward her, apparently too impatient to wait for her to catch up.

"Can you imagine what I've just been thinking?" Maria said. "I've been wondering if this is where we'll spend the winter. Margarita, tell me I'm not giving up."

"Listen, there is news from the river. Romero is angry, come with me." Margarita grabbed her by the arm and tried to drag her away.

"What is it? Is there something you do not want me to see?"

Maria heard the scream and turned back to see the Navajo girl they called Consuela being dragged through the camp by the hair. Romero wrestled her to her knees and hit her with his open hand.

"What has she done?" Maria asked again.

Another scream pierced the still mountain air, one she would remember forever.

"He has cut off her tongue," Maria cried.

The look on Margarita's face sent a chill through Maria. Instinctively she wrapped protective arms over her swollen stomach. "What is it? Please, tell me."

The older Mexican woman shook her head. Her face seemed to show a terror of ominous things to come. "They bring news the *Americano* lives."

HACIENDA OF DON FERNANDO

MacLeod and Sebastian rode tired horses down the hill, with the sun at their backs and the river below.

"Is that the place we're heading for?" MacLeod pointed to the whitewashed cluster of buildings nestled beneath a thick grove of trees and surrounded by a high adobe wall. Two heavy gates provided the only access and both were guarded by men sitting atop the fence.

"It is the hacienda of Don Fernando. He is a friend of Don Cordero."

MacLeod nodded and followed the old man down a narrow trail to the edge of the Rio Bravo del Norte. He let the mare drink while he searched the trees on the far side of the river. Sebastian glanced back once, then continued on toward the gate in the southernmost wall. MacLeod reached down and scooped a handful of the brackish water into his mouth. He washed his face with another, reflecting on the bone-numbing weariness he felt. How much longer would he take it? A question he found himself contemplating a lot lately. He wouldn't spend another winter in that place. No way. He pulled the mare's head up and kneed her toward the far side of the river. Hopefully Sebastian knew what he was talking about when he said they could depend on Don Fernando for supplies.

Don Fernando met them at the gate and threw open his arms when Sebastian told him who they were.

MacLeod dismounted and immediately found himself wrapped in the arms of the hacienda's massive patriarch. The man lowered him to the ground and took his face in his huge hands.

"You are the one they call the *Americano, si?*"

MacLeod grinned sheepishly. "I reckon so."

"Then you are the one who looks for our Maria," Don Fernando said. His eyes glistened with emotion as he turned and invited them into his hacienda. "Please, come, we will eat first, and then you will tell me what you know."

MacLeod followed him across the courtyard toward the main house. Three well-fed women waited by the door as they approached.

They sat in the main room and sipped cups of chocolate while MacLeod filled Don Fernando in on what they had learned at Acoma.

"We didn't get as much information from the priest as we hoped, and what he had heard was a month or so old."

Don Fernando listened without interruption, an occasional nod of his head to indicate he followed the story.

"As much as we can make out, the rumor is that Romero usually goes to this place in the fall to trade whatever he can for guns or powder, when it's available. This time they say he has a Spanish woman to trade. I don't know where the information comes from, or how good it is, but it's the best thing we've heard in months."

Don Fernando stood, walked to his window and looked out onto the open courtyard. He remained silent for some time before responding. "It is strange that this story has passed up and down the river at this time. I too have heard it."

MacLeod scratched his head and wondered where his next bath would come from. It took a moment for Don Fernando's words to sink in. "Why is it so strange?"

"The story is always the same. Usually these rumors we hear are so different it is hard to say they are the same information. But this one is as if someone is causing this story to be spread along the river. Did you know that it is also said that the *Americano* will be there?"

MacLeod jerked to attention, his eyes focused on Don Fernando.

"Now I will give you the last piece of information. It arrived a few days ago, passed along to a few of us on the river who might meet up with you at some point. It is from Santa Fe and is reliable."

"You sure of this?"

"Yes, it comes from a man you know well, Father Alvarez."

MacLeod nodded his acknowledgement. "Go on, sir."

"Miguel Griego left two weeks ago, then another group consisting of many troops left some days later."

"How does this relate to me?"

"Some of the troops spoke about going to a place called Bosque Redondo. It is a place where Indians meet and trade. Do you know of it?"

MacLeod nodded and sipped the remainder of the rich chocolate, then leaned back against the wall. His thoughts rode his mare out across the plains to the Arkansas River and east, toward St. Louis. He saw Jeanette Charbonneau standing on the steps of her house, waiting for him. Winter would be on them again, in a couple of months. Where would he be when it arrived? But like before, when his thoughts wandered so, he remembered all of those who would never leave that place. Those he had buried there and the one who still might live.

"I have to go," MacLeod said. "Someone appears to have gone to a lot of trouble to get me there. I'd hate to disappoint them. And what if Maria is there and I don't show up?" It seems your governor is risking a lot by sending all those troops away from Santa Fe, unless he expects to catch the one person he's afraid of."

"But who?" Don Fernando questioned.

"The Apache," MacLeod said. "You know if you look at their plan closely if would seem they've spread a pretty wide net to catch this guy. I can't see any reason for the governor to do that just for me. And after what the Apache did to the escort troops taking us to Mexico, I can guess the authorities are none too happy with him."

For a moment Don Fernando only nodded. "So you think it is possible they are after him and not you?"

"I think it doesn't matter to me who they're after. If any of it is true, and it brings them all together, then that's the place I want to be. Even if I can't find Maria, I can't go home and leave Miguel Griego alive. Right now there's nothing I want to do more than kill him. I just hope he takes a long time to die."

A look of understanding shone in Don Fernando's eyes. He grasped MacLeod's hand between his own and held it. "If I were a much younger man, I would go with you. It would be most embarrassing for our governor if the stories reached the commandant general that you are still alive. Your existence is a threat to his future. But you are a much larger threat to Miguel Griego. He cannot allow you to live and tell your story."

"So this trap might look like it has been set for the Apache, but it's really to catch me?"

"I would agree to the possibility, but perhaps he hopes to rid himself of both you and this Apache," Don Fernando said. He rose from the seat and spoke to a young boy standing by the open door. The boy scurried off. "I have horses and food ready for you. I do not expect you to return the animals. They are a gift. With this information I have given you, I think you may decide to return to your own country immediately. I will understand."

MacLeod walked out into the blazing sun. Sebastian sat on a mule on the far side of the courtyard. He looked as if he was sleeping. Behind him the heavily laden black mule dozed. MacLeod's mare and the little bay stood stripped of their gear on the other side of the courtyard. They seemed to know they were being left behind. A deep-chested roan with three white stockings fidgeted at the railing, MacLeod's saddle on its back.

"I thank you for your help, Don Fernando. I will think about what you've said before I decide."

Don Fernando embraced MacLeod in his massive arms. "You are a young man, full of love, and desiring that all wrongs be avenged. When you have reached my age, you have discovered that life is full of wrongs. Think hard before you throw your life away."

MacLeod felt the gelding's strength when he mounted. Don Fernando's gift was a costly one.

"Please send word to Don Cordero and Father Alvarez. Tell them I appreciate their help and concern."

Don Fernando laid his hand on the gelding's neck. "*Vaya con dios.*"

Before his emotions overcame him, MacLeod led Sebastian and the big black mule out of the courtyard, toward the Sandia Mountains to the east.

Rio Pecos

They followed the dry creek bed up into the foothills and scrambled through a narrow north-south trending canyon until they crested the range and worked their way down into a wide valley.

Coming down off the side of the mountain, MacLeod could see far out over the plains. Somewhere out there the Pecos River cut a channel in the sunbaked earth and ran south, past a place called Bosque Redondo, where Indian tribes declared a temporary truce and gathered to trade. Don Fernando had made it clear that no one would blame him for giving up his quest and finding the quickest route out of Mexico. But MacLeod had made his decision, and he could only hope they would take their time and still be there when he and Sebastian showed up. Then he would find out if the rumors were true.

A dark-green shape buried in a sea of ochre and brown far to the east stood out for every traveler to see. Sebastian rode toward it and MacLeod guessed it might be a spring, as the green resolved itself into a small grove of cottonwood where two shallow canyons dropping down out of low hills converged.

Sebastian halted his mule and sat watching a circling flock of birds. He pointed toward the trees and sniffed the air, then he shook his head. "No animal."

They rode closer and MacLeod picked up the scent. "Whatever it is, it's been dead awhile."

The roan gelding shivered and had to be urged through the knee-high grass surrounding the stream, spooking a half dozen of the scavengers, who reluctantly took to the air.

The first body lay in the trees. An Indian, lying face down, his naked back covered in a frenzy of flies. Two more bodies lay a few feet from the spring.

"Looks like they've all been shot. Doesn't appear to be Indians' doings." MacLeod rode into the trees and found others.

Alongside the thin trickle of water lay the naked body of an old woman, black circles of blood where her breast had been, clasping an Indian child's doll in her hand.

Sebastian dismounted and walked through the long grass to check on three half-eaten bodies some distance from the stream. MacLeod watched him separate the remains. What was left of a young woman's body lay underneath the others. Sebastian seemed more interested in the body on top of hers.

"Doesn't appear to be one of theirs," MacLeod said, pointing to the boots on the body.

"It is not Navajo," Sebastian agreed.

"Seems the one in the middle was raping the woman, and along comes the third one there and kills him. Then someone shoots the Indian. Actually, it looks like a lot of them shot him, judging from the number of wounds.

Sebastian rolled the body over and sucked in his breath.

"You know this one?" The buzzards had not touched the face.

"He is with Señor Griego."

MacLeod found the tracks of many horses on the outer edge of the trees. He also saw signs that Griego had camped there for more than a day or two. It seemed strange.

The smell of the dead overwhelmed him, and he guided the horse to a spot upwind of the trees. There he found the tracks of many horses. He called Sebastian.

"Too many horses for Griego. There must be twenty or thirty in this group."

"Señor Griego came from there," Sebastian said, indicating a narrow trail coming down the canyon that the stream followed. "These tracks," he said, pointing to a second group, "they are made by the other men who came."

"Zavalda," MacLeod said.

"Others come too," Sebastian said and trotted up the canyon, following Griego's tracks. A hundred yards farther up, the canyon cut sharply to the right and most of the tracks followed the narrow floor. Sebastian appeared interested in the other tracks that came down the sandy side of the canyon and intersected with the first group. Clearly it was not an accident.

MacLeod scratched his head and walked the horse back and forth over the two sets of tracks. Somebody met there and killed those Indians, but was it Griego, or both he and Zavalda.

"Sebastian, you suppose those Indians over there were the ones that Navajo chief was looking for? You know, the ones stopped us eight, ten days ago?"

Sebastian mounted his mule and picked up the lead rope of the big black mule.

"It is them, but no young ones."

"If there were children or young women, Griego would have taken them."

They rode single file back through the trees to where Zavalda and his troops had camped. Sebastian dismounted and picked up a small stick. He used it to break up a pile of horse dung. Without a word he returned to the spring and did the same thing while MacLeod watched.

"What do you make of it?"

"Señor Griego wait here for three, four days."

"What about the Navajo?"

"They come first."

MacLeod leaned out of the saddle to inspect the tracks. "So Griego surprised the Indians and killed most of them, and then sat around and waited for Zavalda to show up and didn't even bury his own man, the cold-blooded bastard. Remind me to do the same for him after I kill him."

Sebastian kicked over the pile of dung. He bent down and picked up a leather strip and threw it toward the stream. It landed a few feet from MacLeod.

For a moment MacLeod studied the piece of leather. Something about it was familiar. He edged the dun alongside it and stepped to the ground, picking it up and turning it over in his hand.

"I'll be damned."

Sebastian looked puzzled.

"See this cut near the end? I started to put my initials on it. Belanger laughed at me and I quit. Means Griego has the furs. That's got to be those other tracks we saw joining them. Don't ask me how he could have found them, because I didn't believe Charbonneau himself could have found them, but I'll bet my boots on it. 'Bout how long ago did they all leave?"

The old man shrugged once more and mounted his mule. "Too many tracks. Up ahead, I will learn more."

48

Behind the troops, a thick cloud of dust rose from the hooves of the *caballada* as they pushed toward the river. Lieutenant Zavalda broke away and walked his horse toward a tent and spoke. "Why did you not wait for us at the spring?"

Griego grinned. "I did not wish to remain any longer, that is all."

"Your men," Zavalda said, pointing to a group by the river. "They do not wear their uniforms?"

"No, we go as Comanchero. They will not know who we are. I think you should go on, and we will meet you later."

For a moment Zavalda stood and stared out at the gathered group. Griego sensed something troubled him.

"I see you have picked up the furs. Is this all of them, or have you sent the governor his share already?" Zavalda said.

"It is not like you to worry about our governor," Griego said. "He will receive his share in due time."

"And these Indians," Zavalda said, indicating a woman and two Navajo children.

That brought a laugh to Griego. "That is what is bothering you and has taken so long for you to question me about. I could not leave them. Keep them until I return. I will find someone who will pay for them."

"In case you have forgotten, Miguel, you promised the governor you would bring him Romero's head."

Griego chuckled. "I will bring him the head of an Indian, and we will tell him it is Romero's. Will you tell him it is not?"

Was the man having other thought? Griego pondered the question for a moment. Maybe it was time for a change, but now was not the time to make an enemy of Zavalda. He threw back his head and laughed. "Do you think I would have gone to all of this trouble unless I planned to kill Romero? Why else would I have need for so many men?"

"Are you positive he will come?" Zavalda asked.

"It is what I have heard. If he thinks the *Americano* is coming, he will come."

"And the *Americano?*"

Griego's heart raced. That was the question he had asked himself since he proposed the plan to the governor. "We will know soon enough. He will come if he thinks she is here."

"But will the Apache bring the woman?"

Griego shrugged. "Who knows what is in the mind of an Indian. If she is still alive, he might bring her, but what does it matter. We will have the Apache and the *Americano*. She is nothing but Romero's squaw now. You would not know her if she did come."

Zavalda said nothing.

"We haven't much time," Griego said. "I will leave now to meet with the Comanche. It has been arranged. If it is not done before they arrive at Bosque Redondo, they will gamble away their silver before I have a chance to sell them the furs. As soon as your men are rested, take them down the river. There is a place where you can wait for my return, but tell your men that they must kill as many as they can with their first shots if it happens. They might not get a chance for a second."

Zavalda moved away from the shelter and pointed back to the tracks his men had made in the sand. "If the *Americano* comes this way, he will see we are here also."

"If he comes this way it cannot be helped."

And what if the woman was there also, Griego wondered. Would she still drive him mad with lust?

Maria felt the first pains on the morning of the fourth day after leaving the *rancheria*. It took her by surprise, although she knew the child would come soon. She stood by the side of her horse until the spasm passed, wondering if anyone had noticed, then Romero's wife cackled. She knew.

Maria mounted her horse with great effort and cradled her swollen belly in her arms. The horse fell in line with the others.

Thank God they had let Margarita come along. Otherwise she would have no one to talk to. She smiled, remembering the look on

Walking Like a Dog's face when she left. He knew she would not be back. She wondered who would keep his cooking fires and keep him warm when the weather changed. The camp had not been the same since word reached them that MacLeod was alive. Everyone walked in fear of Romero's wrath, and they blamed her.

Maria grunted as another spasm gripped her. She looked up at the sun to see how long it had been since the last one and wondered how much farther to this place they called Bosque Redondo. They told her it was at the end of Apache land, a place where the lands of the Comanche begin. Others would be there also, Kiowa for sure, and maybe the Utes from up north, but not the Navajo. They were not invited, since no one would honor a truce where they were involved.

Ahead rode the women who had failed to produce children and were considered unwelcome mouths to feed. Romero needed powder and lead for the few muskets he had stolen from the military, and heavy winter robes for the approaching cold weather. If he got lucky he might trade for a couple of guns from the tribes who raided to the east. Margarita told Maria that Romero wanted a weapon like the one that killed his son. For this he would give them Maria, but not the child.

Several other women rode with the party, but they were along to keep the camp and cook. One that would not return with the others was the Navajo woman whose tongue Romero cut out, the one they called Consuela. Maria watched her stumble along behind the others, a pathetic figure whom no one would help.

Between the spasms, Maria's only thoughts were focused on MacLeod. What had happened to him after his escape and did he ever think about her the way she thought about him? She shook her head as a way of chastising herself for letting these thoughts plague her. She had far more important things to think about, such as this child who would not wait much longer. Maria knew if it was a boy, he would be taken from her and given to another woman who still had milk in her breasts. She had never asked them what would happen if it was a girl.

The next contraction made her cry out. She closed her eyes and clutched the horse's mane to keep from sliding off. She heard the fractured voice of Romero's wife call out and felt her horse being led aside. They helped her slide off of her horse and placed her on the ground in a small depression some distance from the others. She had heard that the women were sometimes left behind and catch up when they could, but apparently Romero would take no chance on losing her.

The child came in the late afternoon, when the sun rode a crimson sky toward the Sacramento Mountains and away from the direction they were heading. Margarita gave her the child while there was still light to see. Before looking at the wailing infant at her breast, Maria caught a flash of hatred in the old woman's eye.

Maria parted the folds of the blanket made from the skins of the desert rabbit and ran her fingers over the face of her son. He opened his eyes to her touch.

A cry of pain and sorrow rose from the desert floor and caused Romero to shift his position as if an enemy had been sighted. He rose and wrapped his long arms around his body as if to ward off his fears.

BOSQUE REDONDO

MacLeod and Sebastian followed the slash in the earth that contained the bitter waters of the Pecos and the tracks of many horses. A scorching sun, with never a cloud to hide it, punished them as they rode the endless miles that MacLeod prayed would end his pursuit of unfulfilled promises. He glanced over his shoulder to see the unchanging face of the old Navajo. The deep lines carved into Sebastian's brow and cheeks resembled the sharp cuts etched into the sides of a dry arroyo. His face was a mask of sand and dust thrown up by the hooves of the animals.

"Any idea how much further?" MacLeod asked as much to hear his own voice as know the answer.

"Maybe tomorrow," Sebastian muttered.

"Maybe tomorrow, maybe tomorrow, it's not far. It's the same answer you gave me a week ago. I don't know why I keep asking."

Sebastian rode up alongside, leading the black mule. "Senior Griego has many, Romero will have many, we are only us."

MacLeod spit out a mouthful of sand, wishing he hadn't used so much spit. "Maybe that's why I keep asking how much further it is to this place so I'll know how long I have to come up with a plan."

Sebastian grunted and shook his head.

They worked their way across a dry wash and scrambled up the other side. Sebastian held up his hand and pointed to a bend in the river half a mile ahead, where thin columns of smoke rose from a number of fires scattered along the banks of the river.

They found a spot where they could watch the camp with little chance of being seen. MacLeod scratched at the dust that thickened his hair.

"Not Señor Griego," Sebastian said.

"You're right, those look like the governor's militia, which makes you wonder where Griego might be. If he is taking the furs to sell to the Comanche, then figures on coming back here to pick up Zavalda and these fellows here, and they all go to this Bosque Redondo, maybe we won't have to contend with half the troops in old Mexico if we hurry and quit lagging." He nudged Sebastian and they crawled back to where the horses waited.

Bosque Redondo lay on a flat, wide plain between rugged walls of sand. The Pecos had spread its precious waters over the area and nursed the growth of many cottonwoods. To the Indians it was the place of the round grove and had become a favorite meeting place of Indians and Comanchero, the band of renegade Mexicans who wandered the southern plains trading whatever they could steal, with the Comanche.

Sebastian grunted and pointed down river to where the travel shelters of the Apache sat like small beaver huts off by themselves. A shiver passed over MacLeod as two Apache rode their horses from the camp toward the main grove of trees. He eased his rifle closer to his body, his thumb unconsciously locating the hammer. If Romero was there, would he have brought Maria?

"The Apache are here all right, but are they the ones we're looking for?"

"Mescalero," Sebastian said, indicating a group of crude thatched huts.

A cloud of smoke hung at treetop level and the sounds of the gathering began to reach them. They passed two wary women gathering wood from along the river's edge.

"They look more Mexican than Apache."

"One, the other Navajo."

"Darned if I know how you can tell the difference," MacLeod muttered.

Two riders burst from the trees and raced their ponies across the flat river bottom toward a lone tree trunk sticking up out of the sand. The lead rider turned too wide and let the other cut underneath him.

Both raced neck-and-neck toward the trees. MacLeod watched in awe as the bareback riders slid to a halt and leaped to the ground.

The main gathering seemed to be coming from the other end of the grove. Sebastian pointed out two Comanche who sat by a small cooking fire, sharing a drink from a water gourd. They eyed MacLeod and Sebastian. One rose and led his horse toward them. He pointed at MacLeod's rifle.

MacLeod shook his head, "No way, amigo."

The Comanche raced back to a tepee and pulled a drunken woman from inside. Her long, black hair hung in a tangled mass over her face but did not hide her mutilated nose. The Comanche pushed her forward and pointed to his horse.

MacLeod kneed the gelding past the woman, who had collapsed on the ground. He wanted no part of a fight at the moment, at least not with that Indian. The other Comanche went back to his jug.

The sour smell of horse urine, mixed with unfamiliar cooking odors, hung like a thick cloud beneath the treetops. Women harangued their slouching husbands, driving them away from the food pots. In one camp three fat puppies were tied to a tree with a leather thong. For a price they would find their way into a pot before the day ended. They passed a group of sullen-faced Kiowa sitting among a pile of buffalo robes and a small stack of knives from a fur-trading post, probably passed along by the Pawnee.

MacLeod watched as Indians passed from one group to another, trading the items they had just bargained for from another group. One staggered off to sit under a tree with a small jug clutched in his hand.

MacLeod chuckled, thinking that when the man woke up, he'd probably go looking for his horse and never remember trading it.

"Comanchero," Sebastian whispered as they rode near a large group with the most to offer. The men looked to be all Mexican, with maybe a couple of half breeds. MacLeod had heard about them, but this was his first encounter. He knew this type would wait for an unguarded moment if they planned any action. They seldom took chances.

The sound of excited voices rose above the general buzz of the camp. Sebastian pointed through the trees. "Apache."

MacLeod gripped the stock of his rifle and urged his horse toward a large gathering in a clearing. He still had no idea what he planned on doing if he came face to face with Romero, but he figured the Apache would make the first move. He reined in behind two Indian ponies and followed. When he turned to investigate a group off by themselves, he saw that Sebastian had disappeared.

Smoke from a fire rose into the canopy of cottonwood branches. Two small children sat huddled to one side of the fire, their feet bound and tied to a stake driven into the ground. Their eyes mirrored a fear MacLeod could almost taste.

Behind a tree, three older women curled their legs beneath thin bodies and busied themselves with camp tasks, while another searched her husband's hair and cracked the crop of lice between her teeth. Another rocked a wailing newborn wrapped in a blanket of milky doeskins.

MacLeod's eye came to rest on the back of a thin figure rocking gently back and forth as if listening to its own melody. Something about the figure gnawed at his memory as he pushed closer to the main group of men bargaining over a group of women for sale. MacLeod felt the eyes on him and knew they were assessing this newcomer, then the eyes slid down to the long, slender rifle he held in his hand and the pistols tucked under the sash around his waist.

MacLeod took in all of the challenging stares but met no one's eyes. He wanted no fight with any of them. He saw those described as Comanchero gather on the far side of the circle. A loose association of Kiowa and Comanche made up most of the others. He pulled the brim of his hat lower over his eyes and casually searched each face.

Two Apaches guarded a small cluster of women sitting off to one side. He recognized both from the long walk into the mountains. Romero had come.

MacLeod touched the gelding and moved around the circle of tension. The squat figure rocking back and forth uttered a low moan. MacLeod shuddered, wondering what could cause such pain, then the blanket slipped off the figure's head and he recognized Consuela. But where was Maria? Had Romero left her behind, or was it possible Romero had lied to him about her being in his camp?

He found a spot where he could observe the group without being noticed and watched as the voices rose in anticipation as one woman was dragged away and another brought into the circle. MacLeod listened to the Indians argue among themselves, their hands dancing with the universal language of the plains. The new captive to be sold stood straight, her shoulders thrown back in seeming defiance, and her long, black hair hanging loose to her waist. An Apache stepped forward and slit the leather thongs of her dress, letting it fall to the dirt at her feet. For a moment the voices of the men fell silent before a frenzy of biding began.

From somewhere in the camp a baby's cry of hunger fought to be heard over the chaos of those bidding on this latest offering. MacLeod watched her turn at the sound of the infant, her breasts hanging loose and full.

The woman continued to turn toward the sound of the child. MacLeod caught her profile outlined against the faces of the bidders. A cold sweat broke out on his face, and his breath came in short gasps. His heartbeat so hard he was certain the others could hear. He choked back a cry of recognition. She was alive, and everything that had taken place over the last few months washed out of his thoughts.

He took a moment to gather himself, knowing this was not the time to lose sight of reality. With Maria here, Romero was also, and waiting. MacLeod casually turned and searched the faces of those encircling the object of their lust. On the second sweep he spotted him, squatting beneath a large tree. Their eyes met.

The competing bidders pushed and shoved to the front to be heard. A tall, barrel-chested Comanche shouldered his way past MacLeod and returned with three horses and a woman who seemed to sense she was a part of the bargain.

Romero shook his head, his eyes never moving away from MacLeod. The circle grew as the word spread, bringing Comanche, Kiowa, and Comanchero, who stood shoulder to shoulder with Mescalero in a restless truce, waiting to bid on the Spanish woman. With a display of wild gestures and shouts, four Kiowa pooled their meager offerings and forced their way to the front to face Romero. Some began to grow angry at his reluctance to accept any of the offers.

MacLeod waited, the muzzle of his rifle casually leveled at the squat body of the Apache. He had identified where each of Romero's warriors were standing or sitting. They were the only ones showing no interest in the bidding.

The big horse answered his urging and moved a few feet closer, only a few steps from the back of the bidders. MacLeod, for the moment, lost sight of the squatting Apache. He took a last inventory of his weapons. Both pistols were tucked into his belt, along with his knife. Three shots, then the knife. It would not last long.

At MacLeod's request, the big roan gelding shouldered his way through the fringe of onlookers until Romero came back into view. His rage cast his face into a mask of hate. MacLeod knew that he was the source, and it gave him conflicting feelings. A man as close to uncontrolled rage as Romero could attack at any time or commit whatever act would satisfy his needs. It also dulled his reasoning. MacLeod felt his own anger rise like a flood. He fought it, knowing he had to control himself. It would be all over soon and one of them would be dead. He couldn't think about Maria or what would happen to her if he failed.

Romero leapt up and ridiculed the crowd for offering so little for such a woman. He circled Maria, pointing out her assets to the serious bidders, then grasped her arm and spun her around.

MacLeod fought to control the terrible weakness that shook his body. She stood, not twenty feet from him, her head thrown back, her eyes challenging the crowd as if to indicate her worth.

51

Maria felt the lustful stares of those surrounding her and the heat their bodies produced in their desire for her. As the bidding continued, she kept track of the ones who appeared to have the most to offer. There were only two left, the Comanche who had pushed his wife into the circle to stand beside his horses, and someone behind Maria whose answering counter bid was in her own language.

Maria flinched as Romero sprung to his feet and came toward her. His sudden chastisement of the two remaining bidders took her mind from the voices behind her. She remembered Margarita's warning, "Beware if the Comanchero buy you. They will sell you again and again."

As the voices of the bidders rose in volume, Romero seized her arm and spun her around to face the Comanchero, seeking to entice him to increase his bid. Maria fought to conceal her fear, remembering that her child lay at the breast of another woman and his life might depend on who bought her. She knew the Comanche would take them both. The Comanchero had no use for a child. Romero had promised this when he looked into the eyes of the child and knew it was not his. But she had lived with the Apache and knew how they thought. The child would grow to become a warrior among the Comanche, and would be taught to hate the Apache. Would Romero want another enemy?

She quickly searched for new faces in the surging crowd. Who else might join the bidding? Her eyes swept over the leering looks, past a lone man sitting astride a sturdy roan, his hat pulled low over his eyes. A long, thin rifle lay balanced across the front of his saddle.

An angry retort to Romero's ear-splitting harangue centered Maria's attention on a heavy Mexican just to the right of the rider. The Mexican appeared to have many of the crowd on his side. He raised his bid by adding two Pueblo children. Time hung like a weapon poised to strike as she waited for the Comanche to counter.

Maria watched the lust-filled grin of the Mexican as he realized she might be his. Others pressed closer to him to offer congratulations, hoping to find favor, and perhaps have her later on in the night. She could smell the sweat from their lice-covered bodies and their foul breath on her neck. She swore she would not allow it to happen this time. No man would again throw her on the ground and mount her like a dog. She would die first. But no, she could not, she would do what they wanted. Who would look after his child if she did not?

For an instant an image danced across her thoughts like the flicker of a distant star, first there, then gone, then it came again and angered her. How could her father have done it? The image became a reality; the rifle held by the man on the horse was his. Hadn't she taken it in her hands herself and entrusted it to her father? How could he have given it to someone else? Her gaze focused on the tall, slender figure, who seemed to sit so casually on his horse and watch.

Then the realization struck her, and her heart felt as if it had dropped into her stomach. It was him, and there was nothing casual about him. She couldn't see his eyes but she watched the muzzle of the rifle track Romero's every move.

Questions swamped her mind. What could he do against so many? Why had he come? What would she do if he died trying to save her? She wished she could tell him to turn around and leave while he could. But she knew he wouldn't.

Maria begged him to raise his head and look at her, just once, just to assure her he recognized her.

Romero grabbed her arm again and held her facing MacLeod. She realized that his presence was known and why Romero appeared so agitated.

He raised his head for a moment and looked at her. He looked different, older, tired, no longer the young man she remembered and fell in love with. Then it struck her how much she also had changed in less than a year. Their love had cost them both and she wondered if it would also cost them their lives.

52

MacLeod wrestled with the urge to look at her again, but he knew he couldn't risk taking his eyes off the Apache. In the brief instant when she mouthed his name and their eyes met, he knew his months of pain and hardship were nothing compared to what she must have endured. Yet, there she stood, naked, her head thrown back in challenge to the mob of men who bid on her.

Romero drew his knife and pressed it against Maria's breast. Beside MacLeod the Mexican Comanchero groaned and raised his bid again.

Then it came to MacLeod that the Apache had no intention of selling her, at least not until after he and MacLeod settled their own private war. MacLeod felt the tension rise. He fought to control himself, reviewing the advice given to him by Stewart and Belanger. He took a deep breath and checked on Romero's two warriors, who were waiting for orders to attack, and decided he was as ready as he could be, although he wished Sebastian was there to cover his back.

"Tell you what I'll do, you sow-bellied runt. You let her go and I'll kill you quick." MacLeod hoped his voice didn't display his fear, but he saw the instant reaction of the crowd.

The Comanchero moved in close to the gelding. MacLeod heard someone whisper, "*El Americano.*"

MacLeod watched Romero's rage surface as Maria translated the challenge. An avalanche of words poured from the Apache's mouth as he pulled her forward and held her between himself and the threatening barrel of MacLeod's rifle.

Out of the corner of his eye, MacLeod saw one of the warriors leave his position and creep forward. But Romero had not counted on the crowd falling back as quickly as it did. MacLeod found himself alone, with an Apache silently moving closer. The fat Comanchero's hand slid down his shirtfront toward the handle of his knife.

MacLeod studied the action of both but what worried him more was the whereabouts of the second Apache, whom he last saw slide in behind the group of Comancheros. He was surprised that Romero would wait to see if his men would kill him first. He saw the grin spread across the face of the Comanchero and knew he had also spotted the two Apaches.

The crowd of bidders moved away from the center of the dispute and sought safety among the trees.

MacLeod waited, hoping the big horse would answer his command when the time came. His eyes tracked Romero, who held his knife at Maria's throat.

Then he caught the movement of the second Apache coming in stealthily and low, a short-handled lance poised over his right shoulder, and knew he was the most dangerous. When the fight began, MacLeod would not have time to swing the rifle back across the saddle or to pull one of the pistols from his belt. MacLeod rehearsed the moves he would have to make, then hope that somehow the Apache with the lance would miss his mark. But at that distance, he had never seen an Apache miss.

The Comanchero raised his eyes and took one last look at the naked body of Maria and the prize he hoped to claim. His hand dove for his knife.

MacLeod drove his heels into the gelding's flank. The big horse leapt forward enough to throw off the aim of the attackers and gave MacLeod a clean shot at the Apache charging him from the left. He didn't have time to aim but it didn't matter. He felt the slight hesitation before the powder exploded at the bottom of the barrel and drove the .50 caliber ball through the chest of the Indian. MacLeod whipped the rifle around, striking the Mexican under the ear and bringing a howl of pain. In a flash MacLeod reversed the rifle and rammed the butt down on the top of the man's head as hard as he could. It sounded like a rock falling into a deep pool of water. The Comanchero dropped to the dirt as if someone had used a sledgehammer on him.

Maria screamed a warning as MacLeod reached for the pistol at his belt. He twisted around in the saddle, causing the Apache's lance to tear through his shirt and slice his upper arm. He jerked the reins, causing the gelding to rear back and throw him to the ground. MacLeod landed hard, forcing the wind from his lungs. The Apache never broke stride as he drew his knife and charged MacLeod, who lay with his knees drawn up to his stomach, trying to fill his lungs with air. MacLeod rolled over, trying to push himself to his feetHe knew his only chance would be to catch the Indian's knife hand before he could strike. At the last moment, he realized he was too slow and fell backward, away from the attack. He felt the turbulence as a bullet whipped past his ear a split second before the heavy crash of a gun split the air. The Apache fell to the ground in front of MacLeod, blood pumping out of his body and forming a puddle on the parched earth. MacLeod dove for his knife in the dirt but couldn't locate it. He spun toward the spot where the shot came from, figuring the shot had been meant for him.Sebastian stood dwarfed beside the black mule, reloading Stewart's musket. The milling bidders in Romero's auction stood momentarily stunned until the cry of a frightened baby again broke the silence.

MacLeod spun around, looking for Romero. The Indian stood frozen, his knife at Maria's throat, waiting.

Slowly MacLeod's right hand explored the damage done by the Apache's lance. He flexed the arm and found he could move it, but only at the cost of searing pain. He wiped the blood from his right hand, knowing nothing could be done for it and sought the bone handle of his knife. The months of anger and hatred for the Apache flooded over him as he rose to his feet and took a step toward Romero.

"William, go, please. Please go while you can. There are too many of them," Maria pleaded.

"Tell him I have waited for this time for many of his moons."

"He will kill you, William. Please go."

"Maria, tell him."

She spoke to Romero through her tears while MacLeod tried to remember the hard lessons taught to him. Romero had the same thick-chested, powerful build as Belanger, but his arms were longer. MacLeod had never won a wrestling match with Belanger and knew that the injury to his left arm would force him to stay away from the Apache. If he had any chance, the fight had to be at long range.

MacLeod drew his knife. He knew one of them would be dead in a few moments. He needed an edge and hoped Romero's hatred would provide it.

"Maria, listen to me. Tell him to come out from behind you. Tell him he can't hide behind a woman."

She quickly repeated his words, giving MacLeod a chance to study his reactions. Romero flung Maria to the ground and dropped into a crouch. MacLeod figured the Apache would come in low, slashing from left to right and hoping to catch him in the belly. But in spite of the lance wound in MacLeod's arm, Romero still appeared cautious and MacLeod didn't want a thinking opponent.

"Maria, I want you to tell him that I am going to kill him like I killed his son. Ask him if he has any other sons for me to kill when I finish with him."

Her words struck Romero like a bolt of lightning. From his throat an animal growl of warning rose until his face stretched into a mask of fury. He charged.

MacLeod barely had time to spin to his left, away from the thrust, and lash out with his foot, catching Romero on the inside of the knee. For an instant Romero's knee buckled. He whipped a backhanded slash at MacLeod, cutting nothing but air.

MacLeod grinned and began taunting him. He knew Romero couldn't understand his words but he could interpret the tone in his voice and the smile on his face. MacLeod hoped he was masking his own fear. The Apache's speed worried him.

Romero tried another slashing lunge and again MacLeod managed to evade the attempt and lash out at the unprotected knee. The knee buckled again, but MacLeod knew he couldn't do it a third time. Romero would be ready for it.

Both men circled to their right and away from the other's knife. MacLeod's left arm throbbed from the wound caused by the lance. He continued flexing the arm, knowing he needed to fight through the pain and use it for balance. He saw Romero reach down and scoop up a handful of dirt, figuring the Apache would probably fake a stab with his knife and throw the dirt at his eyes, coming at him behind the dirt.

MacLeod stopped moving to his right and shifted to the left. For an instant Romero was off balance, with his right hand extended.

With all of his weight on his left leg, MacLeod kicked out with his right and caught Romero's arm. The knife sailed up into the air. Romero stood defenseless, his eyes flitting from MacLeod to his knife, which lay on the ground five feet away.

MacLeod heard the laughter from the crowd encircling the fighters, which seemed to rattle the Apache. MacLeod took up the laugh and motioned to the knife.

"Pick it up old man. I can't kill you unless you stay and fight."

Maria knelt to pick up her dress as she repeated his words. She appeared to add a few taunts of her own, judging by the laughter in the crowd.

With the quickness of a bobcat, Romero scrambled for the knife and spun to meet the charge he expected. MacLeod had not moved but knew he couldn't evade Romero forever. Sooner or later the Apache would get too close and MacLeod wouldn't be able to fend him off or wrestle him to the ground with only one arm. He had to find a way to finish Romero quickly and to do that he had to force him into making a mistake.

MacLeod watched the muscles in Romero's jaw tighten in anger as he dropped into a low crouch and began circling again.

MacLeod followed Romero's movements, gradually forcing him back against the crowd, and all the time taunting the deadly Apache. He knew Romero had to charge soon. He waited, slowly circling, his eyes never leaving those of the man he hoped to kill in the next moment or so. Belanger had always done the same thing to him, trying to make him move first, to make the mistake, and when he did Belanger countered.

MacLeod's left arm hung almost useless. He could no longer find the strength to flex it or raise it to shield himself. He could no longer hear the crowd, or Maria, who waited in fearful anticipation. Every ounce of concentration flowed through him and prepared him for Romero's strike.

Romero slid to his left, crouching low, with both hands spread for balance, the wicked knife held tightly in his right hand. With the quickness of a snake he lashed out, ripping the front of MacLeod's shirt and slitting the skin beneath. MacLeod leapt back, his own knife raking Romero's arm, again surprised at the speed of the older man, but also satisfied at the damage his own blade caused. Romero backed away and surveyed the blood running down his arm into the dirt at his feet.

Through his own pain MacLeod gestured with his left hand for Romero to quit running and fight. It brought more calls from the men placing bets on the outcome. As MacLeod shuffled forward, Romero found himself cornered between two large trees. He tried moving first to one side, then the other, but MacLeod moved with him cutting off any chance of his escape to more open ground. MacLeod saw doubt cloud the Apache's eyes. He tensed, waiting for the charge, knowing it was imminent, and knowing exactly what he would do.

Seconds spun away, then he saw it coming, as if everything happened at walking speed. Romero snarled and threw himself at MacLeod. With the charge, MacLeod fell backward, taking Romero with him and rolling away from the Apache's knife at the same time. As Romero fell forward, MacLeod's knife found the unprotected mid-section of the Indian's body. The knife went in all the way with ease. MacLeod locked his legs around Romero's thrashing body and held on, waiting for his death.

53

Deep in the back of his mind, MacLeod registered Maria's scream, then he felt her hands tearing at Romero's body. Not until he pushed the body of the Apache off did those surrounding them realize what had happened, or who lived.

"I'm sorry I took so long," he said, taking her in his arms.

Maria held him tight, tears streaming down her cheeks. "I knew you would come, but they said you were dead, and then they said, no, you were alive, and sometimes I prayed you would stay alive and go home."

"You mean you didn't want me to come and find you?"

"Yes, yes, I wanted you to find me, but look at me, William. I am an Apache now. That I can never change." She pushed him away. "William, what home do I have that will accept me."

"Your father wants you back and that's a beginning. You can worry about the others later."

She turned away, a sad smile creasing the lines of her drawn face, and saw Sebastian standing by the horses with the guns in his hands. She reached out to him. The old man jerked his head over his shoulder as he spoke to MacLeod. "Señor Zavalda come."

"Any sign of Griego?"

"No."

MacLeod moved to Sebastian's side and took the rifle, seeing that the old man had reloaded it. "We'll need a couple of horses, if you can find them. I think we'd better get out of here pretty quick."

"William," Maria said, pointing toward a group of Comanchero who were moving to encircle them.

MacLeod hefted the rifle and felt for his pistols, but realized he hadn't retrieved the pistols after the fight. Slowly he edged backward, pulling Maria with him, until he felt the rough bark of a tree at his back.

"What is it you want," Maria asked in a voice broken with exhaustion.

MacLeod knew the one who answered would be the leader. He would be the one to shoot.

A Comanchero grinned, glancing over his shoulder at the others who stood with him and pointed at MacLeod. He ran his hand over his mustache and spoke to Maria.

"What's he saying?"

"You have killed one of them and now they want something in return."

"Looks as if the one whose head I caved in was in charge and this one's taking over. Ask him what he wants."

"He wants your gun."

"Tell him he can't have it, and if he comes any closer he'll be the one to die. If I have to shoot him, run to my horse and go with Sebastian. He'll take you back to your father."

"We'll both run, William. I'm not going back alone, never. I'd rather return to the Apache."

A cry of alarm from one of the Comanchero alerted them to Zavalda's approach. They broke away, sprinted to their horses and rode out of the camp. MacLeod watched Zavalda lead his troops into the fringe of trees at the upper edge of the camp. He found his powder and shot bag and pistols. Maria had disappeared.

"For a while I thought you might be a ghost," Zavalda said, grinning. "I think I have chased you over much of Nuevo Mexico."

"You needn't chase me any longer. I found what I was after."

Zavalda looked around. "You found the Señorita de Cordero. She is here?"

"She's here."

"She is well?"

"She's alive. I don't know how well she is," MacLeod said. "Where's the other one? Griego?"

Zavalda shrugged. "He is late. I expected him days ago. Romero, is he here also?"

"He's dead."

Zavalda nodded his head slowly. "How did it happen?"

"I killed him."

Zavalda explained to the men and MacLeod noted a general sense of relief. "Then we can go home now, no?"

"Depends on you, Lieutenant. What do you propose on doing with us?"

At a word from Zavalda, the troops broke ranks and dispersed to find shady spots to rest. He dismounted and turned his horse over to one of his men. "You and the señorita are a problem. I'm sure you can see this. Señor Griego will have a most difficult time explaining his actions concerning the señorita. You he must kill, or I assume you will kill him."

MacLeod nodded. "That's about right, but what about the governor?"

"Well, our esteemed governor will of course take credit for the rescue of Señorita Cordova, and he will report to the authorities in Mexico that he also has rid the land of the Apache. He may even forget about you, and not put you in his report."

"You mean if he puts me in his report he will need to explain my part in all of this?"

Zavalda grinned. "You see the problem he has."

"Griego is another matter," said MacLeod. "I think we had better get out of here before he shows up."

MacLeod watched as the last of the Comanche and Kiowa crossed the river and rode east. He wondered if any of them left the trade fair with what they came looking for.

"I thought you and Griego were together in all this. How do I know you aren't planning on turning us over to him the first chance you get?"

Zavalda pulled one of his men aside and told him to have the men water their horses and check their canteens. Then he walked back to where MacLeod waited for an answer. "I would not say we were friends. He has used my position to his advantage."

MacLeod shook his head and spit out a mouthful of dust. "But you're the one that let him do it."

"Yes, that is so, and I am not proud of it. But now I think I have had enough. Then there was an incident at the spring."

"When those Navajos were killed?"

"You saw it then. He did not need to kill them. It was then that I knew it was enough."

The wail of a child broke the almost serene peace of the cottonwood grove. MacLeod watched Maria return, carrying a bundle in her arms and with another woman at her side leading two horses.

MacLeod turned back to Zavalda. "There's something else I need to know. What happened to my friend, Mr. Charbonneau? Was it Griego who killed him?"

"He and some of his men. Again, it was not necessary to kill the old man. He gave them the information they wanted."

"So Griego killed him anyway, and then went for the furs. Where are they now?"

"That is where he has gone, to sell them to the Comanche."

"That's what I figured. Can I count on you not going back over to Griego's side?"

Zavalda looked off into the distance. "I have decided I can no longer continue aiding him in his affairs. When we return to Santa Fe, I will ask the governor to allow me to return to Mexico. I would like to make peace with my father. It was not good when I left."

"Then we best be leaving," MacLeod said and went to meet Maria. The child had stopped crying. He glanced down at the tiny thing wrapped in soft doeskins and wondered why she had gone back to the camp for the child.

She stood looking at him for some time before she spoke. "William, there is something else you need to know. This child is ours."

MacLeod wasn't sure he understood, at a time when there seemed other, more important things to be done.

"What do you mean, ours?"

"I gave birth to this child, William," she said and offered him the bundle.

He shrank back and saw the hurt in her eyes.

"Please, William, he is your son."

54

"My son?"

"Don't act as if it is not possible."

He still could not reach out to take the child in his arms. For one thing, he had no idea how to do it. "I don't understand."

"William, you do remember what happened the last time we were together, do you not?"

"Maria, how could you ask that question. It's what kept me alive."

The baby began to cry again. Maria lowered her dress and placed the infant at her breast. MacLeod looked away in embarrassment.

"There is much we must talk about, William, of all the things that have happened to me."

He noted the deep sadness in her voice and sought to ease her worries, although he had to admit that he had pushed away those thoughts. "I knew of these things before I came looking for you. We can talk of them later, if you want."

She turned away with the child still at her breast as a hot wind blew through the trees, carrying the dust and sand of the desert. MacLeod lowered his head to shield his eyes. These things she wanted to tell him were the same things Father Alvarez had spoken of. He looked at the child suckling on the nipple of her breast. For an instant the child's eyes opened and looked at him, eyes as blue as his own.

MacLeod leaned across the child in her arms and kissed her on the lips. "Father Alvarez said you would have these things to speak of. He said you would need to do it, and I would need to listen and try to understand. I don't care what happened, Maria. I only care about you."

"Very well, but these things are terrible things. I hope you can listen to them."

"Why don't we wait until we get back to Santa Fe? Right now we've got to get away from here before Miguel Griego shows up."

Maria looked confused. "Why would he come here?"

"He arranged all of this. He wanted Romero to bring you so I would come. I forgot, you had no way of knowing. Lieutenant Zavalda says he must have been delayed selling the furs. Now he's got to try to catch up before we get back to Santa Fe."

Zavalda already had his men in their saddles and ready to leave. A Navajo woman and two children sat on the ground, guarded by one of the troopers.

Zavalda explained. "They are the captives Señor Griego took."

"These are the ones taken at the spring, when the others were all killed?"

Zavalda tilted his head in acknowledgement and MacLeod noted the look of resignation on his face.

"Then we're taking them with us. I'll have Sebastian talk to the woman. I know where they belong."

"We had better hurry then," Zavalda said.

MacLeod helped Maria onto a horse Sebastian had found. "Get going, I'll be right behind you as soon as I find one more person."

He found her sitting in the same spot where the Apache camped. They had left her behind. She sat, her thin body hunched over, waiting to die. He took her arm and helped her to her feet. It was not the same Consuela who had given herself up so he might escape. He led her back to where the others waited.

"We were never able to learn from her what had happened to you. We tried but she would not speak of it," Maria said.

"She saved my life more than once. I'd never have escaped from Romero without her help. A man named Juan told me a little about her, but then Romero killed him. Maybe she'll talk now."

Maria shook her head. "She will never speak. Romero cut out her tongue."

A heavy sadness fell on MacLeod. This woman had suffered so much because of him. "Why would he do that?"

"He did it when he discovered you were alive. He hated you and he feared you. While we ride you must tell me about her," Maria said, smiling sadly. "If she did these things for you, I too owe her."

MacLeod reached up and touched Consuela's cheek, noting the gauntness in her face. "I reckon she don't eat too well without her tongue."

"He never fed her. She lived on the scraps we saved for her. What will you do with her, William?"

MacLeod helped Consuela onto a mule Sebastian held for her. "I'm not sure. Something will come up, I suppose."

They caught up with Zavalda and his troops two miles north of the camp. Zavalda waited for MacLeod to ride alongside.

"One of my scouts located Señor Griego's camp, but they had already left. It looks like they are maybe two days ahead of us."

"You think we'll catch up to them?"

Zavalda shrugged. "They are traveling on the other side of the river. If he is going to Santa Fe, we will see his tracks when he crosses. Maybe he will go north, to Taos, but I don't think he will."

"I don't either, but I can't understand why he didn't show up here?"

Zavalda rode for some time before he spoke. "We have not agreed on many things lately. I think Señor Griego has too many enemies and they are making him very nervous."

"You mean like me?"

"Yes, but I think he meant for Romero to kill you, and then maybe I would kill Romero. This would make him very happy."

"So what happens when he finds out I'm alive?"

A rider trotted up to Zavalda and saluted. They spoke for a moment.

"My scout says there are many tracks ahead of us. They are moving fast."

MacLeod and Maria looked at each other.

"The Comanchero. When they left, they were heading this way," she said.

"Is there another way we can go?"

"No, we have little water and some of the men are already sick from drinking that of the river."

"If these Comanchero run into Griego, he'll know for sure I'm still alive."

"And me also," Maria said. "If we make it to Santa Fe, it will be the end of him."

"It's a big desert. What are the chances of them running into each other."

"There is a good chance. They will go to the spring," said Zavalda. "And so must we. Let us hope they do not remain."

Sebastian rode ahead with the Navajo children and their mother. Maria had explained Margarita's presence. She had hidden when the Mescalero pulled out of the camp and waited until Maria returned for the child.

MacLeod watched Maria shield the child from the glaring sun and wondered why he felt afraid of being the child's father. For so long the end of the nightmare lay with finding Maria, but now a dozen new problems faced him. Would Maria be accepted by her family? What was he going to do with Consuela and the captives, and who waited for him ahead? But his biggest concern was Zavalda. What would the lieutenant do when and if they all came together?

By the time they saw the first hint of green growth at the base of the hills, caution had disappeared. The men walked or rode exhausted horses and thought of little but the cool, sweet water that seeped from the ground a few miles away. MacLeod rode up to Zavalda at the head of the column.

"If he's there, what will you do?"

"We will talk. He will let us drink of the water, I hope. Then we will see."

A scout riding a spent horse jogged up to Zavalda and removed his hat. He looked back toward the spring.

Maria listened to the conversation.

"Miguel is waiting," she said, "and he has many men with him."

DESERT SPRING

Zavalda ordered the men to form up in marching order. "Take the others to the back," he said to MacLeod. "It will be safer there."

"I'm staying up here. This fight is more about me than it is about you."

"If Miguel will not talk, you should take the Señorita Cordero and the child, and try to escape through the canyon. It is very narrow, but there is a trail, and they will be afraid to follow."

The desert floor dropped away, forming a semi-circular flat around the spring. Beneath the trees men rose from their cooking fires and watched the approaching riders. MacLeod noted the smell of death that still hung in the air. He checked the flints on his rifle and pistols, and moved his powder horn and ball bag within easy reach. He flexed the fingers of his left arm, knowing speed in reloading and shooting could mean life or death for all of them.

They walked their horses toward the trees shading the life-giving water. At the narrow opening leading into the canyon, MacLeod could see a pile of bodies from the earlier attack. No one had bothered to bury them.

Griego sat on his horse, his men spread out on either side. Some stood, while others lay on the sand, shifting their muskets for a clearer shot.

Zavalda held up his hand and halted his troops. Griego's men had far more firepower and the Comanchero increased his strength.

MacLeod turned and looked back to where Maria held the child, his son. He prayed that this time they would all walk away from this fight.

Griego shifted in his saddle and checked the positioning of his troops before he called out. "Lieutenant Zavalda, it is good to see you again so soon. I was supposed to meet you at that place, but—" Griego held up his hands and shrugged. "You see my plans have changed."

Zavalda nodded. "My men are in need of water for themselves and their horses. Then we must return to Santa Fe and report to the governor. He will be most pleased to hear the Apache is dead."

"I have heard of this. It is good, but I see you have also captured the *Americano* for me."

MacLeod saw the sudden change in Griego's face before he realized Maria had ridden up behind him.

"The lieutenant is also taking me back to Santa Fe," she said. "Is that not good also, Miguel?"

Griego chose to ignore Maria, but it was obvious to MacLeod that the Comanchero had not mentioned her. Griego's face showed fury and fear. He pointed to MacLeod. "I will take them back to Santa Fe while you and your men rest here by the waters. I will be sure to tell the governor of your involvement. He will be pleased."

MacLeod glanced at Zavalda while his right hand hovered close to the butt of his pistol. This was the moment Zavalda would answer the question of where his loyalty lay.

Zavalda spoke low so that only MacLeod and Maria would hear him. "You and the señorita should go now while there is still time."

"I guess you've answered my question about where you stand, lieutenant."

"My time here has not always been honorable," said Zavalda, turning to face Maria. "I am most sorry for what Miguel has done to you, señorita. I too am guilty of a part of this." He turned back to MacLeod. "Now I must convince Miguel, but I will need your help. If you and the señorita will leave our country, then there is the possibility Miguel's part in this would be overlooked."

For a moment MacLeod thought about Zavalda's proposal. It might work. He and Maria could ride to the Cordero hacienda, pick up fresh horses and supplies, and be on their way to St. Louis before the governor knew they were alive. It left only one problem.

"Lieutenant, Griego has something of mine. If he wants to give it back to me, I'll consider your advice, but right now all I see is a cold-blooded killer, sitting on a horse in front of me, and I can put a ball between his eyes from where I'm sitting. Tell him I want the money he got for my furs. If he gives me what's mine, I'll save his killing for another time."

Miguel Griego seemed to sense his exposure and backed his horse closer to the protection of a clump of trees. "Zavalda, you and your men need to rest and drink. When you have given me back my captives and the *Americano*, I will leave with my men and you can take your time. You have rescued the Apache whore. Her you can share with your men on the way back."

"And what will your answer be to the governor, Miguel, when I tell him what you did to me? Who will he believe?"

Griego spat out a mouthful of blowing sand and ignored Maria's taunt. "Enough stalling. Make your decision, Zavalda."

Only the sound of the restless horses competed with the moan of the wind as both sides waited for Zavalda's answer. His troops held their positions, unprotected, while Griego's better-armed *urbanos* surrounded the spring and lay behind sand barriers.

"Miguel, the *Americano* and the señorita have agreed to supply themselves and leave Nuevo Mexico if you return to them what you have received from the Comanche. This is good for you, Miguel. I ask you to accept this offer and take your men back to Santa Fe."

The tension eased as men began talking among themselves. Many of the governor's troops and the *urbanos* knew each other or were related. A smile creased the folds of Griego's face.

"Let us speak of this, Lieutenant. Come over here and tell me again what you are offering me. If I like it, your men can rest and drink of these cool waters, but you need somehow to assure me that I will not be called before the governor when we return. And the silver, perhaps we can find something to agree on somewhere in the middle."

Zavalda's troops glanced nervously toward the trees where the trickle of water fell into the shallow pool. Swollen tongues flicked out to lick cracking lips in anticipation.

"We have little choice," Zavalda said to MacLeod. "I will go and speak with him."

"That's up to you, Lieutenant, but don't you think you should get your men off their horses and spread out a little, just in case."

"I think it may be a little late for that," Zavalda muttered. "It would only provoke him."

"Suit yourself, but I'm not sitting out here like a turkey sunning himself on a log." MacLeod led Maria toward the rear of the troops, where Sebastian waited with Consuela and the others.

"You know what to do if the shooting starts?"

Sebastian nodded.

MacLeod turned his back on the nearby troops. "I've spotted two men guarding the entrance. I can take out one of them from here, but you might have to handle the other one if he gets under cover. You won't have much time, but you'll have to take a moment to fill your water bags."

Sebastian grunted in agreement. "The Navajo woman cannot speak, but she had been this way before and knows the way."

"Good." MacLeod turned back as Griego's voice rose from the trees in answer to whatever Zavalda had said. MacLeod saw Griego point his left hand toward the spring.

The puff of smoke from Griego's pistol rose before the sound reached out across the distance to MacLeod. For long seconds both sides seemed frozen until Zavalda slowly toppled from his saddle.

MacLeod reacted first, jamming the rifle to his shoulder and firing, cursing himself for not being more patient. Griego fell to the ground but rose immediately and scooted into the nearby trees.

"Go, go," MacLeod cried out, but Sebastian had already grabbed the reins of Maria's horse and raced toward the others.

Zavalda's troops dismounted and sought whatever cover they could find. Two men grabbed the horses and moved out of range as musket fire rattled the still air.

MacLeod whacked the big gelding on the rump, sending him galloping after Sebastian and the other horses. He found a slight depression in the sand and rolled into it as the first fusillade ended and the men on both sides fought their private terror and tried to reload while lying on their backs. From what he could tell, only one of the governor's troops had suffered a wound.

MacLeod slithered out of the shallow depression and inched his way to the top of a low rise. The firing became sporadic. Twice musket balls plowed into the sand twenty yards from his position as Griego split his men and concentrated half of them on keeping MacLeod pinned down. Far to the right, Sebastian led the string of horses toward the canyon entrance as MacLeod sighted down the length of his rifle and fired. Two seconds later a Comanchero, assigned to guard the canyon, slid to the ground and lay at his horse's feet.

MacLeod rolled onto his back and tilted his powder horn over the muzzle of his rifle. He seated a ball and checked on the other Comanchero. He saw him crawling through a mound of rocks, out of Sebastian's sight. MacLeod checked on the line of troopers Griego had set up and decided to test their nerves. He rose to his feet and drew a bead on the Comanchero, fifty yards behind them. Ignoring the flurry of musket balls that sent fountains of dirt into the air in front of him, he held the rifle at his shoulder until the Comanchero turned to investigate the sudden chorus of shots. His ball slammed into the Comanchero's chest. The man toppled over, creating a small rockslide as he slid down from his perch. The effect was immediate as *urbanos* and Comancheros scrambled for protection.

MacLeod turned and moved back from the rise of ground to a spot where a line of creosote bushes shielded him from view. The last thing he saw was Griego directing his men to move deeper into the trees to guard the spring. MacLeod knew Zavalda's troops couldn't last long without water and would attempt an advance against the others, or drop their weapons and surrender. The only way to keep this from becoming a massacre was to cut off their leadership, and that meant Griego. Without him the men would not fight.

Ignoring the pain in his shoulder, MacLeod crawled down the backside of the slope until he was out of sight to those lying among the trees. He figured he had only a few minutes before Griego sent someone out to look for him. Although none of Griego's men had been hit, they knew their muskets were useless at anything over fifty yards. Poor powder, and too little of it, made the fight one-sided, unless they charged him.

By the time he had reached a point where he could work his way back up the shallow swale, the musket fire had fallen off to the occasional shot. Neither side wanted to close with the other. MacLeod figured the distance at a little over eighty yards. He eased his head up over a mound of dirt and looked down the gently sloping desert floor leading to the edge of the trees where Griego's men lay.

One of the *urbanos* casually made his way to the spring to drink, reminding MacLeod of his own terrible thirst. Out in the sun in their heavy woolen uniforms, the governor's troops would be in bad shape. Although Griego was surrounded, he held the spring and could last for days if he had to.

The man returned from the spring, casually stepping over Zavalda's body on his way back to the trees. When another rose from his position and headed for the spring, MacLeod decided no one else would drink. He brought the rifle to his shoulder and fired at a tree only a foot in front of the man. The ball smashed into the tree head high, sending the frightened man scrambling back to safety. A series of shots sent musket balls skipping across the desert floor in many directions. One rolled across the sand and came to rest a few feet away. MacLeod rose from his position and walked over and picked it up, tossing it back at the men in the trees.

Griego quickly assembled all of his men in a half circle facing MacLeod. Another chorus of futile shots rang out.

MacLeod shook his head. He raised his rifle in one smooth motion and sent a ball smacking against a rock behind two *urbanos*. As he reloaded, MacLeod realized the Comancheros had disappeared. They had apparently decided the fight was not worth their lives and slipped out. So much for alliances, MacLeod thought. He made a show of reloading his rifle and checking the two pistols tucked in his waistband.

"Anyone down there understand me?" he shouted.

He saw a few heads nod but no one answered.

MacLeod tried again. "Anyone speak any English? Seems a shame to get killed when I'm offering you a way out of this."

Griego grabbed one of the men and pushed him out from the protection of the trees. The man sidestepped a couple of feet in MacLeod's direction while keeping an eye on Griego.

"*Si*, I think maybe a little," the man said.

"What's your name?"

"Gomez, señor."

MacLeod felt the sun on his back and calculated it was shining in their eyes. If anything it made him appear more menacing.

"Well, Gomez, I want you to tell the others that I have no grudge against them. Miguel Griego is the one I want. Do you understand? I don't have any fight with any of you, just him."

Gomez passed along MacLeod's offer and Griego screamed at his men, ordering them resume firing. One laid his musket on the ground and walked toward MacLeod.

MacLeod's warning came too late. Griego raised his pistol and shot the man in the back, and turned to the others with his second pistol in his hand.

MacLeod tried to feel sorry for the man but couldn't. All of them rode with Griego and killed on his orders.

Gomez looked from MacLeod to Griego, trying to judge where the most danger lay. Griego won. Gomez gripped his pistol.

"Gomez, I can kill any of you from right here. You've got a choice. You can throw out your muskets or you can try to charge me. I figure I can probably kill three or four before you get to me. I can also guarantee Miguel Griego will not be at the front of the charge. So, tell him if he shoots another man I'll kill him right now." MacLeod raised his rifle and sighted on Griego's chest. In the back of his mind he knew he should pull the trigger and kill him right then, but the idea of looking into his face as he did it appealed to him more.

At first nothing happened, only Griego's curses and threats continued, then one man rose and walked toward the cottonwood. Griego's pistol came up but his eyes were riveted on MacLeod's rifle. The man dropped his musket on the ground and went to sit by the spring.

When the last musket lay in the pile, MacLeod lowered his rifle and started down the slope toward the trees. *This is the moment I have dreamed about. This is for Maria, and Charbonneau, and my own months of pain and agony.*

Griego shuffled his feet and sought a route of retreat. He still held the charged pistol at his side.

MacLeod shifted his rifle to his left hand and drew his pistol from his belt. He could kill Griego at that range, but somehow knew that would be too easy.

Griego's arm suddenly shot up, the pistol belching out its puff of smoke. The ball kicked up dirt off to the side of MacLeod. With the shortage of available powder, he doubted Griego practiced much.

Griego's hand seemed to shake as he frantically poured powder down the muzzle of his pistol while the others stood frozen and watched. "I will kill you this time, *Americano,*" Griego screamed as he rammed down the ball and raised his pistol.

Two blasts rolled up the canyon and out over the desert as one. MacLeod held his breath, waiting for the impact. He watched Griego take two steps toward him, then stagger and fall to the ground, blood seeping from his thigh.

MacLeod quickly dropped the pistol and gripped his rifle in both hands.

Gomez held his pistol at his side.

"I've only got one shot, Gomez, but it's yours if you don't put it down now. What's it going to be?"

MacLeod held his breath, waiting. He knew the others would soon realize he couldn't cover all of them. They feared his rifle, and if he had to shoot Gomez, they could easily overrun him at that distance. "I can't wait all day. It's over for him. He's finished," MacLeod said, pointing to Griego who clutched his right thigh with both hands to stem the bleeding. "And when he's gone, what's left for you?"

Gomez looked over his shoulder. Zavalda's troops had moved in and covered the grove of trees. MacLeod had not noticed their approach.

Gomez dropped his pistol at his feet. "I think I want to go home and see my wife."

With an effort Griego rolled over and scrambled for Gomez's pistol. A boot casually kicked the weapon out of his reach as Zavalda's troops entered the trees and surrounded the *urbanos* and the body of their lieutenant.

Maria ran to MacLeod. "I told you to leave," he said. "Why are you still here?"

She wrapped her arms around him and held him. Behind her the others knelt by the spring to drink.

He led her over to Griego. Someone had propped him up against a tree.

She spat on him as he sat in the dirt, holding his leg. "My father will see that you are arrested when we return to Santa Fe."

"I am Miguel Griego, and it will be for the governor to decide."

Maria moved closer to MacLeod. "What are you going to do with him?"

"What do you think the governor will do?"

She laughed. "This pig of a man will be free before I reach Taos. The governor will say it is all a mistake."

"Then we'll have to deal with it ourselves." From his belt MacLeod drew a pistol. He cocked it and handed it to Maria.

"He did far more to you than me. Shoot him wherever you want. If the first doesn't kill him, you can try again."

Griego didn't understand the words but he got the message. He put his hands in front of his face. "No, no," he pleaded.

"Why not? It's the way you shot Zavalda.

"No," Griego screamed.

Maria raised the pistol and pointed it at his head. Seconds passed. The dirt beneath Griego darkened. Maria's two-handed grip on the pistol could not stop it from shaking. The hate on her face turned to tears. "I cannot do this thing. I cannot kill him like this."

MacLeod took the pistol from her hands and carefully lowered the hammer. "Then we'll do it my way," he said.

"What is that?"

"You'll see."

ISLETA MISSION

Before the sun, set MacLeod had Zavalda's body buried with the others in the shade of a large cottonwood far from the spring. Without a word, Consuela and Margarita did their best to tend the wounded.

Maria came toward him as he conferred with Gomez and a sergeant from the governor's troops.

"When will we be leaving?" she asked.

"As soon as that damned sun loses some of its strength. I've got Sebastian making a travois for Griego."

The child in Maria's arms woke from a nap and blinked in the bright sunlight. Maria moved into the shade. "William, sit here please." She pointed to a spot beneath a tree.

"Why?"

"Please, do as I ask."

MacLeod squatted on the ground.

"Now hold your son." Maria placed the squirming child in his arms.

She giggled at the panic on MacLeod's face. "He will not break, and if you drop him, he can only roll onto the sand so he is safe with you."

MacLeod felt the tiny body struggle to find its source of nourishment. He stared down into the pinched face and felt his first wave of emotion grasp his heart.

"But he's so small. Is he alright?"

"All new babies are small, and he is as he should be. Margarita had five of her own and she says he is perfect."

MacLeod gently moved his hands around the baby's body and lifted him up to her. "Never held one before. Still afraid I'll break him somehow."

She took the child. "Do not worry. You will soon not be afraid."

MacLeod and Sebastian repacked the assorted silver bars and coins the Comanche had used to pay Griego for the furs. MacLeod wanted the money transported on more than one pack animal in case anything happened. One promise had been fulfilled, and he had the means to guarantee the second would be also.

By dawn the next morning, the column snaked across the rain-starved land on its way to meet the river somewhere Bernalillo. MacLeod had assumed the unspoken command when Zavalda's sergeant disappeared shortly after the fight. A soldier said he would show up in Santa Fe in a few weeks, after he visited his wife and children.

After two days of living with Griego's howls of pain, cursing, and threats, they reached the river. MacLeod pulled Gomez aside. "Take the men back to Santa Fe and tell the governor what happened.

"What about Señor Griego? They will ask about him when they hear what you have done."

MacLeod shook his head. "Tell the governor you don't know what happened to him, only that he was wounded and couldn't travel."

An hour later the troops filed out of the camp by the river. Sebastian left also, crossing the river on the big black mule and leading the freed Navajo captives. The woman turned to look back at the others when she reached the far side. Then she followed Sebastian toward her tribal lands.

"Are we not to go also?" Maria asked.

"Someplace we need to go first." MacLeod tilted his head toward Griego. "How's he doing?"

"He is very hot, but his wound does not look bad."

The small party slowly worked its way south along the rutted path toward Isleta, where MacLeod hoped to find Father Ramirez. Margarita tended to the feverish Griego while Consuela rode alongside Maria, cradling the child in her arms and cooing to him in her strange new language.

They sighted the Mission of Isleta and its surrounding gardens and orchards late one afternoon. The setting sun spread its golden warmth over the scene. Father Ramirez met them at the gate and escorted them inside the spacious courtyard.

While the others explored the grounds with Father Ramirez, Maria sat on MacLeod's bench and nursed her son.

"In the springtime the smell of the blossoms on these fruit trees is like nothing you can imagine. This is where they brought me after I escaped."

After a brief discussion, a beaming Father Ramirez offered to allow Margarita and Consuela to stay at Isleta. Both wept with gratitude. MacLeod gave the good father a purse of silver coins worth as much as the yearly allowance given the mission by the Church in Spain. It would allow Father Ramirez the luxury of many years of financial freedom.

Two weeks passed before Sebastian rode the big black mule into the mission courtyard and spoke with MacLeod. The next morning they all and rode northwest, into the low mountains. Griego rode, his hands tied to the front of the saddle.

On the afternoon of the fourth day, Sebastian led them over a shallow saddle and down a winding canyon. At the mouth of the canyon, thick bushes sheltered a bubbling spring. MacLeod recognized the man who rose from the ground and came forward to greet them.

"What is happening? Who are they, William?" Maria clutched the child close to her body as the warriors encircled them.

"It's all right. They came here to meet with us."

"But why?"

MacLeod stepped to the ground and went to meet the heavy figure who approached. They embraced. He turned back to Maria, who still sat on her horse. "This is the father of the two children we brought back with us. All of the others killed at the spring were from his village. One of them was his wife. Sebastian and I met him weeks ago when we were on our way to Acoma."

Maria turned and looked back at Griego, who sat surrounded by the threatening warriors. "Look at him. He knows," she said.

"Looks like maybe he does. I think he sees his past finally catching up with him."

"Was this your plan, to bring him here, for them?"

"Either this or shoot him myself, and we've been through that before. To tell you the truth, I didn't think shooting him would be quite enough."

Maria couldn't take her eyes off of Griego. "But they will kill him."

"Yep, you can bet on that."

Griego began to plead as he was led into the middle of the large party. Sebastian finished speaking with the chief and rode back to MacLeod and Maria.

"They will take him back to the village so everyone can watch his death," Sebastian said. "They say it will take a long time for him to die. They also say we are welcome to come and watch."

MacLeod shook his head. "Thank them for this honor. Tell them we will hear the stories they tell of it someday."

As they left the spring, Griego was reduced to a whimpering hulk, pleading with MacLeod to shoot him instead.

"I hope he has time to remember those he did the same thing to," MacLeod said. "I kinda wish I could watch." He nodded to Sebastian and they turned up the canyon.

They crossed the river late one afternoon and spent the night at the hacienda of Don Fernando. No amount of good wishes could overcome the coolness of the women toward Maria. Don Fernando took MacLeod aside and assured him that time would heal the women's attitude.

In camp two nights later Maria surprised MacLeod. "I do not wish to stop in Santa Fe. I wish to go straight to my home."

"But what about Father Alvarez? I thought you wanted to see him? And I have things I need to clear up with the governor."

"No, please take me home first. You can leave me and then see the governor. I do not wish to see any of them, but I ask you to see Father Alvarez and tell him I will try to come and see him soon. He will understand."

"Maria, is this because of the way they treated you at Don Fernando's? Is that what you're afraid of, because he said their attitude would change with time?"

Maria laughed bitterly. "William, you do not understand my people. They have little to do but talk, and when they get together that is all they do. Look at me," she said with tears rolling down her cheeks. "I have this child and I am not married as I should be. I have lived as an Apache wife for many months. What do you think they will do? I will be the one they talk about for many years."

MacLeod moved closer to her and put his arms around her shoulders.

"What will become of me, William? And what is to become of this child of ours, with no father?"

He thought of the same questions but answers came hard. He had to admit that looking at her dressed in a fringed doeskin dress, her long, black hair tangled and unkempt, and riding a horse with a child in her arms, she looked like every Indian woman he had seen.

"Come with me to St. Louis. Surely we can find someone to marry us and nobody will know about the rest."

She shook her head. "It is not a secret that can be kept forever, William. Others will eventually discover it and everything will be the same as here. And you know so little of our Church. They will marry us only if you choose to follow our teachings and become one of us. Father Alvarez will tell you this." Maria placed the sleeping baby on a robe at her side and covered him. "Must you go?"

Although both knew of his promise to Charbonneau, it was the first time Maria had mentioned it.

"I must. This silver belongs to his family, at least most of it does."

Maria curled up on the ground beside the child. It was some time before her sobs diminished and she appeared to sleep.

HACIENDA OF DON CORDERO

Sebastian led, with Maria and the baby on a little mare, and MacLeod bringing up the rear. He saw Don Cordero standing at the gate of the hacienda, watching as they approached. Don Cordero hurried forward to meet them and help Maria from her horse. She held the child in one arm and clung to her father until he held her at arm's length and openly wept.

Together they entered the courtyard, where Maria's mother waited. Maria embraced her gently and passed the child into her mother's arms. The woman quickly turned it over to an Indian woman waiting at her side.

MacLeod could see what she faced. Don Cordero might be master of his land and hacienda, but he would never hold the power to control the thoughts and tongues of the women.

The first storm of the fall began the night before MacLeod planned to leave. He finished packing the animals and entered the low doorway, dripping water onto the rug-covered floor. Maria, holding the baby, moved across the room toward him. They were alone.

"Do you have everything you need?" she asked.

"I think so. Your father has been generous."

"But it is such a long way. How long will it take you to go to this place, St. Louis?"

"I figure I can travel pretty fast by myself, even with the string of pack animals. I think a month or two, maybe."

The question seemed to hang in the air between them but MacLeod knew she wouldn't ask.

"Soon as I get there, I'll see Charbonneau's family, but I figure I won't be able to leave again before spring."

"I know this, William, and I will pray for your safety. I will be safe here with my family, and they will soon learn to live with their disappointments. I do not need others."

A clap of thunder shook the adobe structure. The stock at the railing shivered in the rain, anxious to move and drive off the cold.

"I will be back. That's why I'm leaving my share of the silver here with you. Don't you believe me?"

"Of course, and I will wait for you, but if anything should happen I will understand. You have done so much already."

MacLeod leaned to kiss her without getting her wet. His hand slid down her cheek to the child in her arms. He felt the tiny fingers on his son's hand grasp one of his and hold it tightly.

"I have decided on something else," she said. "I will call him William. William Diego."

MacLeod could only nod. He fought back his own tears. "I plan to stop in Santa Fe and see the governor. I'll see Father Alvarez and ask him to come as soon as he can. I know he will want to."

She could no longer hold back the tears. "William, I do not think you will come back to me, but I will understand. Whatever you decide will be all right. Now please go before I fall on my knees and beg you to stay."

The rain thundered on the roof of the hacienda. MacLeod shifted his feet, feeling helpless in his attempt to convince her he would return. "You told me once about this fellow Don Diego de Vargas and how they sent him up here after the Indians drove everybody else out," he said, not thinking about what he planned to say but just letting it come out. "You also told me about this doll he brought with him, the one you called *La Conquistadora*, you remember?"

Maria gulped. "Yes."

"Well, you promised to show me that doll someday, but you haven't done it yet. I want to see it."

She wiped the tears away with the palm of her hand. "I will take you there when you return."

He turned and hurried out into the rain. As he led the pack animals, laden with supplies and the silver of his dead partners through the arched entrance, he could not bring himself to look back.

Late at night Santa Fe, resembled a celebration that had lasted too long and lost its purpose. MacLeod rode through the muddy lanes between sagging adobe huts, toward the imposing structure of the church. A dog shuffled out to look and barked once before circling in place and sinking to the ground. Occasionally, a lone candle illuminated a window as he passed.

Father Alvarez greeted him with an embrace, and his first words told MacLeod where his thoughts lay.

"I have heard. How is she?"

MacLeod lowered himself onto a low stool and removed his hat. "She is well, at least she seems to be, and so is the child."

"Yes, the child, but she is well?"

"You knew how it would be, how they would treat her. You told me so. That's why I've come. She needs to see you."

The shadows played across the gaunt face of the Church's servant, making it appear a mask of pain.

"Of course. I will go at once. I could not believe the stories I heard when the governor's men returned. The governor is sick over the death of his aide. And Señor Griego, what of him?"

"I didn't kill him, if that's your question? But he's not going to be stealing people no more."

"You are sure of this?"

"I have no doubt Señor Griego won't be a problem again."

Father Alvarez clasped his hands beneath his chin. His eyes appeared to close.

MacLeod waited a few minutes before speaking. "There are a couple of other things I want to ask. The child. Maria is afraid the Church will not accept him."

"I will see to it when I see her," said Alvarez.

MacLeod placed a leather bag of coins on the table. "This is for all you've done. There should be enough here to help in your fight against all the things you see needs changing. One other thing, I would like some of the money used for Lieutenant Zavalda. I heard masses can be given in his name."

Father Alvarez smiled.

"Lastly, would you write to his father? He died for what he had come to believe and for the mistakes he admitted to. He told me he wanted to go home and set things right with his father."

"Yes, I have heard this. I will send it in the next official post. Now you must rest."

SANTA FE

S ounds of celebration woke MacLeod. By the shadows on the
wall he knew he had slept most of the day. He sat up as voices
rose in joyous shouts and laughter. Through the narrow slot in the
wall MacLeod watched the revelers embrace each other as they
danced through the streets and gathered at the far end of the plaza,
where a string of heavily laden pack animals dozed. The people in
the church had emptied into the streets to join with the rest of the
town's residents. MacLeod followed.

A crowd gathered under the awning in front of the governor's office and spilled out into the street. MacLeod shouldered his way past celebrating townspeople and entered the office.

Governor Melgares waddled over and greeted MacLeod like a conquering hero. He led him to the far side of the office. "You have heard of course?"

"Heard what?"

"You have not heard then." The governor clapped his hands together and wrung them. "We are free, we are independent. Mexico is Mexican."

"You mean you no longer belong to Spain?"

"Si, and your friends, they have come. Maybe you know them."

"What friends?"

"*Americanos*, like you. A shout diverted the governor's attention. He turned as someone burst through the door and rushed over to him.

"They wish to know when they can begin to trade, Your Excellency," the man said.

"As soon as they have paid their tax," the Governor said and turned to his new aide. "We must have some sort of tax. They must not make all the profits."

While the Governor worried over an import tax, MacLeod pushed his way outside and headed for the crowd gathered around the piles of goods stacked in front of the Governor's Palace. Then it occurred to him that the governor never mentioned his escape, or asked the whereabouts of Griego. So much for the business of politics.

The trading was already in progress when MacLeod shouldered his way to the front of the crowed. "You come here from St. Louis?" he shouted to the first man in line.

"You bet, but who the hell are you? We were told there weren't no Americans in Santa Fe, least not running free anyways."

"Yeah, well that's almost true. Say, who's in charge here?"

The bearded American straightened and stretched his back. He pointed toward a man in a felt hat near the front of the line. "That would be William Becknell. He's the one in the red shirt."

Before MacLeod could thank him, the man was back to measuring cloth from a bolt and passing it across to the outstretched hands of people who often waited a year or more for goods to arrive from Vera Cruz. If the crowd continued to pour into the plaza, the Americans could go home with empty panniers very soon.

MacLeod approached the man in the red shirt. "You William Becknell?"

"Who would you be?"

"Names MacLeod, William MacLeod."

"I'm Becknell for sure. How'd you get here ahead of us? I supposed we would be first."

"I was with Lucien Charbonneau's trapping party and we ended up here."

Becknell pulled MacLeod to the side and away from the crowd. "You were with Lucien Charbonneau?"

"Along with Stewart and Belanger."

"Well, I'll be damned," Becknell said, taking off his hat and running his hand through his hair. "They here in Santa Fe to?"

"Afraid not. The Indians got Stewart and Belanger, and Charbonneau died later, from his wounds and with the help of some locals."

"Yes, we've heard some rumors about how they treated Americans."

"Tell me about St. Louis. What are they saying about Charbonneau?"

"Well, now, most of us are from Franklin, but from what I hear they figured something happened to the party when you didn't come back last year. We intended on asking around when we got here. Course it was hard on the family, you know, with all the debt he left."

"He tried to return in time, but that's when we started running into all the trouble. But I don't guess it's ever too late to take care of debts. When you're done with your trading, you mind if I tag along on the way back to St. Louis?"

"You're welcome, but are you saying Charbonneau had the money to pay off his debts?"

"He had the furs."

"Well that's good news. We sure can help you take those furs back and help his family."

MacLeod knew he had to trust this man if he was going to travel back to St. Louis with him. "The furs were traded for silver, so there ain't much to carry."

The man pointed at the ground. "You stay right here. There's someone you need to talk with."

While MacLeod waited for Becknell to return, he wondered how long it might take the governor to figure out how much he thought he could charge for his import tariff. Probably not before the Americans were done and were on their way home.

The tall man whom Becknell led over to MacLeod had a touch of gray streaking his mustache. He grinned and held out his hand. "Name's Jim Youngston. I understand you were with Mr. Charbonneau. Too bad what happened, but I'm sure his family will want to know all about it."

"You know the family?" MacLeod asked.

"You bet. I married his daughter, Jeanette. Say, now that I think about it, she mentioned a young fellow that went with her father. Said you were a good friend."

MacLeod grinned and nodded. So Jeanette had married. So much for waiting.

"That's too bad about Mr. Charbonneau, but this news will go a long way to clearing his name."

"So will the money from the furs," MacLeod said, liking the man in spite of knowing he was Jeanette's husband.

"That too. I know Mrs. Charbonneau took it pretty hard when all the people showed up looking for their money."

"Well, now she can pay them off and have some to spare." MacLeod looked over the man's shoulder and saw Father Alvarez at the edge of the crowd. An idea began to form. "How much longer before you start back to St. Louis?"

"Mr. Becknell says a couple of days. We sure can use the rest and see a little of this town."

After a quick word with Becknell, MacLeod found Father Alvarez. The two huddled together for some time, then pushed through the fringes of the crowd and walked toward the imposing structure of the church at the end of the street. He passed a small group attempting to load an ancient cannon. With the amount of powder spilt on the ground in front of the cannon, MacLeod hoped to be far away before someone lit the fuse.

HACIENDA OF DON CORDERO

A chilling wind blew down out of the canyons of the Sangre de Cristo Mountains and raced across the pinion-studded land to remind everyone of another winter's approach. MacLeod tucked his hands under his arms as the big gelding worked its way toward the stark outline of the hacienda. A quarter moon and starlight from a cloudless sky watched over MacLeod as he approached the sleeping guard at the locked gates.

Inside the courtyard, MacLeod lowered himself to the ground and waited for his legs to adjust after nearly twenty hours in the saddle. The flickering glow of a single candle shone out onto the courtyard.

A door opened, revealing the blanket-wrapped figure of Don Cordero holding a pistol at his waist. Behind him others began to show their faces.

"You have returned?" Don Cordero said. "Is something wrong? They would not let you go?"

Suddenly Maria rushed past her father and ran to him. "Why have you come back?" she cried.

He held her tightly in his arms and looked at Don Cordero. "Have you heard about your independence?"

"Yes, word came to us yesterday."

"Is this news good for you?"

Don Cordero shrugged. "It is too early to know. There are some who wish all Spaniards to go home."

MacLeod took Maria by the shoulders and held her at arm's length. "Listen carefully. A lot has happened. There are Americans in Santa Fe. They came from St. Louis with goods to trade and got here a couple of days after word of independence, so now the governor welcomes all Americans. I arranged for the man in charge to take the silver back to Charbonneau's family. I don't have to go back."

"Oh, William, does that mean you will stay here?"

"I'm not finished. I had a long talk with Father Alvarez and I know what you can expect here. It won't be any different if I stay, so here's what I have in mind." MacLeod reached beneath his shirt and pulled out a folded paper. "This here is for a friend of Father Alvarez. They studied together in Spain."

Maria tilted her head. "His friend who he writes to, in Alta California I believe."

"Yes, it's at a mission called San Gabriel Archangel. In this letter, Father Alvarez asks his friend, a Father Sanchez, to help us get started out there. He said he may be recalled to his college in Mexico City at any time and wanted us to have this paper in case he did not see us again."

Tears slid down Maria's cheeks. "But it is so far. How will we find our way?"

"Señora." Sebastian stepped out of the shadows and into the candlelight. "There is a way. I will take you there."

MacLeod pulled Maria back into an embrace. "We have time to think about it. We couldn't leave until the spring."

Maria kissed him on the cheek. "Are you sure this is what you want? You do not wish to go to your home in America?"

MacLeod reached out and took the child in his arms. "If it doesn't work out, Father Alvarez says ships come there from Boston to trade."

MacLeod looked at his son. "What do you say, Diego? Think you might like this place, this California?"

ACKNOWLEDGEMENTS

Many years ago my wife presented me with a beautiful little Adler portable typewriter and told me to follow my dream and write. This is for your patience. Thank you.

I would also like to thank my editor, Larry Edwards (larryedwards.com), for his help in putting this tale together. Also, thank you to Tiffany Lynne at Gray Publishing Services (graypublishingservices.com) for the new cover and interior layout.

OTHER BOOKS BY E. PAUL BERGERON

TWO CAN PLAY
Available at: Amazon

The blood of ancient warriors courses through his veins.

A woman is dead.

A child is taken.

Only his own death would quell the hatred they feel for him. Can Gray escape his past and quench his bitter memories, or will others die to pay for his mistakes. He must answer the question. Does he flee, or fight? But he has sworn an oath to never kill again.

From the Blackfoot reservation in the north, to the barren lands of the Tonto O'odham in Arizona, this story takes the twists and turns that keep Gray alive. Because the man who deals in powdered death holds the key, and only Gray's death will open the lock.

*****

THE SEARCH FOR DIEGO
BOOK TWO OF A LAND IN TURMOIL SERIES
Available at: Amazon

In the bowels of a hostile desert, a woman lay dying. As the last vestige of strength seeps from her body she passed the child into his hands. "Save him—for me. He is all I have to give you," were her final words.

Standing in his way is a fanatical priest who would take the child and save its soul instead. But the Frenchman, whose deadly reputation is built on the bodies of the men who challenged him, has other ideas. Filled with hatred for the man whose son it is, he takes the child from the woman paid to keep it, and passes it into the hands of a beautiful woman from the streets and slums of Vera Cruz.

It is 1823. Mexico has recently gained its independence, with little conception of how to govern this chaotic land. And in that far away place that is Alta California, leadership is based on the whims of the ignorant. It is here that William

MacLeod scours the land in search of his son, while the Church, and those in charge, struggle to banish this foreign intruder from their land.

Love, hate, treachery, and death stalk his path as he attempts to fulfill her dying request.

A thrilling historical novel in this Land in Turmoil Series.

ABOUT THE AUTHOR

You can contact E Paul Bergeron at: edpbergeron@cs.com

As I remember it, life began on top of a load of furniture in a sleigh drawn by a team of horses on a bitterly cold day. My mother was walking alongside in the snow when the moment arrived. She claims it was Valentine's Day, and of all people, she should know.

I attended a one-room schoolhouse outside of the French Canadian town of Mascouche, Quebec, and later in the metropolis of Montreal. At some point, an overworked schoolteacher wrote a note home to my mother to say that someday I would be a writer. The rest of the family laughed.

I spent long winter afternoons and nights reading, and acquired a love of history. I never realized the depth of this love until, years later, I stood on a street corner in old Montreal and read the inscription etched on a brass plaque attached to the cornerstone of a grey, brick building. It read simply, "Hudson's Bay Company." There stood the company synonymous with intrigue and adventure, and, being of French and Scottish heritage, the people behind those adventures were my ancestors. They were the French voyageurs, or coureur de bois, who traversed the mountains and forests, and paddled the streams and rivers, and the Scots who sent them out in search of the fur pelts, which led to the exploration of the North American continent.

I was sixteen when my father found an old farmhouse, badly in need of repair in West Bolton, Quebec. There I spent a year among people who would become lifelong friends. But my father passed away before he realized his vision for the house.

My mother took us back to Montreal, and I soon left school to find a job to help support the family. Then a Christmas phone call came from California, and the invitation to come west took us to North Hollywood, with palm trees and salt sea air--and word that I was too young to work. I returned to school.

I stood in the quad of North Hollywood High with a recent import from Australia, gazing at the parking lot and wondering how the school could have so many teachers. The Aussie informed me that it was the students' parking lot. Life had certainly changed.

I soon discovered California's lofty Sierra Nevada Mountains and streams filled with wild trout holding below the riffles, as if waiting for the dry fly attached to the end of my line. However, those towering, snow-capped peaks beckoned, and I could not care less if the trout were hungry. Life was wonderful.

With the early beginning of a writing life, and being married to an artist, our two beautiful daughters grew up in a home filled with artistic expression. Later, we moved down the coast to a town in Orange County, until it was time to sell a business and find a place to begin the work put on hold for so many years.

We settled in Hayden Lake, Idaho, with a beautiful home a few miles from the shores of Lake Coeur d'Alene. Now I load my Surly Long Haul Trucker bike on the back of the car and drive to the trail whose path winds its way along the Coeur d'Alene River. I find a spot beside a small lake to watch the ducks and geese feed among the lily pads, or sit in a small clearing beneath a canopy of leafy branches, and there work out the twists and turns of the stories I want to tell.

Visit him online at:

Website: http://www.epaulbergeron.com

Facebook: http://www.facebook.com/EPaulBergeron/

www.ingramcontent.com/pod-product-compliance
Lightning Source LLC
Chambersburg PA
CBHW020509260626
47156CB00006B/1938